S'Wonderful

A Symphony of Musical Memories

S'Wonderful

A Symphony of Musical Memories

by

Tony Ireland

Date of Publication:
October 2001

Published by:
John Nickalls Publications
Oak Farm Bungalow
Suton
Wymondham
Norfolk
NR18 9SH

Printed by:
ProPrint
Riverside Cottage
Great North Road
Stibbington
Peterborough PE8 6LR

ISBN: 1-904136-02-8

CONTENTS

CHAPTER 1

'Little Man You've Had A Busy Day'
The Music Of My Early Childhood

When I arrived in 1933 I faced stiff opposition as contender for the event of the year. Jim Mollison had flown solo from Europe to South America, aeroplanes had flown over Everest's summit. Malcolm Campbell had achieved 272.108 mph (with the aid of his car), the film version of 42nd Street, with newcomer Ginger Rogers, had hit town, and the windmill of Mousehold Heath had burned down. Added to this, a stocky little man with a small moustache had appeared on the scene to become Chancellor of Germany. (No, I don't mean Charlie Chaplin!)

Small wonder then, when I turned up at 'Philomel' 65 Harvey Lane, Norwich there were no earth-shattering headlines. Naturally, my father and mother were delighted, as was my mother's sister, Aunt Edith, although she had been hoping I would be a girl: she didn't care much for boys! As it was, I came into a loving home, with parents I was to love dearly all their lives. Also I adored my Aunt Edith, although I confess I was rather afraid of her husband, my Uncle Bert.

There were still world financial problems in the year of my birth, and my father had taken a 10% cut in his teacher's salary in common with many others. As one song of the day went:

No more money in the bank, no cute baby we can spank
What's to do about it, let's put out the lights and go to sleep.

This was barred by the BBC incidentally, as being too suggestive of naughtiness!

Well, I was the cute baby and was christened at St Matthew's church in the parish of Thorpe Hamlet. My parents had decided to christen me Michael, but a teaching colleague of my father's, Miss Ethel Daniels, said, 'You can't give him a common name like Michael: he must have a much more superior name. He must be called Anthony!' Strangely, I have rarely been addressed as such since.

It was a pity that among my christening gifts was not a set of coins of the realm for that year. There were so few pennies minted that a

1933 penny now is worth a king's ransom! I spent much of my youth vainly looking for one.

Whether or not my early flatulent sounds were instantly recognised as the beginning of a musical career I know not, but Aunt Edith used to bounce me on her knee to the strains of crooning 'If you go down in the woods today you're sure of a big surprise . . .' She also bought me a toy glockenspiel with coloured metal keys, although she said it was a xylophone. I proudly went around saying my new word 'xylophone' and playing it to all and sundry, probably causing even the calmest folk to tear their hair and grit their teeth! No doubt they questioned, nay, cursed, the wisdom of my aunt's choice of present.

My father and mother had a wireless and we used to sit and listen to Station IW, and in the evenings I was enchanted by the dance orchestras of the day, especially the pianists. On Sunday evenings there was the announcer welcoming us into the Palm Court of Grand Hotel, to the strains of Strauss's 'Roses From The South', with a trio led by Albert Sandler, then later Tom Jenkins, followed by Max Jaffa.

Another programme, 'Clap Hands, Here Comes Charlie' signalled the appearance of Charlie Kunz, a demure little man from Shrewsbury who had the deftest touch on the piano. No-one could fail to recognise his distinctive style, with his speciality of stringing several numbers in one tempo into a medley. His programme always ended with the song 'Pink Elephants'. Chronic arthritis in his hands brought an end to his playing: a sad thing for his admiring public, and surely a most frustrating one for Charlie.

Carroll Gibbons was an American pianist from Connecticut who joined the orchestra at London's Savoy Hotel and after three years became its leader. He used to broadcast from the Savoy, leading his orchestra, the Savoy Orpheans, from his piano. I loved his piano style, and liked his somewhat lazy American drawl as he announced numbers, or even sang. His signature tune was 'On The Air' but he is best remembered for his lovely composition 'Garden In The Rain'. Carroll Gibbons had class and style, and was ranked high among musicians of the day.

Then there was the clever piano articulation of Billy Mayerl who had an orchestra but was better known for the dazzling piano playing of his own compositions. When I became reasonably proficient as a pianist I bought some of his work; the 'Four Aces' was one album, the most popular being 'Ace of Hearts'. Then there was 'Bats In The Belfry': and the flower series which included his famous signature tune, 'Marigold'. How I loved that one as a small boy! Billy Mayerl called his house in Hampstead 'Marigold Lodge'. Fortunately, thanks to modern technology, recordings of Billy Mayerl playing his own compositions are still available.

Two of the dance bands I remember enjoying were Jack Payne with his signature tune 'Say It With Music', a song by Irving Berlin: and Henry Hall who opened with 'This Is The Time For Dancing', and ended with 'Here's To The Next Time', a tune said to be one he borrowed from a hymn melody. Others I remember listening to were Ambrose ('When Day Is Done'), and Sidney Lipton. There were also two vocal gentlemen who crooned their way into our lives. One called Al Bowlly and the other Bing Crosby.

All the bands played the songs of the 1930s, promoting all the new ones, and I loved 'Smoke Gets In Your Eyes'. My father smoked cigarettes, which was a fashionable thing then! Another hit of 1933 was 'Keep Young And Beautiful', which made me see how pretty my mother was. Other 1933 numbers were 'One Morning In May', 'It's Only A Paper Moon', and 'Stormy Weather', the latter probably reflecting the times we were living in.

I believe the greatest disservice the BBC ever did for the nation was to divide radio into 1, 2, 3 and 4. It widened the generation gap to a point of no return, and today very few youngsters will enjoy, appreciate, or even know, the music of their elders ~ something which I find sad.

My parents had a fairly large collection of 78s and a gramophone on which I listened to classical, and light classical music. My favourite records, however, were those of overtures from the musical shows and operettas. I loved the beautiful melodies from 'White Horse Inn', 'Gypsy Baron', 'Merry Widow', 'Student Prince' and 'Gypsy Princess'.

In 1938, the year after my brother David was born, I was taken by my parents, together with Aunt Edith and Uncle Bert, to a Tea Dance at a luxurious ballroom at Leamington Spa. My aunt and uncle were, by then, living in Birmingham at Acock's Green, and we travelled by bus to Leamington Spa. I couldn't take my eyes off the wonderful bandstand with its musicians, immaculately dressed, playing such superb music, and led by a white-jacketed conductor called Jan Berenska, one of the top bandleaders of the day. Between dances I was persuaded by my family to walk across the dance floor up the great man and ask him for my request. I think of that incident today every time a small boy or girl comes to me at the piano and asks for a request. Anyway, Jan Berenska asked me my name and announced that 'For Master Tony Ireland we shall now play 'The Teddy Bears' Picnic' which, after a round of applause, they played in true Henry Hall style, just like the record we had at home.

Once, at Harvey Lane, I remember watching a swarthy Italian with his barrel organ play at the corner of Gordon Avenue. I had never heard music like it, and was entranced by the sound which seemed to radiate happiness. Added to this curiosity was the organ grinder's monkey, leaping around the onlookers with a little fez to collect contributions. It was a rare sight and I have only seen a barrel organ four times since: once at York museum, another at Thursford: the third which we borrowed in later years to play at a school fete, and lastly, a really beautiful instrument belonging to Edward Murray-Harvey, a musical friend who not only goes around playing his barrel organ for charitable functions, but also has a vast collection of sheet music which he lets musicians have copies of when needed.

We lived quite close to Mousehold, and often my parents would take me at week-ends to listen to the band playing in the bandstand. There were seats all round the slopes, and a larger number of people would sit and enjoy selections from operettas and other light music given by a variety of Norfolk wind bands. I well remember it raining once, and people huddled under umbrellas listening to the march from Wagner's 'Tannhauser', a piece with which I have always associated a brass band on a rainy day ever since!

Next door to number 65 lived a Mr and Mrs Smith (yes, really!) I was taken round to tea on more than one occasion and heard them both sing while Mrs Smith played what I thought was a piano. Imagine my surprise when Mr Smith pushed a panel aside at the front of the instrument and revealed a parchment roll! It was, of course, a pianola, and the greatest delight for me was to watch the keys playing themselves when Mr Smith pressed the given lever. I hasten to add that Mrs Smith did actually play the instrument as a piano for the recital and did not cheat by using the mechanical device. The songs they sang were the compositions of the thirties and their words and melodies echo back across the years still. I think I knew, even then, that I wanted to play one day.

My mother's Aunt Nellie lived with my great grandma at 74 St Leonard's Road in Thorpe Hamlet. I would visit with my mother and take sweets for great grandma, who always wore black and sat permanently in a corner I remember. I was a little afraid of Aunt Nellie but I did like it when she took us up to the first floor where stood a very old piano with yellow keys and candlesticks. She would play, and although the sound was that of an instrument well past its sell-by date, what she did play was lovely. I remember some Ketelbey compositions, but her favourite piece was 'The Robin's Return'. She didn't sing well, but had a harsh, raspy voice, probably on account of her smoking. Years after, Aunt Nellie gave her old piano to the Young Teachers Association who had it kept in a room at Pull's Ferry where they held their meetings. I think, in the end, the old piano died of a broken heart, if not strings and keys.

My parents had friends, Reg and Phylis Thompson, who had met and married about the same time as my own mother and father, in 1929. They had all met and danced together at the Saturday night dances at St Matthew's parish hall, although Phylis had to dance with other men since husband-to-be, Reg, was the band leader! 'Why Did She Fall For The Leader Of The Band?' as the song goes. Without doubt, for his piano touch, for even as a very small boy I thrilled to hear him play what he called 'syncopation'. He had large hands and could stretch a tenth in the left ~ alas, something I cannot do. It was the Billy Mayerl/Carrol Gibbons touch ~ live! I never tired of hearing him play, though I was a bit afraid and in awe of son Colin who was, to me, a 'big boy'. They moved away from Norwich to live in Slough ~ Lascelles Road I think. Heaven knows why! I can think of lots of better places to live, though I expect the good people of Slough would disagree. Years later we went to visit them, by which time their son Colin was an airline pilot, and Reg's sight had deteriorated; I remember that one of his spectacle lenses was black. His piano touch, however, was still as wonderful and even more thrilling to me, for by then I had started to play. He let me look through his great library of music which he was by then hardly able to use. Sadly, I lost touch with them completely and I often think about Reg Thompson and the inspiration he gave me to 'syncopate', although, of course, I had to split the tenth in the left. I do hope his wonderful music library found a good home.

Those carefree days at Harvey Lane were full of wonderment and happiness. I think I even liked my first school at Thorpe Hamlet Infants in Marion Road where my teacher was a Miss Castleton. Our home was always full of the sound of music from the gramophone or wireless, or my parents' singing. My father had been a boy chorister at several Norwich churches and he was proud to tell me that he had 'pumped' the organ at St John's Maddermarket for a penny a time! My mother had the loveliest of voices, and the sound of her singing in those far-off days comes echoing back to me across the years; if I am looking for names of those who inspired me to make music then she is certainly high on my list. In later years, sadly and mysteriously, she lost her lovely singing voice when a bathroom geyser blew up in her face.

One afternoon, in 1939, my father told me that war had been declared. I imagine I was too young to understand, and my brother's great capacity for silver-tongued philosophising had hardly begun to develop at age two-and-a-half, and we were left at the brink of an era which was to change our lives, and millions of others, drastically and dramatically for ever. The writers of popular song were about to change to an altogether different theme in their thirty-two given bars, and I find it somewhat ironic that such beautiful, yet sad and sensitive, songs should have been borne out of such a tragic epoch.

Thirty-nine years later, on holiday with my family in Normandy, I visited the war cemetery just above Omaha beach. As I stood in the morning sun, looking at the seemingly endless rows of crosses, the Ted and Moira Heath song 'That Lovely Weekend' filled my thoughts. It was the words of a young girl, so in love with a young man who had spent a precious few hours with her before leaving for war; a song, incidentally, banned by Auntie Beeb for inferring that the two had spent the weekend together and had done things not quite according to somebody-or-other's rules!

> *I haven't said thanks for that lovely weekend . . .*
> *And now you are gone, dear, this letter I pen,*
> *My heart travels with you 'til we meet again.*
> *Keep smiling, my darling, and someday we'll spend*
> *A lifetime as sweet as that lovely weekend'*

But those lying there beneath the velvet green lawns and the beautiful surroundings, bathed in the morning sunlight, never had that chance. I wept unashamedly and uncontrollably.

CHAPTER 2

'I Love A Piano'

The old Music Hall gag tells us how one of Tchaikowsky's symphonies was written in four flats because the family had to move three times to avoid the rent man! We moved in 1939: no, not to some far away place to avoid any rent man, or even the little German with the 'tache, but across to the other side of Norwich to 541 Earlham Road, which was again called 'Philomel'. My father had received promotion ~ at least, I think it was promotion ~ to Larkman Lane school and it was becoming just a little difficult for him to nip home to Harvey Lane from there for lunch. I will always think I left just a little part of me behind at 65 Harvey Lane where life had epitomised the thirties, with the people, the fashions, the cars and, of course, the music.

I was sent to Avenue Road school and very soon reached the primary department with the fearsome Mrs Lilian Hughes at the helm. She taught singing herself and we learned many of the old hymns such as 'Summer Suns Are Glowing', and 'Glad That I Live Am I'. She made us learn some quite difficult songs I remember: 'Where The Bee Sucks', 'Song Of The Jolly Roger', 'Good Morrow Gossip Joan', and a beautiful song called 'The Faerie Song' from 'The Immortal Hour' which I loved, though never knew why 'faerie' was spelt so. I concluded that people in a bygone age weren't particularly good at spelling! Mrs Hughes could play the piano very well indeed and could sing at the same time, something which I have always both admired and envied.

I imagine that music was Mrs Hughes' main subject when she studied to be a teacher: she also took what was called percussion class and all the class were dealt out an instrument to hit ~ tambourines, castanets, triangles, bells, wood blocks, and *drums*. Yes, drums, which you hung around your neck and beat with small drum-sticks. I used to strain forward with all sinews to the very ends of my fingers to have a drum when instruments were held aloft, but invariably I ended up with a triangle which dangled on a string and proved to be uncontrollable with a mind of its own when it came to trying to strike it with the metal rod. We read the music from huge sheets hung over a blackboard, each instrument indicating its own cue to come in by a different colour. To begin with, the cacophony that issued forth gave the impression that everyone was totally colour-blind and Mrs Hughes became extremely cross. However, after some practice things began to improve, though I do remember being somewhat scared to strike my instrument in case it should be at the wrong point, particularly with the wayward triangle! It was all very interesting though, and contributed greatly to my musical education.

My father loved music, as did my mother, although neither of them played an instrument. Apart from all hymns, father loved the music from 'Cavalleria Rusticana', particularly the Easter Hymn, and the children's choir singing 'Nymphs And Shepherds'. My mother loved to listen to people such as Kathleen Ferrier, especially singing 'What Is Life?', and Helen Hill and Grace Moore. She would also enjoy 'The Slaves Chorus' from 'Nabucco'. I suppose their love of music was something they wanted to pass on to me, and indeed my brother also, and it must have been with this in mind that my father bought a piano. It was a new one, from the Co-op, marked with the name 'Amyl' and cost £75.00 ~ a large sum of money then. Undoubtedly, my parents wanted us to have chances in life that they had not been given.

With a piano installed in our lounge and a young potential genius straining at the leash, my father managed to persuade Miss Nina Warmoll to tutor me in the art of playing the pianoforte. Miss Warmoll lived at No. 1 Maud Street, off St Philip's Road, close to the Dereham Road. In those days there were not many cars and Miss Warmoll travelled by 'bus every week from Maud Street to Earlham Road to attempt to teach me the rudiments of music. She charged my father 15/- for ten lessons, plus the cost of any music, though she didn't seem to charge him for the 'bus fare. I liked her from the outset for several reasons: she smiled when she talked, she seemed to have the patience of a Saint (a necessary virtue in a piano teacher!) and she played the piano beautifully. Furthermore, she called me 'Tony' and not 'Anthony' like Mrs Hughes at Avenue Road. Miss Warmoll was somewhat buxom, with her hair tied back in a Victorian bun, and with rimless spectacles on the end of her nose.

My first music book was 'A Child's Primer' which was the starting book for thousands like me, and I seemed to take to the piano from the start. Nina Warmoll taught me scales and arpeggios without the use of a scales manual, and I actually enjoyed running up and down the keys playing the scales of C, E and others. I always had trouble with the chromatic scale (and still do): that is, the scale that uses all the notes, both black and white, in consecutive order.

In the beginning I found playing enjoyable, and practice sessions were not so bad until it came to warm summer evenings when all my friends were outside playing. It was that then piano practice became a chore and I probably skimped a lot of it. I love the bit of Victor Borge where he is describing the childhood of Tchaikowsky when he says, 'Peter was born in Votinsk. On summer evenings he did not play in the streets with all the other little boys of Votinsk ~ because when he was eight his parents moved to St Petersburg!'

Like many other pianists I learned pneumonics. The spaces of the music staff spelled F-A-C-E, and the lines of the treble were E.G.B.D.F. ~ 'Every Good Boy Deserves Favours'. Nowadays, due to the fact that 'favour' is classed as archaic, it is substituted with 'football'. Well, what else? I suppose aspiring girl pianists learnt the same pneumonic then and never considered that it was touching on a male domain. The spaces in the bass staff were A-C-E-G, which was 'All Cows Eat Grass'. Not a particularly awe-inspiring statement.

One day I received my first real piece of music; that is to say, not an exercise type of piece in a book, but a folded sheet music copy of a piece called 'Sur la Glace de Sweetbriar', which I proudly told my parents meant 'On The Ice At Sweetbriar'. My next proud moment was showing Miss Warmoll my own composition I had carefully written out on manuscript entitled 'The Saturday Waltz'. I remember how she helped me to reconstruct with chord work and various bits of alteration, and how she encouraged me to go on. It was my first venture into writing music which perhaps was how I came to write operettas in years after.

Miss Warmoll's concerts were well known and people flocked to the Baptist Church, Dereham Road, and enjoyed listening to the talents of her pupils in the church hall. Proceeds were to the Baptist Church, which was where Nina Warmoll worshipped. As a very young pupil

I took part and for the beginning of the concert sat on the front of the stage playing Ludo with my friend Graham Packer. I don't quite know why we were doing this; perhaps we were meant to be decorous, or just an amusing aside for the front row. At one point I had to stand up and recite a poem. It was without script and was entitled 'I Bought My Mother A Wooden Spoon', being the first line of the poem. I don't remember how it went on, but did manage to complete it without fault or prompt, being beamed at by my proud parents. I do remember some very fine piano playing at the concert in question, and in particular from a 'big boy' called Brian Spelman. I knew I wanted to play like he did and told Miss Warmoll so, 'You will one day,' she said, 'if you practise hard.' I was always being told that by my uncles and aunts, and others, as well as Miss Warmoll. There is a lovely story of the music student lost in London and chancing to meet Sir Thomas Beecham, 'How do I get to the Albert Hall?' he asked Sir Thomas. 'Practise, my boy, practise,' replied the great man.

Concerts were not always held in church halls however. Miss Warmoll arranged with parents of her pupils to have informal concerts with tea in their homes. Two such concerts I can well recall: one was at 28 Whitehall Road in Norwich, the home of Mrs Woodcock, her daughter Sonia being one of Miss Warmoll's pupils. Each pupil had to play a carefully rehearsed composition in a set programme arranged by our teacher who was present, after which there was the reward of tea. This was not the days of big macs or slices of pizza, but sandwiches, cakes and, of course, jelly and cream. I seem to remember that most of the pupils were girls ~ creatures whom I found giggly and annoying at that age. Naturally, just a few years on, my opinions changed and, indeed, in my mid-teens I fell hopelessly and helplessly in love with Sonia Woodcock, my first 'puppy love' which hurts worst of any when it ends!

I went with my parents to other concerts, and at one I listened to some superb playing by a Mrs Giles whose name I think was Mollie. She played the shortened version of the 'Warsaw Concerto' which was popular at the time, it being played on film screen by Anton Walbrook in 'Dangerous Moonlight'. I listened to Mrs Giles, totally enraptured, and knew I wanted to play like that some day.

I was taken to the circus, and whilst I enjoyed all the acts, I really had eyes only for the wonderful band, all colourfully dressed and making such a wonderful sound. Like all small children, I was amazed how the horses in particular kept in time with the musicians, but of course learned years afterwards that it was the other way round ~ the band kept in time with them.

Walt Disney hit the headlines with 'Snow White And The Seven Dwarfs', and my parents took me to see it ~ my first film. I thought it was wonderful and was bowled over by Frank Churchill's music. Of course, I didn't know it was by Frank Churchill then, but learned that years after, when I bought the Song Album. I suppose today such films would be tame stuff, what with 'Star Wars' and similar films filling young minds, although I do believe Disney is still popular with such productions as 'Jungle Book', and 'Mary Poppins', even though the great man has long since left us.

At Avenue Road school music was a very important part of education as I have said, all thanks to the headmistress Mrs Hughes. A very skilled violin teacher called Leonard Ward visited the school each week to teach some pupils the art of playing the violin. I did not express much interest, but my brother began lessons at a very young age with Mr Ward and proudly brought home a school violin and bow in a somewhat battered case and commenced practice. I suspect all parents on first hearing the sounds produced by their prodigy immediately have misgivings about the choice of instrument. In years after, when I became a head of school music, parents would express such feelings to me. However, as time went on the sound improved and tunes began to replace parrot squawkings! There had been a number of excellent pupils of Leonard Ward at the school: I remember the school listening entranced at the playing of Paul Doe in assembly. He went on to become a splendid musician. Others were Colin Clouting, whom I met so many years later when he was head of music at the Hewett school: Donald Sparrow, John Martin, John Dawson, and John Winsworth, the latter coming into my life later both as violinist and bass player. I suppose the most famous was John Bacon who was a contemporary of my brother David and, indeed, they played their violins together and were the top two in Leonard Ward's orchestra. John went on to become a very proficient violinist and was leader of the Welsh Symphony Orchestra and, I believe, was with the Berlin Philharmonic. My brother, alas, didn't continue with the instrument, even though Mr Ward had told my father that David was the better of the two. One wonders what he might have achieved had he gone on with his tuition: 'Practise, my boy practise . . .'.

The little German with the 'tache began bombing raids on Norwich ~ well, not him personally of course, but it meant disruption to our school lessons, and in a most orderly fashion we tripped down into the underground shelters built in the playground. Once inside we chanted arithmetical tables and had general knowledge quizzes, but we also sang, unaccompanied of course since the air-raid shelter was not equipped with a piano! Actually, if there had been a piano down there it wouldn't have survived long since those shelters were very wet at times. I suppose the singing wasn't bad really but I do recall the hideously monotonous strains of 'Ten Green Bottles' and 'One Man Went To Mow'. I was quite thankful when the all-clear sounded and we were able to surface again and back to sanity. Naturally we all knew it would re-commence the next day and the infernal men and their dog would go mowing once more. I can never quite forgive Adolf for many things . . .!

Sometimes I would catch the 'bus home from school which meant waiting for it at a stop at the corner of Havelock Road, off Earlham Road. One sunny afternoon as I stood there I heard the most beautiful piano music coming from the house on the corner. My mother had always told me that staring was rude, but on this occasion I was transfixed as I made out a lady dressed in black playing a grand piano in the room facing the road. She was playing the most wonderful music, and with a touch that only the best can achieve. I stayed listening until the 'bus came but a long time afterwards I caught the 'bus home just to wait by her house and hope to hear her play, and to think 'One day I want to play like that . . .' Years after, I met her. Her name was Beryl Cross and she played the piano for all kinds of functions, and accompanied all kinds of performers in and around Norwich during her musical career. Of course, I never mentioned how I used to listen as a schoolboy to her playing, which would have been touching upon the sensitive area of a woman's age ~ something I would never do.

At home I loved to listen to radio, and in particular the bands. 'Music While You Work' was a popular programme each day for those who were working for the war effort, and the songs of the forties flooded the airwaves. There was also a programme called 'The Organist Entertains' which was music played by the theatre organists of the day, and I particularly liked Reginald Foort, Reg Dixon, and Bobby Pagan. Our favourite programme was 'Children's Hour' and my first introduction to classical piano music came for Helen Henschel who would play and talk about music. I loved her signature tune which was the 'Berceuse' from Faure's 'Dolly Suite' and she told us that Dolly was the name of Faure's little girl and the suite was written for her and was nothing to do with dolls. If ever I was ill in bed my mother would let me listen to the radio and the music would give me the greatest possible enjoyment; I particularly remember how I would lie looking out of the window at the beautiful blue sky with fluffy clouds and listening to the wonderful opening strains of Vaughan Williams' 'Fantasia On Greensleeves'. Even today when I hear it played I am reminded of days of lying and looking at summer skies. At Christmas I heard John Masefield's 'Box Of Delights' with the wonderful music of Victor Hely-Hutchinson's 'Carol Symphony' and loved every moment of it.

I expect every family has a musical uncle ~ one who sings. Our family was blessed with two, no less. They both had very fine voices in the baritone-bass range. Uncle Herbert, my father's brother, would belt out 'Song Of Songs', 'You're Mine' and 'You Are My Heart's Delight' on Saturday evenings, or other occasions when the family got together at my Aunt Violet's house in Buxton Road, Norwich. Aunt Violet was my father's sister, and she was married to my Uncle Godfrey, the other singing uncle. His stentorian voice would thunder out 'Friend O' Mine' and 'The Floral Dance' and it became something of a contest between the two, possibly to see which one could shatter a window or wine glass! Uncle Godfrey belonged to a concert party called 'The Jolly Boys' and would go round entertaining at various clubs and smoking concerts. Thinking about it nowadays, with smoking cigarettes and cigars such taboo, it is a wonder to me that the concert parties were able to utter any musical sounds with a room filled with noxious fumes! I believe Uncle Godfrey's concert party consisted of two singers, a pianist and a comedian.

So it is that I remember nights at my Aunt Violet's home with songs around the piano. Her piano was an 'Amyl' like our own, and was to come into my life again later.

Both my uncles shared another thing, apart from their singing voices: they loved to gargle and lubricate with malt and the barley, which I assume did wonders for the vocal chords and loosened them up for each performance as it were. Strangely enough my own father didn't drink, not because he had any religious feelings about alcohol: it was just that he didn't like the stuff!

During the war years my mother's half-sister, Flora (Nell), came to live with us to escape the blitz in London. My brother and I were very fond of her, and because she was so much younger than my mother and father we almost looked upon her as a big sister. She worked in Norwich and, naturally enough, brought home young men admirers to Earlham Road to visit our family. Some were English, and some were American since we had quite a few USA personnel in the city at the time. At least two of Flora's boyfriends played the piano and many evenings were filled with the sound of beautiful piano playing. Sometimes it would be late and my brother and I had to go to bed, but I would listen to the sound coming up the stairs to our bedroom and being enchanted, again by the familiar 'syncopated' sounds. I lay there, listening, and thought 'One day I want to play like that . . .'

I loved the songs sung during the war and knew them all. The radio was a wondrous source of music then, and there were some very fine bands that played, and singers that poured out all the favourites: songs like 'I'll Be Seeing You', 'A Nightingale Sang In Berkeley Square' and 'We'll Meet Again'. I find it incredible that such beautiful songs were born out of such a terrible and tragic time.

In 1945 the war ended and there was great rejoicing; at the front the rejoicing was the ending of hostilities and the lads coming home. In our household my father, and more particularly my mother, were rejoicing because I had gained a scholarship to Norwich School.

CHAPTER 3

'The Music Goes Round And Around'

n September of 1945 I went to Norwich School, following in the footsteps of a boyhood hero, Viscount Horatio Nelson. I was put into Parker House, named after a bishop who stuck his nose into everything and from whom we get the expression 'a nosy parker'.

If I was looking for a school with a musical tradition, a strong music department, and a large orchestra, it was certainly not to be found at Norwich School. Certainly there was a choir led by an excellent choir master and organist named Henry Blakeney. If he was indisposed then the organ was played by Mr Beckwith, another fine organist.

Norwich School was highly academic and music played only the whisper of a part in its life in those days. Boys who wanted to play an instrument made their own arrangements ~ or at least their parents did. Aspiring violinists and viola players went to Miss Elsie Edmund's house in the Lower Close and many became very fine musicians. I knew of no boy who learned a brass or woodwind instrument however. I remember during one lunch break how there was great excitement by the gym at one end of the playground. Dozens of boys were gathered around the doorway and the open windows listening to three fellow pupils making the most wonderful jazz music on the piano, saxophone and drums. I listened, enthralled at the sound, and realised they hadn't a note of printed music between them. I cannot recall who the pianist was, but the very versatile sax player was Johnnie Byles, and the very talented young drummer was Rex Cooper, both of whom I was to meet later when school days were done. Of course, the number of boys crowding round increased and I believe the jazz came to a stop when the then headmaster, Andrew Stephenson, intervened. Perhaps he thought the large audience might get out of hand, or maybe he didn't like that particular brand of music making. In my young mind, however, the seeds of jazz music had been sown.

There were a few more excellent musicians came out of Norwich School and in years after made their mark in their different ways. In the field of classical music came Angus Watson, a fine violin and viola player whom I met years after when he was examining music pupils in my care at Princes Street Church where music exams were conducted. Two dance pianists come to mind in Roger Cooke, who ran a very fine trio, and Johnny Lofty who later took up the sax and ran various small combos. There was David Huke, a fine musician who I believe became a well-known organist and choirmaster in London, and Brian Harvey who played both violin and double-bass though, as musicians witticise, not at the same time! Another friend was Colin Campbell who became a splendid drummer.

In the meantime, my lessons with Nina Warmoll continued, although I cycled to her home at Maud Street for my weekly lesson. The house, standing on the corner of Maud Street and St Philips Road, was white painted, tall, and very elegant. Miss Warmoll's music room was exquisite: she had a beautiful piano which looked a lovely piece of furniture and played like a dream. On the piano was a metronome ~ Denis Norden once said musicians keep them instead of garden gnomes ~ and against the wall to the left of the piano stood a music cabinet. This fascinated me as when each drawer was pulled open the front of the drawer dropped down to reveal all the sheet music there to take out easily. It was a very beautiful piece of furniture and I often wondered what became of it. I imagine an Antiques Roadshow expert would put an astronomic price on it today. The piano had an adjustable stool, something which I have always wanted.

In another room lived Miss Warmoll's mother whom I rarely saw and who would often call for her daughter who would have to leave and go to see to her needs. Occasionally Miss Warmoll's brother from Gidea Park in Essex paid a visit and I met him on a few occasions and found him a very charming man. Miss Warmoll herself was very fond of her niece, Margaret, and often visited Gidea Park to stay with the family.

Nina Warmoll was in some way related to Sir Alfred Munnings, the famous artist and painter of horses. One day I went with my mother to have tea with Miss Warmoll at Lyon's restaurant on The Walk in Norwich. As we were having tea Miss Warmoll produced from her handbag a drawing in pencil (or possibly black ink) of a cat done by Sir Alfred and said it was for me. It was signed by him and I took it home with me. Sadly, through the mists of time as they say, the drawing was lost. I wonder what it would be worth now? If only I had realised its value then, but life is full of 'if onlys', as I know only too well.

Miss Warmoll inspired me to carry on with my piano playing in many ways, although I have to say that I didn't practise as much as I ought to have done. I would tell her about pieces of music I had heard on the radio that I liked and she would produce the sheet music for me if she thought I could manage it. Pieces would be added to my library of music, and the cost added to my father's bill which he never seemed to mind. I liked what was termed 'light music', and I remember having 'Parade Of The Tin Soldiers' by Jessel, and 'The Grasshoppers' Dance' by a gentleman called Bucalossi. Later on I played 'Chanson De Matin' by Elgar, and 'None But The Lonely Heart' by Tchaikowsky which I found both sad and very moving. I was featured in a school concert held at Norwich Maddermarket and Nina Warmoll patiently coached me to play Rubinstein's 'Melody in F', the tattered copy of which I still have ~ marked with her hand-written notes.

Miss Warmoll was a very fine pianist and occasionally she would play to me, either one of my pieces as it should be played, or something from her own repertoire. Her playing seemed so easy and effortless, the mark of the professional, and I used to sit back and take in her beautiful playing in wonderment.

Then came the day that I found I could play without music. I'm never quite sure how it happened but it just did. Perhaps memory played its part, perhaps the study of scales, arpeggios and chords came into its own, or perhaps I received some divine inspiration! I can't say, but I found it very exciting when it happened. I don't think I rushed off to tell Nina Warmoll, although I had already found myself playing from memory some of the pieces she set, which she didn't seem to discourage as I knew some music teachers did.

Like all my fellow pupils I took exams. I wasn't good at exams at all, and all examiners seemed awesome and even frightening. As a matter of fact I still held that impression when, in later years as a music teacher, I took pupils to their exams. I did scrape through my exams, and also my theory exam, but I hated them nevertheless. I remember that one of my examiners was the composer York Bowen who gave me some words of encouragement when I told him I had composed a few pieces. Sadly, pressure of school work forced me to end my lessons with Miss Warmoll which I realised afterwards was something I would live to regret. I later met her several times and we would stop to have a chat and hear about my progress and about my family. She was an exceptionally gifted music teacher and I think she inspired me more than any other person with my musical life, and I am very proud to think I was once her pupil and she my teacher. She was still teaching shortly before she died in her ninetieth year.

My teenage years were very full and I developed this love of jazz that I spoke of. My friend, Graham Packer, who in the end didn't play anything at all, used to come with me down to Willmott's store and try out 78s galore in their listening cubicles. They were mostly jazz, although sometimes a popular song caught our fancy and we'd try that. I think the staff at Willmott's got a bit tired of us taking a cluster of records to listen to and then buying only one!

On Sundays we attended Holy Trinity Church and I became Sunday school pianist, taking the week's hymns to Miss Warmoll for practice purposes.

Graham and I decided to go to dancing lessons and we went to Elm Hill dancing studio run by Eileen Page. Each Saturday evening we would go there, clutching our half-crown fee and the Pink-un football paper, and sit at one end of the room while all the girls sat at the other! Eileen Page would then try and cajole us into dancing a waltz or quickstep with some girl or other. Sometimes Eileen Page's husband, Laurie Singer, would come along and, sergeant major fashion, frog march the boys onto the dance floor to dance with a girl they positively detested. The music was all Victor Silvester which although boring, was perfection in tempo and which was to be my guide for dance tempo when I became a dance musician. Victor Silvester had two pianists playing at the same time, the one playing the basic melody and the other improvising or extemporising on the melody: they were brilliant.

When we were able to dance a bit and not give the appearance of having two left feet we went to dances and, of course, began to show some interest in girls! I think the most elegant dancing place in those days was the Arlington Ballroom, just off Newmarket Road. It was a touch of class, and the orchestra was first rate led by violinist Frank Kelly. I went to some private parties there and it was always the tops for me: I particularly remember there was a lovely grand piano.

Our family went for a week's summer holiday each year to Gorleston-on-Sea. Whilst we were there we always paid a daily visit to the Floral Hall where there was a lovely swimming pool. The attraction for me was the ballroom where you could sit round the edge and watch the dancers going round the dance floor to the music of Eddie Gates at the electric organ. Eddie was blind and lived in Norwich at St Matthew's Road. He had become blind at the age of three after having measles. He was superb on that organ and with the mike used to announce the dances and have anniversaries and spot prizes and such like. One day I went and told him it was my parents' wedding anniversary (August 1st) which he announced and my father and mother had to get on the dance floor and waltz to 'The Anniversary Waltz'.

When later on I became a teacher, Eddie's daughter, Eileen, was one of my pupils. Whenever I met Eddie I only had to say his name and he knew it was me, something which lots of other musicians used to relate. He was a splendid musician who was so well known and loved by many. He ended his career playing the organ at the crematorium.

My Aunt Flora went back to London after the war and married Bert Colman who was a pianist. Well, he had to be, didn't he? We went to London to visit them living in my grandmother's house near the Elephant and Castle. They had a huge upright piano which had three pedals. Victor Borge, in one of his acts, says, 'I'm often asked why a grand piano has three pedals. Well, it's easy really; the middle one is to separate the other two.' With Bert's piano the middle pedal, when depressed, took the action away from the felts so that you got a jangle-box effect, rather like Winifred Attwell used to achieve. That piano was in fact so huge that Bert said it had to be hoisted up and brought in through a window. I do wonder what happened to that fine instrument.

Bert himself played without music and I used to be amazed at the keys he would play in. He seemed to play all the black notes, and I realised he was playing in keys such as Gb and B for a lot of the time. He had a trio and they would go around parts of London doing dances, although he had nearly given it up by the time he married Flora.

In 1950 our family moved again, this time to Thorpe Hamlet ~ to 111 St Leonard's Road, the very road where my mother had lived as a girl. After the move my mother became ill and went to live with friends. For a time I was sleeping at the old house alone, and one dark night I was awakened by the wind banging the window shutters. I took courage and went and closed the shutters and was about to return to the bedroom when I distinctly heard the sound of the piano downstairs. I froze, with my thoughts racing. Of course, had common sense prevailed I would have realised that no intruder in his right mind would start running his hands over piano keys, unless he happened to be a compulsive pianist unable to resist the ivories! The next few moments would have received an Oscar for a Hammer horror-type movie. I went slowly down the stairs, heart thumping, and gingerly opened the sitting room door. There, scampering over Amyl's keys, was a tiny kitten! It had somehow managed to get in though an unshuttered window and thought it would be great fun to give me a literal rendering of 'Kitten On The Keys', a fiendishly difficult piano novelty number from the twenties which became the signature tune of a very fine pianist, Kay Cavendish. Naturally I breathed a huge sigh of relief, and, indeed, laughed out loud as I deposited the intruder in the garden and returned to sleep.

Several of my friends at school started to organise dances at church halls which, I suppose, were the forerunners of discos since the music was supplied by gramophone playing, in the main, the inevitable Victor Silvester. I had become a member of the church Youth Fellowship where very often I played the piano, and I think it was there that my friends persuaded me to play for the dances. Initially I played solo, but I realised that for dancing I needed other musicians, not only to make more sound, but to add some rhythm to the whole thing.

So it was then that I recruited a drummer who was at Norwich School called Roger Hook, a trumpet player called Richard Brown who was at the rival City of Norwich School, and another Norwich School friend, Chris Spalding on the violin. We had a couple of practice runs and then played for the school dance. It probably sounded terrible, but we were showered with praise and not rotten fruit, and were asked to another, this time at the CNS school. I felt that the sound was a bit thin and realised that what was needed was a saxophone, or at least, someone playing one. By this time, of course, Johnnie Byles had left school and I knew nothing of his whereabouts. Somebody ~ I can't recall who ~ told me about a sax player named Jack Wilkinson who might come along and play. I wrote down his address, which was 17 Angel Road, and I cycled down from St Leonard's Road to find him. I didn't know anything about him, nor what I was really expecting of him. Here was I, a raw schoolboy musician, about to ask a much more mature man if he would come and join my 'band' for a school dance. Frankly, I was worried and a bit nervous!

As it turned out I had no need for any worries at all. He came to the door, a short, slightly built figure, somewhat shy, but with such twinkling eyes and wonderful smile that I knew I liked him from the first. He asked me into his front room, a room I was to know very well over the next years, and he asked me how he could help. I told him about the dances and the other musicians and that we simply had a few sheets of music and played for quick-steps, some fox-trots, and waltzes, with a few party dances thrown in. Jack readily accepted the invitation to come and play but apologised profusely that he didn't read music! I said I didn't think that important and we arranged that he would come and play at the dance without any rehearsal and fit in as best he could. He wasn't very sure where the CNS actually was, but would be there, never fear.

I was nervous, excited, and apprehensive about having a band playing for the dance which included a sax player with whom I had never played, never heard, and didn't really know. I don't recall how Jack got to the school, but he was there all right. I have an idea in the back of my mind that he had a friend called John Bussey who lived in Salisbury Road who had a van, and I think it was he who supplied a microphone and amplifier; but I can't be sure. All I do know is that as soon as Jack Wilkinson began to play his sax with the other musicians I just marvelled at his ability and the dexterity of his playing. As for the young dancers, they went wild about the sound and called for more and more. To them it was something new, from the dreary records to a live band, albeit dreadful in quality to an expert, but real music coming from instruments they could see. When the dance came to an end we were surrounded by admirers, and in particular Jack who, I was to learn afterwards, was never one to like lots of words of praise. We parted that night with his promise that he would always come and play his sax whenever I needed him, if he were free. I now knew where he lived and I had only to call round. He had no telephone for in those days telephones were not common in our homes. I had found a man who was to play a very big part in my musical life; Jack Wilkinson, one of the nicest men I ever knew. A sentiment that is echoed by many musicians I know.

Of course, I had but one thought I mind now. I must form a proper dance band, give it a name, organise rehearsals, get some cards and printed notepaper and, more importantly, get some engagements. Without having the faintest idea how it would all work out I had the stationery done and the cards printed. I called the band 'The Maxinas', a name I fancied after seeing it printed on the cover of an old time dance album among a list of dances. The cards were placed in various places for the public to take notice of this latest phenomenon, and lo and behold, along came our very first engagement, the first booking for The Maxinas, our first step into the world of dance bands.

CHAPTER 4

'Let's Face The Music And Dance'
The First Gig

A young couple came to the house one dark evening who said they were getting married and wanted a dance band to play for their wedding reception. As I remember, my father seemed to speak a lot on my behalf, extolling the virtues of the Maxinas and how they would be ideal for the occasion. That he had never actually heard the band play didn't seem to be of any import and he really ought to have had an accolade for being my Mister Ten Percent. I never considered at the time that my father could have moonlighted from his role of headmaster to be an entertainment agency. Certainly in time to come my mother was to be my telephone secretary with the most wonderful charm and PR that any boss would cherish.

The wedding pair seemed to be duly overawed by my father's appraisal of the band and agreed at once to the price. They gave us the date, the time and other details and went off happy to think they had secured the services of Norwich's own Glenn Miller and his entire band ~ well, three others. As for me, well I was over the moon: our first 'gig', for you see by now I had learned some of the dance band jargon and went around using it freely like a man of many years experience in the business.

The venue for the reception was the Roxley Hall on the Yarmouth Road at Thorpe on a Saturday evening. There was a major set-back for me, however: my new found friend Jack Wilkinson was booked elsewhere and couldn't play. He recommended his friend, Brian Halesworth who played the clarinet and I duly went to see him. He agreed to play, although he admitted that his 'busking' ability was limited and nowhere near Jack's. (Here you will notice that I have used another piece of dance band vocabulary. In those days it meant the ability to play minus music but nowadays has come to mean entertaining pedestrians in city centres and a cap on the ground for contributions). Brian said he would bring along his music library together with a list of things he could busk.

My next problem, believe it or not, was obtaining a drum kit for Roger Hook. No, he hadn't one and if he were to be the drummer for a wedding function, then he really would need a set of drums, plus an odd cymbal or two. He did actually have a pair of drum-sticks but that would have been like having a steering wheel and no car. For our two school dances, Roger had 'borrowed' or hired a set of drums from a shop in Magdalen Street owned by a Mr George Capps, a sallow faced man who seemed to have difficulty in smiling I remember. On those two occasions he had taken the drum kit out of the window and rented it to Roger, rather like a pawn-broker in 'The Glenn Miller Story', only in that case it was a trombone. Mr Capps' shop was full of various musical instruments, all for sale at prices none of us could afford but in dubious state of repair anyway. This time the drum kit was for sale only and definitely not for hire; Capps was adamant and we were stuck with a king sized problem. Into the picture stepped another father ~ Roger's father, who was a detective inspector with the City Police. Roger explained our problem to him and Mr Hook reassured us that we would have the drum kit, never fear. He was as good as his word and within the hour the huge bass drum, together with the side drum, hi-hat and cymbal were at the Hook's house. Now I have no idea how Inspector Hook achieved such a miracle; whether or not he had some mystic influence over George Capps I shall never know. All that mattered to us was the we now had a set of drums and even a set of brushes which Mr Capps had thrown in.

We arrived at Roxley Hall on bikes, since none of us had any other transport, wearing our best suits and bow ties and all eager to play. Roger was towing the drum kit on a home-made trailer which would have doubtless given George Capps an apoplectic fit had he known.

We set up on the stage with the help of my friend Graham Packer who had come along to assist and enjoy himself. I suppose he would have been the forerunner of a modern day 'roadie', although Graham on the occasion was acting unpaid.

We tried to give the appearance of being highly professional by tuning up with the piano, an instrument which would have been given around seven out of ten by me in my present day ratings. Pianos I have met in my career have had rating which have ranged from full marks to minus figures, something to which I will refer later in this book. Tuning up does have a purpose of course as well as sounding highly technical. I remember much later on in my career that I was playing with Paul Donley's Yare Valley Jazz Band and a dancer came up to Tony Cleary, the bass player and said, 'I notice that you didn't tune up at the start of playing.' Tony, who is a marvellous wit said quietly, 'No, we tend to do that afterwards.'

The hall was packed with guests of all shapes and sizes, each clutching a glass of something or other and watching us with expressions of curiosity, suspicion and it has to be said, some doubt. The bride's father, a portly man with an extremely red face with nose to match and what appeared to be a great capacity for brown ale insisted that we 'give 'em something lively. They love something lively. You get 'em started and there'll be one or two who can give 'em a song.'

Now this last remark is one guaranteed to cause a shudder among musicians, since most of us in our fraternity have had occasions when trying to follow or 'back' many a dubious vocalist has been either difficult or well-nigh impossible.

However, things began well enough. Everyone danced around happily though I was quite intrigued with some couples who managed to negotiate a quick waltz clutching a small baby between them at the same time.

The bride's father kept urging us to 'keep it lively' and by way of encouragement sent trays full of beer to the stage. Had we consumed it all, we would have been found drunk in charge of bicycles and in Roger's case, in charge of a drum kit. Graham had found a seat behind the piano and also a fire bucket into which he promptly poured the beer. When the bucket became full, he emptied the contents out of an adjacent window, presumably on to unsuspecting yet possibly grateful flowers and the whole system began again.

The aspiring singers began to besiege the stage just as the bride's father had promised. An enormous woman was pushed onto the stage by her admiring fans.

'Go on Ada ~ give us a song!'

Ada laughed uproariously and thumped me hard on the back.

'What shall we give 'em love?'

I really didn't mind although I did know she had given me a rather sore spot between my shoulder blades.

'Do you know 'I'll Be With You In Apple Blossom Time?'
Even today when you're asked such questions there's always that devilish streak in you to answer 'Why ~ what's happening then?', but of course you don't. There was a spate of those quickfire answers with song titles when people went into music shops. Gems like: 'Have you got 'Red Roses For A Blue Lady?'
'Sorry, this is a music shop not a florists.'
and . . . 'I'm wanting 'Someone To Watch Over Me'.
'Aren't we all dear?' and so on and so forth ad infinitum or probably ad nauseam.
Anyway I told the good lady that I did know her song and foolishly ventured to ask her what key she might like.
'Ooh, I don't know nothing about keys dearie. Just you follow me and we'll be all right.'
Well, Ada set off and we struggled to follow. Every so often I would find a note she had discovered and would hold it in triumph, only to lose sight of it in the next bar. Eventually I came close to her key which seemed good enough but the other problem was her sense of timing which was practically non-existent. We'd all keep losing half a bar or so and then making it up later on in all the wrong places. As she came to the end, Ada crescendoed to a shriek amidst roars from the admiring crowd. They howled for more, quite naturally. Ada gargled with a light ale and began another number. It was worse than the first: none of us knew it properly and that certainly seemed to include Ada. We made valiant efforts to keep in time and tune and just when it seemed that the song would die the death, Ada went into her dance routine. Raising her dress high to reveal long pink bloomers, she cavorted all over the stage while the guests went wild, encouraging Ada to achieve contortions she might have reached in former years. The result was that she collapsed in an exhausted heap among the drums, whereupon the bride's father suggested it might be a suitable time for an interval, so that the cake could be cut and Uncle Fred could take over on the piano.
So it was to a background of quaint janglings of numbers with indeterminate beginnings, middles and endings from Uncle Fred that we made our way across the floor to the tea room. In all probability

when church fetes were functioning, what was actually served in this particular room was tea ~ but not so on this occasion.

Two large barrels of beer stood on the floor with their taps at the ready and two petite ladies, dressed in their wedding finery, though quite obviously not in compete control of their faculties, invited us to help ourselves.

'You'd best pour the drinks,' one of them said to a six-foot tall Roger, the drummer. 'You're a lot taller than I am.'

'Have some wedding cake,' said the other. 'It tastes good with beer. Here ~ dunk it in ~ like this.'

Whereupon, the two women, giggling away like five-year-olds, proceeded to saturate their pieces of wedding cake in draught bitter and gulp it down. Lots of other guests were doing the same thing but somehow none of us chose to sample this particular delicacy.

At last Uncle Fred was removed from the piano and the second half got underway. It seemed as though the various beverages being consumed were having effect in different ways. The people dancing seemed less sure of their steps and tended to cling hard to each other, presumably to prevent each other from falling over.

A non-dancing gentleman, however failed to sustain an upright position and just fell flat on his face without any pre-announcement. It took four men to carry him out into the fresh air of the evening. Several others followed suit and it seemed as if there were more outside than in at times.

I was fascinated by one cameo being acted out along the line of chairs at the side of the room. A small lad, about six years old I suppose, had a box of matches and taking one from the box, set light to the beard of the gentleman next to him, presumably his father, who was apparently sleeping off the effect of his thirst quenching. On the stage we watched. When the reaction came, it was a beauty. With a roar like a wounded moose, the sleeper beat out the blaze with one hand and belted his heir with the other.

All this time we couldn't help noticing that even though it was growing quite late, the bride and groom made no attempt to leave. They danced on in wedding clothes like the other guests although perhaps a shade closer and they did take a turn at dancing while holding a baby which we all supposed was good practice for the future.

The bride's father grew more and more excitable and his nose seemed grow redder. The dancers whirled on, some more guests achieved prostrate floor positions, glasses and bottles skidded about, the beer literally flowed, with our own supply continuing to make its way through the window and the caretaker of the hall began to look somewhat threatening.

Desperately he went though the motions of clearing away, but as fast as he marshalled chairs into the centre of the room with the idea of sweeping up, they were scattered again. All he managed to do was surreptitiously clout a few charming little junior guests now and then.

The bride's father, with a great beaming face and a bulging wallet came and paid me and once more Ada advanced upon us. This time she gave us a rendition of 'If You Were The Only Girl In The World' with the dancing couples and triplets joining in. The bride's father, not terribly sure of his directional stance, came to the piano to pay me again.

'But you've already paid me,' I said.

'Oh, nonsense boy,' he said, 'here you are.'

He brandished a bunch of notes which I took and immediately handed to the bridegroom who seemed surprised but not ungrateful.

The noise grew tumultuous, even though only a quarter of the guests were still in action and we began to wonder if this gig would end at all.

'End? We've only just begun!' shrieked Ada as the bride's father sidled round the piano, his face resembling a harvest moon.

'I'll settle up with you now,' he muttered, seemingly afraid the others might hear.

'You've paid me twice already,' I hissed. I was beginning to think that if all gigs were going to be as lucrative as this one, then we'd certainly come into the right business. A further fistful of notes followed, despite my protests.

'You've already paid me,' I said.

'Ah, that was for last time, only don't you tell my old woman,' was the mysterious reply.

'Well naturally I won't,' I promised. I hadn't the faintest idea what he was talking about but anyhow it was another bonus for the surprised bridegroom who must have thought that weddings were based on piecework.

At last, the caretaker in ugly mood ~ to match his appearance ~ told the company that he had sent for the police which suggested to us lads that it might a good time to leave. Not to leave the assembled company without any music I persuaded someone to revive Uncle Fred, who made his way to the piano by sheer instinct.

As we bade our farewells, the bride's father asked me whether he had paid me enough. I assured him that he had but he insisted on presenting me with his top hat which I was forced to wear as a sign of goodwill as we cycled away just as the police arrived.

It had been our first gig and most certainly one that we would never forget. I had always fondly imagined that the world of the dance band musician was full of glitz and glamour like the theatre world.

I rather think that wedding reception brought me heavily down to earth.

CHAPTER 5

'Such A Lot Of Living To Do'
Out Into The Working World

In 1951 I did something which was probably stupid and I should never have done. I ruined my educational prospect by walking out of Norwich School and getting a job at Norwich Union Fire Office. Why, I shall never really know.

I had hoped for a place in the NU Publicity Department and had been to see the charming Mr A P Cooper there who told me it was jobs for dead men's shoes and that I needed to go to London to study art.

Everyone seemed to go to Norwich Union; my furious headmaster was both rude and disdainful about such people but I went like one of the sheep he spoke of and started working there in the Motor Insurance Department.

I have to say that I hated everything about it all; the banal work which included filing, some extremely rude clerks, some very disagreeable departmental managers and their deputies and some very strange people with some extraordinarily weird habits.

Everything? Well, no not quite.

You see, I found there were quite a number of musicians there disguised as insurance clerks. Some I found and some of them found me; by that I mean that by some means or other they discovered that I played the piano and might just be useful for a gig or two somewhere.

The visits of musicians to my desk grew more and more frequent until my boss, Mr Fred Leeds said, 'You know Tony, this is an insurance company and you are employed as an insurance clerk ~ not as a musician.'

Although I respected what he said I did feel it was somewhat misdirected, especially when I knew of all the activities the clerks were involved in during office hours that had absolutely nothing to do with insurance.

At the desk next to me was a lovely man called Geoffrey Nicholson. I had become obsessed with finding out the titles of songs where I only knew a snatch to two of the melody. I would whistle or hum the tune to Geoff and he would tell me the song title. He was brilliant and I very rarely caught him out.

As soon as he had told me the name of the song, I would write it down and pop off after work down to Willson's Music Bazaar by Castle Steps and order it. They got to know me in there and would always wait in dreaded anticipation of what I was going to order next. Billy Willson himself was a grand old boy, going blind, who had been a fine musician in his day with a very popular local accordion band. I used to spend a lot of time and money in there and would enjoy my chats with Billy who was very well known to many Norwich musicians.

I hadn't been at Norwich Union very long when a very tall, quietly-spoken chap came to me and introduced himself as Roger Vickers. He said he had a band, that he played sax and would I play piano for him on Saturday at Barford Village Hall.

I knew where Barford was since I had cycled there many times from our Earlham home but I ventured to ask him how we would get there. When he told me he would take me on the back of his motorbike, I knew I would have to tell a lie to my parents for in no way would they allow me to go on the back of any motorbike.

I told them Roger had a car and would be taking me, something which I hated doing but I really did want to go and play. I forget now where he picked me up but we went on his bike, he first having told me how to travel pillion but I was terrified for the whole trip and vowed I would never do it again.

Barford Village Hall reminded me of a chicken shed with a stage and a few coloured lights dotted here and there. The 'dots' were all from sheet music with Roger occasionally playing his tenor sax reading over my shoulder.

We were a trio with a drummer, although I can't recall who it was. I don't remember an awful lot about it, except that Roger was quite pleased with what I'd done and said he would ask me again and I do remember that I got paid!

Of course I had now entered the real world of dance band musicians and I decided to buy the current magazine for such people ~ 'The Melody Maker'. In it were various articles about musicians and bands, instruments and music for sale and all the dates of well-known British and American bands.

The most intriguing part, however, were the ads of musicians offering their services. I was fascinated that so many sax players 'doubled' on violin, for example but the bit that really caught my eye was the mystifying word 'Ace' after each of the pianist's names who wanted work. I never really found out what it meant but assumed they were able to read anything and busk anything.

It was a superb weekly paper which in after years was to become a gutter rag.

Roger Vickers did ask me again to go on a gig, this time to Deopham near Wymondham, again at the village hall. We didn't go by motorbike but by car which belonged to his Norwich Union friend Gerry Cooper. The car was an Austin Ruby and into we stuffed ourselves and a whole lot of gear besides.

I recall that we encountered the usual wreck of a village hall piano and in this particular instance I opened the top of it to gain more sound and a huge swarm of moths flew out. Needless to say they had trimmed much of the felting with the result that the instrument sounded as if it were suffering from a dose of pleurisy. This, coupled with the fact that the music rest had been crudely repaired with string made my performance somewhat under par. However, the dance went well and since nobody commented on the piano playing, I assumed they were all used to its eccentric sounds.

Other musicians started to come into my life and I imagine that it was the word getting round that I was a pianist and available for dance gigs.

There was Jack Leggett whom I first knew as an accordion player and seemed to have a complete disregard for 'dots' and play everything and anything. He was a likeable chap who seemed to get plenty of work and I went with him a number of times. He suddenly produced a lovely new alto sax which he played as though he had been playing it all his life and really quiet well. Rumour had it that he had flogged his grandmother's war savings bonds to buy it, though I don't know how true that was.

Later on, Jack formed a bigger band called the Jack Rogers band (the Rogers part was from Roger Vickers who had joined him) which he led on sax and went to play at USAF bases.

There was Dave Norris, a drummer who had a small band and worked during the day at Chadd's, a gents' outfitters in Bedford Street. I went to play for him a few times and had an enjoyable time. I remember he had a very small drum kit which one jocular musician described as coming out of a Christmas cracker.

Tony Howard was another well-known Norwich musician who at one time had his father playing piano for him. He asked me to play for him at an RAF station. I remember we went by coach since he was taking a number of girls as partners for the servicemen.

Tony was a sax player, a very strict musician and I at the time was somewhat raw and naive. On the coach, as we went, he came and asked me if I was in the Union. Of course I said 'Yes', thinking he meant the Norwich Union where I worked. It seemed to satisfy him and I played without much incident except that all his music was proper band arrangements and not sheet music, something completely foreign to me. The result was that I didn't make a very good job of things and that it was obvious my best was not good enough. It goes without saying that Tony Howard never asked me to play again.

I had a similar experience with another fine band leader called Bert Priest when I 'depped' for his pianist at the Gala Ballroom in Norwich. The orchestrations were difficult and I struggled through.

Sometimes I met some very easy-going musicians who were really a delight to work for.

There was Joe Thoroughgood, who ran a band called the Joe Scott Trio. He played drums, I played piano of course and Derek Page played the guitar. I did one or two very enjoyable engagements with Joe and Derek, one in particular I remember at a country club near Brundall, a place where I believe Joe was trying to get a foothold. There was wine, food and girls in plenty and we had a super evening, Joe being such a laid-back fellow to work for and Derek was both a fine guitarist and a quietly-spoken gentleman.

My father, sensing how ill my mother was, decided to sell the house in St Leonard's Road and buy a house in Eaton Rise. At least he managed to buy a plot there and persuade a local builder to put up a house. The idea worked, thankfully and my mother recovered from her deep depression and when we moved into number 60 Ipswich Road she had regained much of her former zest and brightness.

There were often ads in the musical column of the Eastern Evening News which read something like:

> *'Pianist wanted to join local band; must be willing to rehearse, gigs waiting. Write . . . whoever, wherever.'*

It was my reply to such an ad that brought sax man Alan French to my door, accompanied by his drummer whom I ever only knew as 'Darkie' a nickname that I assumed was on account of his somewhat swarthy complexion.

They came from Bergh Apton, a place I'd barely heard of then and they spoke with lovely, soft broad Norfolk accents, although it has to be said that Darkie only echoed every word that Alan said.

They seemed to be quite enthusiastic about forming a dance band and said they had some definite bookings in the pipeline.

I played a few things on the piano just to show I could actually manage more than just a five-finger exercise, at which they grew quite excited ~ well, as excited as most reserved Norfolk people can get.

So it was that I went and played a few gigs with the Alan French Band at various village hops with the usual array of pianos ranging from the ailing to the chronically sick. I often think that it's a great pity the Japs didn't make electronic pianos in the forties instead of war: what a difference it would have made to music, to say nothing of the countless thousands of lives saved.

Alan was a very happy, laid-back musician who played his silver plated tenor sax quite well though without any vibrato. I remember his smile which extended from ear to ear and that Darkie remained the strong, almost silent type for as long as I knew him. I lost touch with them completely, although I did still have the Bergh Apton address and I often used to wonder what became of them. Since writing this book I have met up with Alan again when we looked at each other in a music shop (where else?) and in only a short time exchanged our life stories. He now lives at Swainsthorpe and still runs a duo, playing accordion and not sax.

Billy Beales was a plump, jolly avuncular sort of chap who played the alto sax, amongst other instruments. He was 'resident' at the Gothic Club, then situated on Hall Road, not far from the Tuckswood pub.

I played piano for him several times, accompanying his somewhat dated sound on the sax. A kind of whinny that Jack Wilkinson used to call the 'Nanny Goat' sound. I think it was achieved by lip or possibly throat vibration or as I have heard elsewhere by knee jerking.

Anyway it contributed to a rather quaint sound which amused some and satisfied others.

In the dance interval, Billy would have his refreshment and his rolled cigarette and chat about the years gone by which was like listening to musical history. His usual pianist was his wife Elsie whom I met much later in life and who also had a sister Dolly, a very fine cellist.

Billy would insist on calling me John (actually my second name) which was rather confusing to other musicians on the night who either knew me or whose name was John anyway.

I think Billy gave up playing when he found the music not to his liking and I saw him several times after that at his market stall in Norwich.

One day I received a call from a chap I knew by name only ~ Bill Burn, a drummer whose wife ran a dancing school I believe.

Would I play solo piano for afternoon tea at the Cliftonville Hotel, Cromer and afterwards with his band for the dinner dance there in the evening?

I agreed to go, Bill duly collecting me on the Saturday lunch time and off we sped in his two-seater coupé with the top open. I think it was an MG, cream in colour with a beautiful walnut fascia and with a capacity for very fast driving.

Under a blue sky dotted with white cotton wool clouds we hurtled through the villages in the direction of Cromer yelling conversation at one another above the whistling wind which buffeted us on our way. By the time we reached Cromer I looked like Worzel

Gummidge, my head was completely numb and I had practically lost my voice.

Bill introduced me to Tom Bolton, the hotel owner after which I went to do something about my hair which had all the appearance of having undergone electrical shock.

I made my way to the hotel lounge, placed a few selections on the piano and gingerly started to play to ladies and gentlemen of the upper age bracket who accompanied my playing with percussive clinking of cups, saucers and spoons and the occasional demure smile. It was sedate, elegant, a little of a passing age but nonetheless very pleasant for me, for it was my first real experience of being a hotel lounge pianist playing what I liked best. It was apparent that my audience enjoyed my music, since many stopped me afterwards to express their thanks while others reminisced about the shows they had seen in their younger days. The only thing spoiling my enjoyment was that I felt decidedly unwell which I concluded had been brought about by the journey there.

After the tea session Bill took me to the dining room which had a small ballroom floor and a stage in readiness for the dinner dance. We prepared the stage for the band which was to consist of Bill on drums, me on piano, a sax player and a bass player who lived locally. We were given a meal in a small room adjoining the kitchen, after which we played for the dinner dance, responding to the many requests from the diners.

I had a birthday card recently which showed a couple dining at a restaurant, their table close to the pianist. The gentleman diner is saying: 'Do you take requests?'

'Certainly,' says the pianist, 'what would you like?'

'I'd like you to stop playing.' is the reply.

Well, we played all the requests and the dancing stopped around 11pm I guess. Afterwards in the hotel car park we went to Bill's car where he put up the hood, much to my relief. I had been dreading the return journey minus any cover, but mercifully there were some drops of rain falling and it was none too warm either.

Bill told me he had some business to attend to in the hotel and left me with the car radio and a copy of 'Melody Maker'. I could only hazard a guess as to what his business might have been at that hour of night, suffice to say that he returned to the car about one and half hours later (yes, one and half hours) looking both dishevelled and somewhat guilt ridden.

We drove back to Norwich without too much to say to each other, he clearly finding difficulty in explaining away the business he had been conducting and I, both angry and feeling too ill to say a lot.

In the next few days that followed I was quite ill with a mild dose of something or other and I resolved never to go in an open tourer again. As for Bill Burn, I never saw or heard of him again.

What of the Maxinas?

Well, there didn't seem to be much work about for bands that could only manage to get about on bikes, in modern parlance I needed some wheels ~ other than my bicycle wheels of course.

It seemed as if the Maxinas were fading away, but there came the day when, wonder of wonders, the Norwich Union wanted my musical services. I don't mean the entire Norwich Union organisation, of course, but the Olde Tyme Dancing Department whose chief administrator, head instructor and general tour de force was a Mr Donny Land, who during the daytime did something or other in the Norwich Union Life Offices.

He was an Olde Tyme dancing fanatic, a martinet for perfect tempo and like a Regimental Sergeant Major, it was woe betide anyone who was out of step. He gave the impression of practising his dance steps while he walked, an impression that I quickly formed when he approached me ~ yes, me, a junior filing clerk on the first rung up to General Manager of the whole outfit.

He understood that I ran a dance orchestra called the Maxinas which had naturally stirred his excitement and curiosity, since it was the name of ~ yes, an Olde Tyme dance! As he talked to me, I soon realised that he thought my orchestra was Olde Tyme and that we were fully acquainted with all the dances from that era. Now at that point I could have said 'no, we don't play that sort of music', but I didn't, especially when he started to mention playing for regular Olde Tyme dances and actually getting paid for it.

I decided to bluff it out and assured Mr Land that we were very capable of doing all he wanted; after all we had played the Gay Gordons and a Barn Dance, so the rest would be simple, dead easy.

He began to recite a catalogue of dances: Boston Two Step? Oh yes. Dinky One Step? Easy. The Lancers, the Floradora Quadrilles? Oh yes (what the heck were the Floradora Quadrilles?)

Mr Land, well pleased with my apparent confidence agreed that the Maxinas and I should meet him and Mrs Land the following Wednesday evening in the Norwich Union Life Office canteen and go through the dance programme for content and tempo (I expect that should be tempi to a purist).

With that, he turned on his heels very deftly and went off down the corridor doing a practice run of a waltz cotillion or something similar.

Of course, at once Fred Leeds wanted to know what Donny Land was doing talking to me and still with my veins full of bluff and counter bluff, I told him it was business in connection with the Norwich Union Life Office and strictly confidential. Well, so it was but Mr Leeds, always one to have the last say, suggested that in future any business should be conducted out of office hours.

Straight after work I headed for Willson's Music Shop and Billy Willson himself who stared at me through his thick specs and said in his usual inimitable way, 'Tony, you've taken on something there and no mistake. Anyhow, you'll need these for a start,' and he handed me Volumes 1 and 2 of Francis and Day's Olde Tyme Favourite Dances album.

'Now pop upstairs,' he said, 'and see if Norman has got any records by either Harry Davison or Sydney Thompson.'

I did so and bought a record of Sydney Thompson and His Orchestra playing the Lancers which I hoped would give me some idea of what we would be expected to do.

On the following Wednesday evening we met up at the Norwich Union canteen for a run-through of things with Mr and Mrs Land. I had Brian Harvey on violin, Richard Brown on trumpet, Roger Vickers on tenor sax and a drummer whose first name was Maurice, though his surname has gone into the mists of time.

Roger and Richard had bits scribbled out of my two albums and Brian read over my shoulder while we put ourselves entirely in the hands of the master and his wife as to introductions, tempos and finishes. Of course, we really hadn't a clue but we strove to look and sound professional and I made the odd musical aside which I hoped would sound highly knowledgeable and technical. There were many stops and starts with Mr Land pointing out errors here and there but with the help of some encouraging smiles from Mrs Land, we seemed to come through what was, I suppose, an audition.

Donny Land set the date of the first dance which was to be at the canteen and realised we had got ourselves a booking.

We duly played for the said dance and apart from finding the Lancers and the Quadrilles the most testing of all the dances, we came through it very well and were engaged for another.

I think the best part of the actual evening for me was seeing the array of Top Men of the Union, dressed in their dinner jackets with their wives in splendid evening gowns and jewellery and all dancing to my band, my orchestra.

I recognised a great number of them and it gave me the greatest satisfaction to beam at them as they danced around, occasionally seeing a look which said 'Now where the blazes have I seen that young man before?'

We did quite a number of those Union dances and became very popular with the customers.

Gradually I noticed a few more smiles during office hours from some of the Top Men and I began to think that perhaps life at the Norwich Union Fire Office may not be that bad after all . . .

However, these small sparks of illusions were soon shattered when I was sent for by a certain Top Man who told me that having reached the end of my 'probationary period' with the Norwich Union, it was generally felt that I 'was not suitable for a permanent position there'.

I did not go down on my knees and plead to be taken on, nor did tiny tears glisten in my eyes but I did agree that he, in his profound wisdom was very probably right. Of course I could have said other things but my mother had always tried to bring me up to be a gentleman and I thought it prudent to leave it at that.

Faced with expulsion to be cast out into a cruel world I wondered where the next chapter in my life would lead me.

That question was very soon answered by King George VI. Well, not by him personally, you understand. He sent me an invitation in a brown envelope to choose to be one of his soldiers, sailors or airmen, serving him and the entire country for two whole years in what was known as National Service.

CHAPTER 6

'Some Day I'm Going To Murder The Bugler'
On His Majesty's Service

As my train crawled over the undulating, unfamiliar snow-covered countryside, I began to reflect what had happened in my life so far.

I'd been blessed with a lovely father and mother, a nice happy home, a younger brother and a good education both at home and at school. The latter I had ruined, having cut it short to go out and earn some money. I had been an obvious square peg in a round hole or the other way round at the insurance company and had completely wasted many months getting nowhere. The only real success had been with my music but I knew very well there was no future in that, professionally speaking and as for my other interest ~ art, competition in that field ran high too.

My father was a good teacher and now a headmaster who had entered a profession that did some good in the world and he was a respected figure in society. Well, perhaps not entirely by some of the parents he had to have dealings with sometimes, but generally speaking he was liked and admired and indeed, loved. So what should I do? Where would I go next?

I was roused out of my thoughts and daydreams by hearing shouting. I was to hear a lot of shouting in the next few weeks and this was just the beginning; we had arrived at a place called Warrington and I was bound for a spot I had never heard of called Padgate. On the icy cold platform the shouting grew louder and lots of young men like me were herded into cattle trucks and driven through the town of Warrington with thousands of cheering people (well, not really) out on to snow-covered roads and on to the infamous city of Padgate, which was to be our home for a week before going to our first posting ~ we knew not where ~ for 'square bashing'.

We were emptied out of the trucks to be greeted with more shouting from blue-coated gentlemen all intent on giving their instructions simultaneously which became somewhat chaotic. The whole thing reminded me of the old Norwich Cattle Market I had been taken to by my father when I was a boy.

That week saw us up each morning at an unearthly hour, wash in freezing water, parade in icy conditions, taken on a conducted tour of the camp with landmarks pointed out such as water towers from which several airmen had jumped to their deaths, fed on sliced bread spread with tomato ketchup and fitted out with costumes consisting of shirts that either strangled you round the neck or had room for your hand to slip inside; trousers and great coats that swept the ground; berets that sat on your heads like Melton Mowbray pies and boots that Doc Martin would have sold as rejects.

The shouting went on all that week but the blue-clad gentlemen assured us that they were like saints compared with those we would meet at our next holiday camp and that life at Padgate was a vicar's tea party by comparison.

With that happy news we all looked forward to moving on. To where? To a place in the snowy mountains of Staffordshire called Hednesford which bore all the charm of Stalagluft 111. I began to make rapid mental plans about an escape tunnel as we were marched through the snow to an enormous reception lounge ~ well, no: a huge RAF hangar and there the shouting I mentioned was magnified by the enormity of the place without any thought given to the acoustics by its architect I suspected.

There, inside, were more blue-coated gentlemen with shiny white teeth, huge mouths and throats, massive lungs which bawled out words, some of which were undecipherable, many unfit for print here and were clearly splendid graduates of the Royal Air Force Charm School.

I do not wish to dwell too much upon such 'gentlemen' but one could have been forgiven for thinking they would have been better suited to their task wearing black uniforms bedecked with swastikas. However, that is not the purpose of this book; so what of the music?

Well, some of it began at an ungodly hour on a tannoy relayed to each billet, which, if you were very unlucky, was positioned directly above your bed. I think they had one rather cracked record which followed Reveille of Les Paul and Mary Ford singing 'The World Is Waiting For The Sunrise' obviously singled out by some charming NCO with a completely warped sense of humour. The other side of the record which we would hear every night was 'How High The

Moon', clearly another choice of the same NCO, both sides being played every day until you could see visible signs of delirium coming from some of the inmates ~ sorry, conscripts.

On the very first morning at parade came the question from the sergeant I'd been anticipating.

'Any musicians here, step forward!'

I'd heard all about this one: you step forward and you're told the station piano has to be shifted.

'Remember,' said my informer, 'in the RAF never volunteer for anything.'

Nevertheless, despite such warnings I stepped forward with several others.

'Instrument?' was the question barked at everyone and the replies came in variety:

'Tenor horn' 'Clarinet' 'Trombone' 'Saxophone', 'cello' ('cello?') and from me 'Piano' which gave cause for a Glaswegian gentleman with two chevrons and a fanaticism for Heart of Midlothian FC to pull a face and repeat the word quite loudly and unpleasantly just as if I'd said 'UFO'.

His sneer quickly disappeared however, when the sergeant said to me, 'Report to Sarnes' Mess this evening at 1900 hours to play for the NCO party' and to everyone else, 'Report to Warrant Officer Wilson now.'

I ventured to ask if I should go with the others to WO Wilson and despite a further disparaging look from the Hearts fanatic, the sergeant indicated that I should go since the WO might have a use for me. The Warrant Officer at the Music Hut was tall, wavy-haired and smiling ~ in fact the first real human being we'd seen for many days. He actually spoke like a human being too and used English words we could understand ~ a pleasant change from the uncouth foulness of the parade ground gauleiters.

He thought the cellist might try a tenor horn and I might be at home with clash cymbals seeing that pianos are not usually featured in military bands. I accepted this great post of responsibility with glee and took my place alongside the rest of the percussion section.

Music was dished out and a practice session began with the WO conducting with his baton in the right hand and drawing on his cigarette with the left. I'm not sure which of us was following which hand but the resultant sound was horrible. I think the overall effect made WO Wilson nervous, for he chain-smoked for the entire session, literally lighting one from another in brown nicotined fingers.

There was great joy among all the newly-found musicians that band practice would be every morning instead of 'square bashing' with the others but my heart sank when he said this would not include the percussion. My dismay was short-lived, however, since he came over and asked me if I knew anything about dance music and dance bands. He seemed delighted when I told him yes: you'd have thought I'd been Geraldo in person. He asked me to go with him, along with my cellist friend to a nearby hut where, he explained, was a dance band library which needed some sorting.

This must have been the understatement of the year, for in that building was a massive amount of dance music, probably enough to stock Chappell's and Boosey and Hawkes together ~ and the muddle! It looked as if someone had mistaken it all for paper money loot and thrown the lot in the air anywhere and everywhere. Some sorting? 'It would take weeks,' I said.

'Well,' he said, 'you haven't got weeks. You two have got three days to sort out a programme for a dance in the Sergeants' Mess on Saturday. Collect up as many parts as you can and I'll organise the other musicians. You're obviously the pianist and you (to the cellist) can play bass.'

With that he left us and we gaped at each other in disbelief. Frankly, we didn't know where to begin amid the mountainous piles of band parts. A typical stack would contain 'Vienna City Of My Dreams;' for 1st alto sax, 'Stumbling' for 2nd violin, 'Brazil' for double bass, 'Gay Gordons' 3rd trombone and so on and so on. Still, something had to be done, so we set to our task albeit a mammoth one if not impossible.

Our section corporal, a gentleman by the name of Blake, who was probably an escapee from Borstal, was not best pleased to learn that I would be spending my time at the Music Shed rather than in his company. He showed an instant dislike of me from then on but a distinct liking for my mother's cakes and other goodies which

45

arrived by parcel from time to time. He was apparently under the impression that my mother had baked them for him, whereby he would commandeer any parcel that arrived addressed to me and devour the contents in his room, sharing them with his NCO colleague from Glasgow. I had the last laugh, however, when he broke open a parcel in readiness for his late night festivities, only to find that it was filled with 'Cherry Blossom Boot Polish', 'Silvo' and polishing cloths.

The news came that the King had died in his sleep.

Things began to happen at a furious rate in preparation for the funeral service on camp. The band practices were doubled, if not trebled, buglers were summoned to practice and everywhere there were bunches of RAF personnel rehearsing things with flags, rifles and bayonets.

It was a bitterly cold day for the funeral parade and service with a watery-looking sun and a north wind that whipped around that parade ground like fingers of ice. I took my place at the back of the band next to the big drum, my clash cymbals at the ready and we broke into 'Abide With Me', a hymn that I have always found very moving, especially at Wembley Cup Finals, prior to the yob era. There were readings and prayers, several on parade crashed to the ground either due to the cold or poor circulation and it was all rather solemn. The whole ceremony ended with the parade led by the Station Band and me playing Davies' 'RAF March Past', which I think I must have heard at least once on most of the days I spent in the RAF.

Due to the King's death, the dance was cancelled but the following week I went and played a giant NAAFI piano in the Sergeants' Mess for three nights. I hasten to add not for three nights without break, although the sergeants and their crowd seemed to want me to play non-stop and permanently, plying me with an array of drinks which, in the accustomed manner, littered the top of the piano.

Of course, I didn't escape marches altogether, although I must admit that when I had to, I had considerable foot problems. Occasionally the corporals would encourage us to sing as we marched and I remember striding out to:

'I love the sunshine of your smile,
I love the laughter in your eyes
In ev'ry dream of you,
You are the one I idolise'

and thinking, as I looked at our corporals ~ no, I somehow can't apply the words to you gentlemen with the best will in the world.

The cancelled dance took place the following weekend in the Sergeants' Mess as the 'band' with an incredible line-up of musicians took its place, together with a strange concoction of music. I was on piano, a reasonable instrument of about 7 out of 10, the cellist had reverted to his cello since he couldn't play double bass, a clarinet, a tenor horn, a dubious sax and a very makeshift drummer on an equally makeshift set of drums. The amusing bits were the odd assortment of band parts which gave rise to some very strange sounds, which although harmonious were distinctly unbalanced and in places disjointed. By that I mean that certain passages in some numbers were unaccounted for and empty, there being no-one having the part. The other amusing thing, to me at any rate, was the military way the MC that ran the dance. I think he was a Flight Sergeant, a regular serviceman and his life was totally regimented, with the result that everything had to be done with military precision such as the interval would be exactly 17½ minutes long and so on. My friend of more recent years, Jimmy Skene, told me of an RAF officer who wanted to know why all the trombonists in the band did not have their slides out at exactly the same length together? Almost unbelievable!

As usual, the drinks flowed during the evening and some personnel began to dance with distinct swaying motion while others started to vocalise involuntarily. Of course, there were the requests: there always are. 'Do you do requests', you're asked. The temptation is always to reply 'Only if we're asked' but you have to resist such things. Once in a wicked moment I gave that answer and the gentleman said, 'Oh I see,' and walked off.

The best 'request' story was told by Spike Milligan when he was trumpet player in an army trio playing at the Officers' Mess Ball. A somewhat inebriated officer came up to him and asked the same question.

'Do you do requests?'

'Yes,' said Milligan, 'we do. What would you like us to play?'

The Officer replied, 'Oh anything you like.' Priceless!

Despite the weird combination of the band, we were thanked profusely and the dance was acclaimed a success. 'Could we book you again?' 'Well, of course.'

I should have mentioned that we did get paid ~ with money, no less.

WO Wilson wanted me to carry on sorting the dance band library, along with my long-suffering cello friend and I would have done so had it not been for the fact that I developed Quinzies, having to be hospitalised for some time and very soon afterwards came the end of the holiday at Hednesford. I had to be hidden behind a wall at pass-out parade because I had missed all the rehearsals, having been ill. There was a threat of being deferred for a month until next pass-out but I believe WO Wilson stepped in and the idea was scotched.

I found myself posted to RAF Scampton in Lincolnshire where at the time they were filming 'The Dam Busters' since it was the home of 617 Squadron which had been led by Guy Gibson's Lancasters. I draw a veil over that period of non-excitement in my life which saw me having to visit RAF Cosford for a medical concerning my foot which eventually led to my discharge from the RAF and National Service.

I had to explain to all and sundry that I had not crashed a Vulcan bomber, overturned the Station Ambulance, seduced the Station Commander's wife or failed to salute an officer while wearing a rain cape in a thunderstorm.

Actually I had committed the last offence but escaped court martial with a dire warning and three days' CB.

Thus it was to the surprise of my parents that I turned up at Ipswich Road with the news that the RAF was not quite right for me and I was not quite right for them.

My father asked me what I intended to do now and deliberately misconstruing his question said that I was going for a drink with the lads.

However, on a more serious note, next day we had a long talk and I told father I wanted to make something of my life, to do something useful and use the talents and skills I'd been blessed with. Both the

Top Man at Norwich Union and my Wing Commander at Scampton had accused me of being lazy and work shy, accusations which were simply unfounded.

Sure, I didn't put my heart and soul into things in which I had no interest whatever ~ who does? When I'm involved in something where I can use my body and mind fully and see a wonderful end product, then there is no-one works harder.

My father telephoned his old college at Borough Road, Isleworth in Middlesex where he was told there was one place left for the new academic year and subject to a few formalities, I would be entered as a student for September 1952, just thirty years after he had entered the same hallowed halls.

CHAPTER 7

'We Said We Wouldn't Look Back'
The Salad Days Of College

Interviews with lecturers in the first few days at Borough Road were to get to know students' interests, strengths and weaknesses and to see what made us tick. You had to select two 'special' subjects, in other words two subjects that you studied in depth aside from all the other things. Many people wondered why I didn't opt for special music and indeed, friends, long after college life have queried me on it. Looking back now, maybe I should have done and maybe it was another big mistake in my life. Who can say? All I know is that I took English and Art as my special subjects and Music as one of my basics.

Doctor Wardale was Professor of Music who, on interviewing me, asked me if I had any favourite composers to which I replied Gershwin and Lehar. I don't think either was listed in his own musical Who's Who and despite my murmurs of 'Rhapsody In Blue' and 'Merry Widow' his face bore an expression of total vagueness and bewilderment as if I were delivering my answers in colloquial Hindustan. I rather think that had I decided upon Music In Depth it would have been a mixture of Chamber music, Baroque fugues and motets and heavy opera with a few madrigals thrown in. Whilst I think all these aforementioned are splendid forms of music, they are not for me which really answers the question I spoke of earlier and why I chose English and Art instead.

The good doctor had auditions for the college choir to which many of us went along, some hoping to show off their vocal talents and others out of sheer curiosity or bravado. One of the first songs we took was 'Drake Goes West', a particularly rousing song for a male voice choir, since I should have stated at the commencement of this chapter that it was an all male college with therefore no sopranos, altos or even falsettos or castrati ~ as far as I knew of course.

During the singing of 'Drake Goes West' Doc Wardale went around listening closely to each individual student, sometimes smiling in pleasurable satisfaction or sometimes with a distinct wince. I have to say that as he listened to me, he had the appearance of a man who, having just lost a filling, had bitten into an ice cream. In sotto voce he suggested to me that I might either like to mime the songs or find an alternative activity at choir practice time. I was quite disappointed, since I fondly imagined I could sing but I have had other critics of my voice since so I do have to accept it might be better to mime or seek other activity as Doc Wardale suggested. A couple of terms later when he came to watch me take a music lesson on teaching practice, he complimented me on my lesson and my musical abilities but asked me why I had not sung the 'Tonic Sol-Fa' to the children. He then looked hard at me and you could see him suddenly recall the night of the lost filling, his question answered for him. 'Ah . . . yes,' he said, nodding knowingly and walked off.

Naturally there were other students curious to know how I had escaped from the RAF, since I was indeed the second youngest member of the student force. The very youngest, I believe had convinced the conscription authorities that he had citizenship of some obscure foreign protectorate and was therefore ineligible, something many students clearly envied and wish they'd somehow engineered. I simply said I had been given ignominious discharge having been found guilty of passing classified Air Ministry plans to a foreign power and left it at that. However, since there were many who half believed me I had to own up to the real truth of the matter, in case one or two of them wrote home about it.

I soon found a good number of friends, several of whom played the piano which led us to the two college music rooms which each contained an upright around 8 out of 10 for both. Outside lecture hours we would get together and make splendid sounds, sometimes one of us playing while at other times playing duets. Roy Kitchener, who came from Olney in Bucks, could busk a lot of things, Peter Turner, who became head student in my second year could play most of 'Warsaw Concerto' by heart and Brian Hooper, a fine pianist who never actually took up a teaching post after qualifying but joined the South African Police Force, all shared with me a love of music.

We would spend many happy times there and even on occasions take one of the uprights into the second music room and have eight hands in harmony. The sound was simply great and needless to say attracted crowds of students in to listen. Curious to know what was happening, Doc Wardale came over and told us the pianos 'shouldn't be used for such things' and 'in that way' and 'such unseemly goings-on would have to stop'. Some students, more mature than I, thinking he was joking, said as much but he made it quite clear that the pianos were for the music students' practice and not for the kind of 'things' we were doing. However, we did manage to pop in now and again to have a bit of fun but it was never quite the same.

Every college has its own pub, its 'local' and Borough Road had 'The Chequers' in Old Isleworth with its wonderful chessboard sign hanging on the wall. I often wonder if 'The Chequers' is still there.

In the lounge was a piano, though I can't remember how good or how bad it was and any one of us who played was forcibly sat at it and the songs came thick and fast, particularly on a Friday night or after a rugby match. I must say I learned some incredible songs, most of which were easy to play, the tunes being rather predictable but it was the words that were so outrageous and extremely funny.

Some were totally banal such as 'Bluebells Are Bluebells' and 'Lloyd George Knows My Father' (to 'Onward Christian Soldiers') and almost as awful as 'One Man Went To Mow'.

Of course many of them were not the sort of thing you might hear at vicarage soirees and there were times when the landlord had to ask the students to 'keep it down' for the sake of other customers in the bar. Most of the songs had robust choruses which were chanted lustily by us, ably led by a strong Welsh contingent among our numbers. One favourite was 'Lily The Pink' cleaned up twenty or so years after and used by the group 'Scaffold'.

I imagine Doc Wardale would have been delighted with the overall sound and harmonies, though it's doubtful if he would have been impressed with the lyrics. I have happy memories of playing through all this with the familiar beer glasses ranked upon the top of the piano and the din reaching tumultuous level by the end of the evening.

Weekends in college were awful with many students who lived near going home and leaving the place deserted with a skeleton domestic staff providing 'get what you can' meals. It was because of this state of affairs that found me going up to London either by Southern Railway from Isleworth or by tube from Hounslow to spend the weekend with Nell (Flora) and Bert Colman at number 22 Gladstone Street near the Elephant and Castle. They always made me so very welcome with such warm hospitality, lovely meals, drinks galore and a 'tuck box' to take back with me on a Sunday night. They also had an early 9-inch TV ~ a novelty to me in those days.

Bert still had his massive upright grand with the three pedals and how I would enjoy playing that, but the greatest highlight for me was going on a Sunday morning to one of Bert's locals, after he had collected various bits of monies from clients around Lambeth, Kennington and Newington Butts ~ Bert worked for a bookie in Lavender Hill.

Sometimes we went to a pub called 'The Duke' just round the corner from Gladstone Street not far from the Imperial War Museum, others to 'The Cricketers' near Kennington Oval but best of all to the famous 'Elephant and Castle' itself a huge relic of Victoriana. Inside it was a sight to behold with Bert's pals all gathered around a table littered with glasses and bottles, the London accents coming thick and fast everywhere and the smoke haze filling the air. Across the far side of the room, barely visible through the smog, was a band. Yes, a band endeavouring to make itself heard above the noise of laughter, talk, bottles, glasses and more talk. Contrast that to today when people can't hear what each other is saying or even yelling above the multi-decibelled din from an electrified group. It's interesting to note that the aforementioned band used a piano in its line-up, a rare sight today where electric guitars abound in number.

The band's break came at 1 o'clock which I know because the radio was turned on for the familiar cry of 'Wakey Wakey!' followed by Billy Cotton's band playing 'Somebody Stole My Gal' to the delight of the patrons of the 'Elephant'. Billy was a Cockney lad and everybody's favourite in all the London boroughs.

I met some members of his band once, which was a co-operative, who said it was the happiest band they'd ever known and that them Billy was 'King Cotton' ~ what a lovely epitaph for a lovely man. I remember he had a splendid trumpet player called Grecia Farfell and his vocalists were Kathy Kaye and Alan Breeze, the latter in retirement becoming Mine Host at the 'Buck' at Flixton near Bungay.

53

My closest friend at Borough Road was David Williams whom I met on my day of arrival and instantly liked. David, who hailed from Leicester was a great film buff by which I don't mean he was just keen filmgoer but that he had studied the whole art of film making and the motion picture industry. With his tremendous enthusiasm he formed a college film society, attracting many students as members and becoming its secretary and general factotum, which entitled him to two regular seats at the National Film Theatre by Hungerford Bridge. I used to accompany him to see some very old and rare, sometimes 'way out' footage of British, American, French and other countries' films, all of which was most interesting, with the further additional explanations and tales supplied by the knowledgeable David. He decided to hire some films for the college society, the first full-length feature being a silent picture called 'The Cabinet Of Doctor Caligari', an early horror movie. There being no soundtrack, David asked me if I would play the piano for the two showings he had planned, with a quick résumé from him on the content, there being no time for a preview.

I agreed and that afternoon and evening joined the ranks of the old 'silent cinema' pianists as I plunged into heavy minor chords for the terrifying bits and quicker running movements for the chases and softer lighter strains for the romantic moments and innocent bits. It was a wonderful experience for me and the glow of pride and pleasure I felt when the lights went up to applause added to my own personal satisfaction ~ something I did not realise at the time would be repeated in years to come.

David Williams was well pleased with the entire showing, promising there would be further films over the year which would be ably accompanied by yours truly.

College dances in those days came thick and fast with the venues at Borough Road or more popularly at girls' colleges such as Whitelands at Putney, Maria Grey, Maria Assumpta, Roehampton, Philipa Fawcett, Avery Hill and Stockwell, where male students would survey the girls and choose a likely partner, occasionally for life as did David Williams with his lovely wife, Rosemary.

There were often bands for the dances but as often as not the girls of a college such as Whitelands would ring us to say they couldn't afford a band so would we take one over? It was as though they thought we had one in kit form ready boxed to provided at the drop of a hat. Would one keep it in a band box, I wonder? Oh dear . . .

Well, we did in a way ~ have a ready-made band I mean. Another Tony ~ Tony Webb was the enthusiastic drummer who brought his kit along to wherever the dance was being held with loads of students acting as his bearers, carrying side drum, tom-tom, hi-hat, cymbals and the bass drum which was strapped to the neck of a mischievous rogue named Phil Rudkin, who always insisted on it being his charge. Tony was ably supported by other student instrumentalists, plus me on piano. The greatest fun was transporting the instruments to the various colleges on the train, either Southern Rail or tube. Railways officials would frown or curse, while passengers would tut-tut or worse. On arrival at ~ say Putney, we would all process along the platform in safari style with instruments honking, banging or clashing and Phil Rudkin bringing up the rear keeping rhythm on the bass drum (or nearly). Then it was out of the station and up Putney Hill to Whitelands College to be greeted by cheering females as we approached. I need hardly say that I was among the marching band not carrying a piano ~ that was in situ in the college hall.

Our little band played for the dance which was a lot of fun and as always, the musicians were popular with the girls who tended to form unofficial fan clubs with the result that one or two 'went missing;' from time to time during the evening.

At the end of the evening with the gear all packed up, it was off to the station to catch the last train back to Borough Road with the musical procession wending its way up College Road in time to Phil's muffled bass drum accompanied by a dozen cries of 'Sh!' in vain attempt not to disturb the surrounding community.

It was painfully obvious at the college dances that many of us hadn't a clue about dance steps, looking embarrassingly awkward with two left feet and forever apologising to your partner after planting them both on hers. What could be done about it? For although there were probably plenty of dancing academies around the Hounslow area, student grants did not run to such extravagances.

Into the picture stepped our hero, second year student Dick Stannard who hailed from Downham Market in my own county and one of the few Borough students which whom I have kept in touch with since.

Dick was a superb dancer as well as an athlete and since he, like all of us, was training to teach, then it naturally followed he could teach us ~ for a fee, quite naturally I have to add.

Down to the gym they trooped, small men, tall ones, fat and thin ones, some built like lumberjacks but all having two left feet, to go through the rudimentary steps of the quickstep and waltz, with the more ambitious learning the fox-trot. There being no females in college, they danced with imaginary partners or sometimes with Dick dancing the part of the lady (he was very versatile) until came the day they were able to match his versatility (well, nearly) and dance with each other. Of course, if it happened today, half a dozen sleazy tabloids would plaster it across their pages with whacking great headlines leaving nothing to the imagination with 'sensational pictures' to match.

Now who do you suppose was supplying the music for these ballroom dancing classes? No, not Victor Silvester, not even on record. Yes, little old me, sans drummer or other musicians but on my ownsome, giving Dick the various tempos he wanted, stopping and starting, recapping this bit here, that bit there and helping the dancers, under Dicks superb guidance, to discover their lost feet. And what did I get in return, apart from my now familiar self-satisfied feelings? *Free* dancing lessons from Dick and, as I recollect, five shillings per session!

Someone (I forget who) thought we ought to have a variety concert in which those who had the talent should show what they could do to the other students. Naturally enough, I got hauled in as pianist but having a good pianist friend in Roy Kitchener, I worked up a duo act with him in which we did a lot of clowning around, spraying it liberally with lots of corn such as, 'This is our first Opus ~ opus as you like it.'

I presented a mime cameo of a little lad giving his first recital with the music upside down and a few wrong notes sprinkled about, followed by Roy doing some bits of Victor Borge with a finale of us playing 'Black And White Rag' as a duet.

There were several other acts, the most memorable being the impressive Colin Dewberry, member of the Magic Circle with his very sophisticated act which I accompanied on the piano. It was a foretaste of a part of my life which was to come later, involved deeply in the world of magic and magicians. Colin was suave and slick with a beautiful opener, 'A magician is known as a mystic ~ here's me stick,' and he produced his wand. 'See, I give it two taps ~ one hot and one cold,' and there appeared a vase of flowers from nowhere. Beautiful stuff!

The student body went wild about the concert with the result that it went 'on tour' to the girls' colleges (well of course) and received rapturous acclaim everywhere. Show business began to stir in my blood, the roar of the greasepaint, the smell of the crowd beckoned.

That stirring rose higher when I was asked by a group of senior students to be their pianist for an Olde Tyme Music Hall to be given as a 'one-off- trial at the 'Castle', a huge pub in Tooting, West London. Danny Newton, who was the chairman, was the organiser assisted by Roger Taylor, Walter Midgeley and others. The girls were from Maria Grey College, costumes were made or borrowed, music produced from everywhere and anywhere and rehearsals got underway in the Music Room. They were all so good and I thoroughly enjoyed the practice of the songs, songs that I hardly knew but was soon to come to know and love.

Came the evening of the show, a Monday night. We crowded into the tube train where we donned make-up, moustaches and side-whiskers (yes, me too) much to the surprise and amusement of fellow travellers. There was the short step from the tube station to the 'Castle' where we were put into a cellar to change, a curtain being rigged up for the girls who had already arrived, to change behind. Everyone was excited, nervous and raring to get on the stage; they all looked stunning and with make-up and costume were different people. It was time to go on: Danny opened the door at the top of the cellar steps and strode onto the stage to huge applause. He took his place at his table, white gloves and gavel in hand with a broad smile asked his audience to welcome their orchestra for the evening ~ at enormous expense 'Maestro Professor Polowski!' More applause and on I went to sit at a giant upright with lighted candles dripping tallow. I glanced at the audience, many of whom were in Edwardian costume! My, the patrons of the 'Castle' had done things in style!

One by one the artistes were introduced, again at enormous expense to deliver their songs which began with verses telling a story, followed by a chorus familiar to all and echoed by a vociferous clientele. There were comic songs, wistful ones and even sad numbers, all delighting a highly appreciative audience.

Derek Howes got his tongue round 'She Sells Sea Shells On The Sea Shore' with incredible dexterity as he added:

> *The shells she sells are sea shells I'm sure*
> *And if she sells sea shells on the sea shore*
> *Then I'm sure she sells sea shore shells.'*

As he reached the chorus for the last time, he indicated to increase the tempo which ended up in a race between the audience, Derek and me. In the second half he followed that with another favourite Edwardian tongue-twister called 'Does This Shop Stock Shot Socks With Spots?' which of course grew more and more preposterous and hilarious as it went on.

There were so many songs it would be impossible to list them all but I do remember 'Gingah, Gingah, The Colonel Of The Nuts' sung by somebody in a military get-up, 'The Boy I Love Is Up In The Gallery' by a demure young lady in crinoline and the amusing tale that began:

> *'Last week down our alley comes a toff,*
> *A nice ol' geezer with a nasty cough'*

~ entitled 'Knocked 'Em In The Old Kent Road'.

Planted among the audience were a couple of student 'Edwardians', Roger Taylor being one I recall.

'Mr Chairman,' he called out, 'My brother, a London bobby is the strongest man in the world.'

'Oh, and how is that?' queried Danny.

'He can hold up the traffic with one hand,' replied Roger.

'I don't think I wish to know that,' says Danny but before he can continue there comes another.

'I say Mr Chairman . . .'

'Yes, what do you say sir?'

'Where do women have the most hair?'

'Honolulu!'

Great laughter and guffawing drowning out 'I don't wish to know that . . .'

More songs followed with a 'special' from the Chairman himself with the hat going round the audience.

On my right by the small stage hung a huge painting stretching the length of the wall depicting an enormous garden in which stood or sat dozens and dozens of Edwardian Music Hall artistes. They were all there ~ Marie Lloyd, Vesta Tilley, Dan Leno, Little Tich, Harry Champion, Florrie Ford and so on and so on, some better known than others. Underneath was a silhouette guide to the identity of each one which took ages to study but I promised myself I would do so when next we were there.

That was to be sooner than we expected, however, since the landlord, overjoyed at our performance, to say nothing of his night's takings asked (nay demanded) our return, not just the following Monday but as many Mondays as we could manage. We partly agreed, not being too sure about Mondays later on which might in the run-up to either Teaching Practices or worse, examination finals. The landlord seemed most happy, with the promise that he would not only advertise the show well with the opportunity for patrons to come in Edwardian costume, but would add his 'bit' to the night's takings.

In the cellar, as we changed, an excited Danny counted the hat's contents sharing it out among us, I believe our number being about twelve. Everyone praised my playing which gave me the greatest joy. Everybody likes to be praised and all too often pianists and other musicians get forgotten, perhaps taken a bit for granted. Would I come back next week? You bet I would: wild horses wouldn't stop me.

For many Mondays we performed at the 'Castle' with new songs and routines, fresh banter with, by now, the audience joining in, many fully geared out in wonderful costume, men and women alike. Occasionally Danny would invite someone to come up and sing and

I remember so well an old man, coming up saying, 'You see that figure in the painting? That's me, that is. I knew them all, everyone of them.' I didn't recognise the name but he was there all right. He volunteered to sing his 'speciality', the song that had brought him some notoriety in those far-off days; sadly, he had no music and the song, totally unfamiliar to any of us (me especially) was most difficult to follow, although I did my best and the audience cheered us both at the end, perhaps a touch sympathetically.

I loved those Monday nights. I loved what I was doing: helping to make people happy by my talent. The Music Hall songs were wonderful, tuneful and clever, sometimes slightly bawdy, sometimes filled with pathos or nostalgia but I loved them all. In those weeks I 'grew up' as an accompanist, learning so much about the business, learning how to follow people's little habits, nuances and even eccentricities, learning the pauses, the stops, the accels, the dimins and the rits and through it all getting the greatest kick out of doing something really good and doing it well.

My mind often returns to that time and I wonder what became of all those people, the audiences, the great garden painting and indeed the 'Castle' itself.

Gilbert and Sullivan's 'HMS Pinafore' was the musical choice of the Dramatic Society with some help from the Music Society. Brian Hooper, a Grade VIII pianist was chosen to be rehearsal pianist and I was to 'dep' for him when he was indisposed or in other words, somewhere along Richmond towpath with a young lady. The fair sex do happen to favour pianists it seems ~ well, some anyway.

It meant that I was often faced with some fiendishly difficult passages of music to read, some of it at considerable speed and turning pages (always my weak point) made it doubly difficult. Let no-one ever say that Sullivan's music is simple stuff!

The production itself was a great success with Brian actually playing the piano for it with me turning for him and/or ready to step in, should he faint, feel ill or have an uncontrollable desire to nip off down to Richmond towpath. As it was, he and I 'doubled' on making up the crew of 'Pinafore' each night, smearing bodies from neck to waist with Leichner Numbers 5 and 9 and here I add hastily that it was the male members of the crew. So it was 'Hello sailor, come and have a rub down' and after getting the worst off our hands, we made our way to the 'orchestra pit'. It was certainly the 'roar of the greasepaint' followed by 'the smell of the crowd' for us, but nonetheless, a tremendous experience I wouldn't have missed for anything.

Money, or rather the lack of it, has always been a student problem and I was certainly no exception to the rule, continually wondering where the next ten bob note, half-crown or even shilling was coming from. My father, bless him, would pop a pound note in with his letters occasionally, my mother too when she could afford it and Bert and Nell would often slip me a few bob when I left them on a Sunday night, though I knew they could hardly afford it.

There was only one thing for it and that was to go out and earn some extra cash doing the one thing I knew I could well ~ yes, play the piano. The Osterley Hotel was just across the Great West Road which ran behind the college and one lunch time I made my way there and had a chat with the landlord, the Osterley in reality being a very large pub. It had a piano, a grand no less that wasn't in bad condition (about 7 out of 10) for a pub. Coming straight to the point, I asked Mine Host if he needed a piano player (it tended to be a piano player rather than pianist in pubs) to which he surprisingly replied that he did on a Saturday night as his regular pianist (piano player) could only manage Fridays. Of course there was no signed contract for me but he did ask if I'd play something to show that I had more to offer than 'Chopsticks' and within a few minutes it was agreed I should start on the Saturday night ~ for money!

This Saturday night several fellow students came over, including friends David Williams and Dennis Jeffries to give me moral support and as is customary, ensuring that my glass was never empty. Students are beer drinkers, draught or bottled ale being a reasonable price then and not at the mortgage price level of today. The evening was uneventful but the landlord, clearly impressed, asked me to play on Fridays too and discretion, being the better part of valour, I didn't venture to ask about his 'regular' although a couple of patrons did speak rather disparagingly about him.

A couple of weeks later, whilst I was playing, a gentleman came to the piano, as I thought to request a number, but instead asked if he could talk. At first I had visions of going into a small back room and, with coat collars turned up, speak in muffled tones about some heist or other. Clearly I'd been going to the Essoldo Cinema too often.

It turned out he was a band leader with a great problem for the coming Saturday night, having a big society dinner dance to play for with his five-piece band and his pianist off sick. He asked me if I could read and busk, had I got a DJ and would £8 be all right for payment? My answers were Yes, what is a DJ and did you really say £8? He quickly enlightened me as to what a DJ was and of course I hadn't got an evening dress. As to the pay, yes it was £8 which in 1953 was quite a sum; in fact it was half of what Norwich City Council had allowed me for my first year's grant! He said he would put matters right with the landlord of the Osterley, insisted on my begging, borrowing or stealing a dinner suit and promised to pick me up at 6 o'clock on Saturday at the corner of Wood Lane, near the college grounds.

Where was I to get a dress suit and more to the point, one which would fit a near six-footer like me? Dennis Jeffries said he had one at home in Walthamstow which would have fitted but although he went home at weekends, it was this very weekend I needed one. Frantically I asked around and eventually someone suggested Eugene, whose surname escapes me now. He was a strange fellow, lame in one leg and nicknamed 'Prince' Eugene since it was said he was related to the Archduke of Liechtenstein, whose portrait hung in his study. Eugene said he would be happy to lend me his dress suit, which he fetched from a cupboard for me to try on. Trying it on took me back to the 'kitting out' session I had experienced in the RAF, since Eugene's suit fitted me in very few places, the sleeves of the jacket and trouser legs being at 'half mast' so to speak. Still, it was a dress suit nonetheless which I had not stolen but admittedly begged or borrowed, courtesy Prince Eugene who supplied me with a bow tie to complete the ensemble.

At the agreed rendezvous I was duly picked up and we went off in the leader's car, bearing two of his musicians, drum kit, instruments and me. We headed down into the beautiful Surrey countryside and from the conversations in the car, I realised that these chaps were top class semi-pros, one of whom had played with some of the 'name'

62

bands, something which scared me stiff. Would I cope with the music, how would I fit in, would I . . .? My questions came to a stop as we pulled in for a drink at a pub called 'The Cricketers', a 'stiffener' before the gig since we were in good time and where we met two more of his band. We were heading for a very upmarket hotel and country club called 'The Pantiles' at Bagshot, near Sunningdale, in the heart of which the band leader called 'Millionaire Country'.

When we pulled into the car park of 'The Pantiles' I could hardly believe my eyes: there were Rolls, Bentleys and Mercs in ranks, some with liveried drivers cleaning them and ladies and gentlemen going into the front in full evening dress, toppers and all (well, the gents that is). We went in via a back door which led to a small stage bearing a piano and a microphone and were met by the manager who was taken on one side by our leader, who clearly had to explain my presence and have me vetted. The manager looked a bit sour regarding me as though I were carrying some contagious disease or other which made me feel even more ill at ease, stuffed into Eugene's suit as I was.

We set up the band and I was dished out with some 'orks', a few words of instruction from the leader, who played saxes, some words of encouragement from the drummer, trumpet player and bass player and the music began. I just about survived that first half of intermittent dancing, the diners getting up to waltz or whatever round a fairly large dance floor space in what I would describe as quaint dance steps, there being very little co-ordination of rhythm, footwork and music, something I was going to witness later in my life when I moved in aristocratic circles.

During the interval several ladies and gentlemen came to speak to me, possibly because they were aware I was a young, raw 'dep' and wished to offer words of encouragement but others to request certain songs special to them, all of which I sensed was not pleasing the sourpuss in charge. I then tasted champagne and for the very first time ~ caviar, provided as part of our refreshment in the break. In the second half of the evening we busked most things, partly because I was not coping well with the orchestration sight reading but mainly because we were catering for so many requests. At the end of the dancing the band leader, to his credit, thanked the 'young pianist' for stepping into the breach, which drew a hearty round of applause from all, including the sourpuss, albeit grudgingly.

When the car reached college at around one in the morning, I was politely thanked and paid as promised. Feeling very tired, rich and fairly satisfied, I crept into my room, thankfully shedding Eugene's suit which was fairly treating me like a ligature under my armpits and other places. I'd learned a lot that night, I'd seen a lot and I'd rubbed shoulders with some very rich, top people ~ well, nearly.

The very next week at the Osterley I had another visitation, this time from a gentleman of distinct Hebrew origin, looking a bit like the film actor Abraham Sofaer. After he had sat listening to me play, he came and introduced himself as a member of the Isaac Wolffson organisation, of which I knew precisely nothing but tried to give the air of one who knew every one of the board personally and was my daily opening topic of conversation.

'Doubtless you know that the corporation owns a chain of furniture stores which trade as Jays or Smarts,' he said to which I nodded as though it were common knowledge.

'From time to time,' he went on, 'we have special promotions, such as beds or dining suites, a fortnight of intensive selling of one particular item with a big publicity campaign launching it. Anyway, in the coming weeks the company is promoting its pianos in most of the West London boroughs, a big sales drive which I (and here he proudly stuck his finger to this chest) have called 'Piano Fortnight'.'

He paused, waiting for me to look suitably impressed, which I tried to do and continued, 'This is where you come in, son.'

'Me? I play pianos, I don't sell them.'

'Quite right, son,' he said taking swig of his Scotch. 'The Sales Staff do the selling and you ~ you do the playing.'

He sat back, folded his arms and surveyed me with a satisfied smirk which said 'Well, what do you think of that? Brilliant, eh?'

Perplexity must have been written all over my face for he quickly went on, 'We've got this wonderful piano, you see, made entirely of glass . . .'

'Glass?'

'That's right. It's going to stand right in the window where all the shopping public can see it ~ and hear it, because . . .'

'I'll be playing it.' I was ahead of him.

'Exactly.'

My mind was spinning wildly, filling itself first with visions of me at a glass piano with an audience of shoppers and secondly, realising all the problems and snags involved. Even while I thought of such things, my Yiddishe friend was saying, 'Now you start next week at our Chiswick branch. You know Chiswick?'

'But I'm a student at the college over the way. I have lectures to attend and so on. I couldn't work all the week for you.'

He at once assured me he would only need my services on one weekday ~ Wednesday, the heaviest shopping day, from 2 until 5.30 with a break for tea. Ten shillings for an afternoon plus a free cup of tea. How did that sound?

Again I thought fast: lectures on Wednesdays ended at 12 noon and the afternoon was 'Private Study' which meant a quick bite, change into my blazer and grey flannels and catch the 'bus to Chiswick.

'I'll do it,' I said simply.

'Good,' he replied. 'It's a Smarts' shop in the High Street. Be there at quarter to two and make yourself known to the manager.'

With that, he left after first buying a drink to seal the deal.

On the Wednesday I arrived at Smarts in Chiswick High Street, feeling nervous ~ no, terrified and introduced myself to the manager and his assistant, who led me to the front of the store where in the window, standing among half a dozen pianos was the 'glass special'.

'There, what do you think of that?' asked the manager clearly glowing with pride and satisfaction.

The instrument was composed entirely of pieces of mirror glass, each about one inch wide and three inches long stuck on in a uniform way all over it, front, back, sides, top with even a stool with legs in similar style. I suspect my jaw had dropped considerably on seeing it as I surveyed it in sheer disbelief.

'Beautiful, isn't she?'

'What? Well, certainly different,' I said, realising that tact had to prevail if I were to secure the job.

I ran my fingers over the keys, mentally giving it about 6 out of 10, which I next did with the other pianos in the store, recognising none of the makes as I did so.

Within a few minutes I began my employment and was playing all sorts of things as they came into my head, although I was somewhat distracted to see my own image appearing in the 'cut glass' facing me, my ten fingers and thumbs performing a reverse image directly beyond my hands.

Gradually I became used to it, even starting to enjoy myself when I suddenly realised, as I looked, there were people crowding into my vision, mirrored in the piano and who where gathered, listening and looking outside the shop window. I almost lost my nerve but told myself to 'pull yourself together', that they were my public and that I'd better put on a good show. When I duly finished my selection with a flourish, there was a round of applause from the onlookers, some outside with others in the doorway and I positively glowed.

So I went on through the afternoon in similar vein, all the time my audiences changing. There's a line in the old song 'If I Had A Talking Picture Of You' that goes: 'I would give ten shows a day and midnight matinee . . .' a figure which I was definitely exceeding that afternoon, although I had no plans for a midnight matinee.

After a well-earned cup of tea and biscuit at about quarter to four I resumed my place for the last session. Very soon I sensed an audience of giggling schoolgirls, stopping on their way home which slightly unnerved me. Now I did have a slight head cold which may have been exacerbated by my nervous, somewhat embarrassed feeling but I began to be aware of a runny nose which was culminating into a dewdrop. Yes, a decided dewdrop, right in the middle of a selection of songs, at which point I could nothing about as it hung there at the end of my nose. I was well aware of it by now and, horrors of horrors, so were the giggling females with the faces pressed to the window eagerly watching its progress and awaiting the drop. Desperately I tried sniffing hard without success and resorted to a hurried finish of the music, leaving the piano for the rest room, red-faced with embarrassment with a bunch of females left laughing fit to burst.

When I finished at 5.30, the manager complimented me on an excellent job done, though as I remember there had not been one enquiry about a piano, let alone a sale, and asked me if I would be willing to come in all day on Saturday, 10 until 5.30 with a lunch hour for £1. I knew full well it meant skipping a Saturday morning lecture but the prospect of a whole pound made me say yes. I left with my crisp ten shilling note, heading for the ABC Restaurant which I soon learned meant Associated Bread Company, where I had sausage, egg and chips, a cake and cup of tea for 2/3d, good food and value for money. I noticed Arthur English in there, almost unrecognised by the customers and as I walked to the Underground, saw that he was appearing at Chiswick Empire.

I returned to play at Chiswick on the Saturday which as you can imagine was a long and tiring day, although a satisfying one with many people saying how much they enjoyed it and others asking for special favourites. The management was pleased, something that counted for much and doubly so that day since they had sold a piano!

The same routine continued in the following week, after which the whole 'show' entitled 'Piano Fortnight ~ Come And Try Our Superb Range', emblazoned across the window, moved on to Hammersmith, glass piano and all with me as Musical Director!

After Hammersmith, it was Putney, then Wandsworth, Feltham and on to Ealing Broadway. There, the management went a bit too far and relayed my music through loud-speakers into the street! The shop, Jays, was opposite Ealing Town Hall where all the typists and other office staff kept sending across with requests for songs of the day and other favourites. In the end the Chief Clerk of the Borough telephoned the store complaining of work disruption and the speakers were duly disconnected.

The most exciting thing happened at Ealing late on the Wednesday afternoon when four gentlemen came into the shop and asked the manager's permission to speak to me. One of them asked me if I could play trad jazz and could I manage a twelve-bar blues, the latter being something I'd vaguely heard of, but only that. He asked if I'd like to come over on Friday night to the 'White Hart' at Hayes and sit in with his band, though he was quick to add that I'd have to make my own way over to Hayes. I said I'd see what I could do, although I really saw no way of going and with that, they left. During the conversation there were no introductions as I remember but I had a vague idea I'd seen two of them before somewhere and said as much to the manager.

'Don't you know who they were?' he said in amazement. 'It was Chris Barber, the short fair-haired one was Monty Sunshine, the dark-haired one was Lonnie Donegan and the tall one, the bass player.' (Jim Bray).

I had been asked by no less a jazz man than Chris Barber to play at Hayes' foremost jazz spot and knew there was no way of getting there. Ifs and buts abound in this life and I wonder what might have happened to mine if . . .

As it turned out, the Chris Barber Band played for the Summer Ball at college that year and I did actually sit in for one number.

The pianos show moved on to Hounslow, too close for comfort as Mr Porter's song says and one afternoon there I had to dive into the back of the shop when I caught sight of the Vice Principal, Doctor Page approaching: a close thing!

The last borough to be inflicted with the piano performance was the pretty town of Staines, where to my surprise the glass piano was absent. I was told that it had mysteriously vanished as if into thin air in transit from one store to another. Throughout the whole circuit there had always been enquiries from customers asking if they could buy it and I could only suppose that one of them, mortified at being unable to purchase it, had gone to elaborate lengths to own it at any price! I often wonder what became of Joanna Glass . . .!

Each year the college had a Rag, which meant all kinds of events taking place in Isleworth, Heston and Hounslow with students dressed in strange gear doing charitable things to raise money to buy the mayor a new gold chain or something (well, not really). Come to think of it, the way we dressed in Rag Week would probably pass every day unnoticed these days.

Rag Week culminated with a colourful procession of floats through the boroughs, inevitably some bearing bands, either 'home-grown' or from round about the area. I sat at a jangly upright with Tony Webb bashing out his drums while one or two other hopeful musicians (perhaps that should be hopeless) added their bit. We were joined very soon by members of the Crane River Jazz Band led by a young cornet player called Pat Halcox, who was later to become trumpet/cornet lead in Chris Barber's band. The whole thing was tremendous fun with huge crowds lining the route giving their cash to the cause on a memorable sunny afternoon and the music from our float just wonderful ~ well, I thought so anyway.

In the evening there was the Rag Variety Show at the Dominion Cinema in Hounslow, all the stage-struck students doing their 'thing' including one called Jim Tickle (yes!) who did a marvellous impression of Carmen Miranda, fruit and all, Colin Dewberry as Mr Magic and Roy Kitchener and I fooling at the piano. We loved it, the audience loved it (I think) and everybody had a marvellous time.

In 1954, just before I left Borough Road and my college life behind me, I happened to be in London and stood on the opposite side of the road facing the Vaudeville Theatre where in huge letters it said 'Salad Days ~ a new musical by Julian Slade'. In songs about student life, Julian Slade had summed it all up: the laugher, the fun, the friendships, the magic of it all, our 'Salad Days', which I wouldn't have missed for anything.

> *'We'll never be able to break the spell*
> *The Magic will hold us still*
> *Sometimes we may pretend to forget*
> *But of course we never will.*
> *We mustn't look back, no we mustn't look back*
> *Whatever our memories are*
> *We mustn't say those were our happiest days*
> *But our happiest days so far!'*

CHAPTER 8

'Hometown'
Return to Norwich

Despite pleas by Tony Webb and one or two other musicians to me to stay in Middlesex or the London area with the idea of keeping together as a semi-pro outfit for gigs, I opted to return to my native city. I had applied for a teaching post in Middlesex, Norfolk and Norwich with the result that I was called to three separate interviews for jobs in the Primary sector and offered a place with all of them, presenting me with something of a dilemma.

After some deliberation, I chose to teach in Norwich, mainly because lodging at home with my parents was infinitely more comfortable and cheaper than a rented accommodation either in the wilds of Norfolk or more certainly in the London area. Added to this was the ever-smouldering idea that I still wanted to play piano in the dance or entertainment work in and around Norwich where I knew so many musicians.

I had 'gone down' at the end of May 1954 with the summer before me back home in East Anglia but with which is known today as a cash flow problem. What to do about it? Almost on the brink of signing up as a waiter at a local holiday camp, I had a telephone call from the City Education Office, asking me to cover for a sick teacher for the rest of the summer term ~ with pay, albeit unqualified rate. My cash problem was solved and one particular wheel had come full circle: the headmistress of the school was Miss Grace Varney, my old class teacher at Avenue Road Primary!

Tony Webb telephoned to say he had a residency lined up for a trio near his home at Farnham Common which needed a pianist to make up the trio. Could he persuade me to come? Even when I told him I couldn't and given my reasons, he insisted on giving me time 'to think it over'. I'll give Tony eleven out of ten for persistence, bless him and I was flattered to think that he thought so highly of me or my playing ~ or both. Indeed, when he had concluded some days later that I wouldn't be joining him in what was a most attractive and lucrative hotel engagement, suggested that he might apply to teach in

Norfolk and move down to the area. He never did actually, though I fully expected him to turn up on my doorstep any day!

One wet afternoon, quite soon after my return, I chanced to meet a pianist friend of mine in London Street named Peter Stone. We chatted about the music business, comparing fortunes and he happened to tell me that Brian Green was looking for a pianist and that he, Peter could not do it since he was going abroad to Australia. At that time the name of Brian Green meant nothing to me but Peter filled me in, telling me that Brian was a splendid trumpet player who had just won the 'Carol Levis Discoveries Award' in London but was presently working at Lennards' Shoe Shop at the top of London Street.

At Peter's suggestion I went into the shoe shop and asked to see Brian Green. It transpired that I had spoken to the manager, Joe Eden who turned out not only to be Brian's boss but also his drummer. Brian appeared, a tall, good-looking chap with rimless specs, crinkly hair and a whisper of a moustache. I told him I had met Peter Stone only minutes earlier, that I played piano and understood he was looking for a chap like me.

It was close to closing time and at 5.30 I went with Brian and Joe in Brian's car to his mother's home in Waddington Street, where there was a piano. I played a few numbers, some requested by Brian which seemed to impress them both, with the result that Brian asked me if I'd like to join them for the summer season at Potter Heigham Dance Hall in the middle of the Broads (not the dance hall but Potter Heigham). It was going to be Wednesdays, Fridays and Saturdays ~ 8 'til 11 and 11.30 on Saturdays with 'Union Rate' pay. I mention the pay here because within days I'd had to join the Musicians' Union since at that time they had a Mafia like coverage of Norfolk and if you didn't belong, then you might go home one night and find your piano shot to pieces.

The season began, the bandwagon being Brian's little Series E Morris car which wound its way through country lanes to arrive at Potter Heigham Dance Hall, situated just by the infamous bridge where tourists waited to see sailing boats crash their masts, their owners having omitted to lower them. The hall itself was nothing more than a great black wooden shed having some filthy windows, two toilets, a soft drinks bar and a high stage at one corner on which stood a giant upright of indeterminate vintage.

When Brian said he would like me to meet Harry, I really thought he was the caretaker, for he wore a dirty black overcoat, trousers, scarf and hat to match so I was more than a little surprised to learn that he was the owner.

Harry had very little to say, apart from telling me that Brian was 'a good boy' and he spoke in words of one syllable with about six being his usual limit, given some colour occasionally by an odd Anglo-Saxon expletive.

Joe set up his drums, Brian erected a wooden music stand bearing the letters BG, while I donned an ill-fitting maroon band jacket and sounded out the giant piano, being hopeful of every note functioning. It was then that I was introduced to the fourth member of the band, the one who I would say qualified to be the person least likely to be a musician, let alone one in a dance band. He was George Milligan and as I understood a millionaire and director of a construction firm called Tooley and Young's, 'big' in the Broads area. He lived at East Ruston Hall, I think, had a manservant, a fleet of valuable vintage cars, usually drove a Mercedes sports car, had a mother living in London and played the accordion and occasionally the alto sax. He'd played with Brian on and off for some time 'just for the love of it' and was the unpaid fourth part of the quartet but I hadn't the courage to mention Musicians' Union in front of him.

Two things stood out immediately about George: one was his sheer flamboyance of dress, for what little there was of it was dazzling in appearance. His sport shirt had all the colours of the spectrum woven into it, rather like Lloyd-Webber's 'Joseph', while his bright green shorts were so skimpy they gave cause for discussion if not speculation. The other thing about George that was such a part of his 'stock in trade' and which would hardly be associated with a dance hall musician was his incredible Oxbridge accent, so perfect as to think he was the originator of the 'How Now Brown Cow' elocution series.

George was a delightful fellow who thoroughly enjoyed his music, could play the accordion very well and the alto sax rather less well. In Harry Drake's eyes he was the 'Lord of the Manor' and would have touched his forelock to George, but in fact didn't possess one to touch. Each week he would appear in one of his vintage cars and I remember he had the first Wolseley ever made and another beauty called an Invicta, always matched with another vivid shirt and colourful briefs. During the evening's playing he would request that we played 'We'll Gather Lilacs' as a quickstep which he loved and Brian loathed.

There was no question that Brian was good on that trumpet, being versatile enough to play like such men as Harry James, Bobby Hackett and Louis Armstrong which of course delighted the great crowds of holidaymakers who had filled the hall. At the time, Eddie Calvert had recorded 'Cherry Pink And Apple Blossom White' with the gimmicky glissando at the beginning of the open phrase, something which the public thought both clever and wonderful that Brian dismissed as simple, drifting into it with ease and leaving the dancers, especially the girls, swooning.

As a matter of fact, most pro trumpet players regarded Eddie Calvert as rather ordinary and there was a great story told to illustrate this. The superb trumpet player Bobby Pratt who played with, among others, the Ted Heath Band, was, sadly enough, often in hospital. When he was recovering from an op, the nurse apparently said, 'There Mr Pratt, you'll soon be up and about and be able to play like Eddie Calvert', whereupon, word has it, Bobby had a relapse.

Joe Eden was a stocky Lancashire man, likeable though quick-tempered and it has to be said, not a particularly good drummer. His biggest fault was playing the bass drum and the side drum together on the first and third beat of each 4/4 bar with the result there was no lift in the rhythm which tended to slow as a tune progressed. Brian, with great patience tried to show him and for a time it would be correct but soon lapse back again, leading to sharp word exchanges on stage which I have always thought highly unprofessional.

How did I make out? Reasonably well, considering the piano. As it was, the season was enjoyable, sometimes a bit frantic when Brian left it rather late to get to Potter Heigham which meant a hair-raising drive there and sometimes a trifle aggravating when the women took over. I said the girls swooned when Brian played but he could charm them off the trees without the aid of his trumpet, often disappearing during the evening we knew not where and sometimes after the dance was over too. The evening would end, as was customary with the last waltz, although at Potter Heigham there was the unusual added feature of Harry Drake emerging from the gents' toilet, bucket in hand, to then enter the ladies' which he always preceded by taking off his black hat and re-emerging with a second bucket. This done, he would cross the floor to the microphone and to the assembled dancers thank 'Brian Green and his lovely, lovely band and see you all next time' ~ his longest sentence of the day or even the week.

With the kit left covered with a cloth (would you dare do that today?) we would take Harry home to Repps where he lived with his wife, who was the local headmistress, he having paid Brian first. Of course, George Milligan had beetled off to his stately home where his two permanently employed car mechanics would put away the vintage model he'd used, ready for servicing next day. Brian once told me George had taken him for a spin round the Norfolk lanes in his Rolls Royce Silver Ghost averaging 100mph with George looking at Brian half the time as he talked. Brian did say how grateful he was to get out of the car alive.

During that season, which lasted until about the end of September, I got to know both Joe's wife and family and Brian's wife Cynthia and their family, although I, being a bachelor at the time and younger anyway, did not expect to meet them socially. Brian had very little in the offing following the season at Potter Heigham but assured me that Harry Drake had engaged the band for the next summer and I would be pianist; this meant that I was to see him only from time to time during the winter months.

Scanning the musical ads one night I saw that somebody was wanting to form a band and out of sheer curiosity I telephoned the number. I spoke to a Mrs Pearce who put me on to her son Richard, who asked me to be at the 'Unthank Arms' in Norwich the next evening for audition.

The landlord of the 'Unthank' indicated by thumb that I should go upstairs where I opened a door into a room in which there were some chairs, two or three ceiling lights of low wattage, an ancient upright and two sombre gentlemen, one seated at a set of drums, the other nursing a banjo.

'Richard Pearce?' I said.

'Mr Ireland?'

The first sombre gent rose from behind the drums to his full six foot height to shake hands and I wasn't to know at the time that his greeting and handshake were the introduction to a long and lasting friendship that has endured to the present day; moreover, I couldn't have begun to guess at the time what an amazing musical future lay in store for both of us.

Richard, who quickly became 'Dick' introduced his banjo-playing friend, Denis Howes, who had been unofficially baptised 'Lonnie' by musical associates after Lonnie Donegan of the Chris Barber Band. Denis, who turned out to be an ex-Avenue Road lad, was shortish with black wavy hair, quietly-spoken with a nervous laugh and allowed Dick to do most of the talking. I was to discover that Dick had some very strong qualities, the three most outstanding being his drumming ability, which was exceptional and sometime electrifying, his infinite thirst for bitter, mild or both and his great capacity for talking.

He told me that he and Lonnie worked at Montague Burton tailors in Norwich, where there were not exactly thrills by the minute, had decided to 'break out' as it were, go in search of some musicians and form a band. Their quest had produced some strange encounters: they had been to the house of a well-known semi-professional pianist whose wife had answered the door and was clearly his agent, secretary and spokeswoman.

'What kind of music do you play?' she snapped.

'Well, er . . .'

'Is it modern, mainstream or what?'

'Well, er . . .'

'How many in the band?'

'Well there's him (Lonnie) and me so far.'

'I don't think it sounds like him; he is the poor man's Bill McGuffie you know.'

With that, she shut the door.

In Bracondale the two went to the house of a lady who said she played the saxophone, which she produced from its case and put to her mouth. No sound issued forth whatever as she blew, first gently, then stronger until she was going purple in the face with Dick and Lonnie fearing she would burst a blood vessel. After further attempts with renewed vigour and the saxophone remaining resolutely mute, she said, 'I can't understand it. It was perfectly all right this morning.'

Now Dick, at that time would never have admitted to being a musician and his musical knowledge was somewhat limited but he did venture to ask her if the gold cap on the mouthpiece ought to be removed before playing commences.

'I may be wrong,' he said politely, 'but perhaps that's the reason it's not working, though of course as I said I may be wrong.'

It turned out that he was right but I think by that time the good lady was rather too puffed to play.

We waited for other would-be members of Dick's band to arrive ~ a lady accordionist and violinist but the door remained shut on our trio and as the time ticked on, it became clear that this was it: banjo, piano and drums, not the sort of line-up that your average impresario was bursting to engage. We played a few old numbers together to raise spirits, I mentioned one or two musicians who might be interested but by closing time nothing much had been planned or resolved and we went off into the night, totally unaware that we would come together in a relatively short time.

I had taken up a teaching post at Thorpe Hamlet Junior School on the east side of Norwich, under the headship of Mr Stan Sinclair, a Glaswegian, in a brand new building along with other new members of staff. I was immediately slotted into the role of Morning Assembly pianist, given an upstairs classroom with a piano, a set of New English Folk Songs (which were anything but new) and forty-two ten-year-olds in my charge.

Because I was able to play the piano it was assumed that I could handle anything musical and was soon given a large group of youngsters to whom I should teach the recorder, an instrument I knew nothing of at all. As it was, I had to be about three steps ahead of the children with progress to say the least, rather slow and to the ears of other members of staff, painful. One of the staff, a Mr Darrington was completely tone deaf, though quite how the cacophonous recorder sounds affected him I cannot say. I remember him telling the staff how much he had enjoyed 'The Third Man' with Orson Welles, but the film was completely spoiled by 'that awful din in the background'. He was, of course, referring to the zither playing of Anton Karas which was not only both haunting and atmospheric but was at least three-quarters of the essence of the whole motion picture. Darrington could not recognise one tune from another and only knew a hymn at morning prayers by its words. A great man (I forget who) once said 'I must confess that I am tone deaf. The only tune I know is God Save The Queen and I only know that because everyone stands up.' I don't know what it must be like to be tone deaf. I've witnessed quite a few people in more recent years, who judging by what they are listening to, most certainly do not have an ear for music, but that is not quite the same thing.

There's a wonderful story related by Sir Brian Morton, one time chairman of Harland and Wolff in Belfast, when he was presenting the prizes on speech day at a school in England. After the ceremony, the boys began to sing 'When Irish Eyes Are Smiling' as an obvious compliment to him. The singing lacked everything: tunefulness, harmony, cohesion, finesse. He noticed a lady on the platform wiping her eye with her handkerchief to brush away a tear and thinking she had become emotionally overcome, said to her, 'Are you Irish too?'

'No,' she replied, 'I'm a music teacher.'

Our school caretaker was a Mr Vic Smith, who when he was not caretaking, was putting on greasepaint and variety shows with a concert party around Norfolk's fair county. He would include a number of talented people in his line-up such as Gertie Freeman, a soprano who was his sister-in-law; there was Stuart Leslie, a comedian, Peter Matthews, who did lightning sketches on large sheets of paper mounted on an easel, Len Rudd who sang, did magic and played the guitar, Gerald Morter (Called Geraldini) who did magic and Eric Palmer, a Norfolk comedian.

Vic compered the show which went to village halls around the area and persuaded me to join as the pianist. All of them were good in their own way: Gertie had a lovely voice and sang such favourites as 'Sunshine Of Your Smile' and 'Little Grey Home In The West'. Stuart Leslie told a good joke, while Peter Matthews' drawings were brilliant. He would end his act with a challenge to four members of the audience to each place a line on the sheet of paper and he would come up with a picture of a Scotsman playing the bagpipes, which of course he managed every time. Len Rudd dressed up in a Roy Rogers outfit and sang cowboy type songs, while Geraldini performed some skilful feats of conjuring. My favourite was Eric Palmer, dressed as a Norfolk yokel with florid face and stentorian voice who would have his audience laughing helplessly at his Norfolk stories and sketches, always ending his act with the same song that I would accompany until I knew it off by heart.

It was a repetitive type of ditty, the title of which eludes me, which had lines that went:

> 'Father had a farm, real nice farm
> I'd a farm, he'd a farm
> Big farm, a little farm
> An' the green grass grew all around, all around
> An' the green grass grew all around.'

The second verse would be the same as the first, except that 'farm' became 'bull', then followed by 'farm'; the third verse would be 'pig', followed by 'bull' and then 'farm' and so on, rather like 'The Twelve Days Of Christmas'. As the catalogue of things on the farm grew longer, Eric would increase the speed, his audience in stitches and I desperately trying to keep up with him. Came the 'molto rall' at the end with the 'green grass grew all around' and Eric bowed to rapturous applause. I never actually saw the great Sidney Grapes, the Boy John but knew of his splendid acclaim, of course; I doubt if he was better than Eric Palmer.

Vic Smith was a versatile compere and performer with a fine singing voice with one particular favourite song: 'That Lucky Old Sun' which he used to announce was a Negro spiritual, which of course it wasn't. He did a double act with Peter Matthews, who, painted up just like a ventriloquist's dummy, sat on Vic's lap and performed a hilarious routine, Peter doing a wonderfully convincing impersonation of Archie Andrews. Vic's finale was to appear in long gown, wig and long gloves and in falsetto give a commendable rendering of 'I Was Never Kissed Before' whilst he circulated among the men, making cow eyes at them. This always seemed to be received with great hilarity, nay ecstatic laughter from both sexes (and probably a third) but I never could understand why, though there is no accounting for taste.

I must have worked with Vic Smith for at least two years but lost touch after he left the school to join the one at Coltishall RAF Station. He kept his concert party going with other pianists such as Vic Delf, Ted Cutler and Ted Hardiment playing for him. I kept in touch with Peter Matthews who went to live and work in Austria at Karnten, but I hardly saw anything of the others after that.

I joined the Norwich Conservative Club, not for any political leanings but because they had three splendid snooker tables there and I was to become, like many others, the victim of 'a misspent youth'. I had played snooker at college, was rather hooked on the game and the St Giles Club seemed the ideal place. It was at the club that I met two very fine singers and a violin virtuoso.

Reg Tyrell was a quiet, soft-spoken man who had married late in life with a wife and son he worshipped. He told me that he played the violin 'a bit' and we arranged for him to come to my parents' house to practise with me. His playing lacked practice but I soon realised what a splendid violinist he was, particularly going through the Kreisler repertoire with great dexterity. We gave a few 'private house' recitals I remember at some friends of his in Constitution Hill but I was unable to persuade him to 'go public' since he seemed to be so diffident and hypercritical about his performance.

His violin was one he treasured, not for its monetary value but because an Arab had made it for him from pure white wood after his violin which he took with him on active service in North Africa was blown to pieces by enemy shells. I often wonder what became of that remarkable instrument which Reg held so dear, the gift of an Arab craftsman.

At the Conservative Club was a piano around the 6 out of 10 mark which I tried out, much to the delight of some members and probably to the disapproval of others. One such member of the former group was Reg Willis, commercial rep, born at Great Yarmouth, wandered to Gloucester like Doctor Foster and with a fine rich bass-baritone voice. He would stand by the piano as I accompanied him to such great songs as 'I'll Walk Beside You' and 'Old Man River' but his best, in my opinion was 'Friend O' Mine' with its tremendous ending: *'Let me be there, let me be there, Friend o' Mine'.*

He drew deserved applause from bar members which immediately signalled drinks for Reg and me, followed by an encore.

I knew Reg and his wife, Ann, as friends and when he died, kept my friendship with her.

George Armes, I think, was one of the most remarkable men I ever knew. He was built of the stuff that legends are made of and in his lifetime he was a giant among men. To say he was a member of the Norwich Conservative Club would be a great understatement since although he was not a committee member, was to most of us the Norwich Conservative Club personified. There is no doubt he was a wealthy man, having taken over, with his brothers, a sawdust business from his father William Armes, known as 'Kidney' on Bishop Bridge, Norwich. I'm not sure how wealthy George was but he always had a 'fistful' of notes and paid in cash for everything. He was 'Mr Generosity' himself and on entering the Conservative Club bar would order drinks for everybody from Bill, the steward.

So how does George Armes fit into my musical life?

When he found in me a young, capable 'tinkler of the ivories' (not my favourite expression) he at once demonstrated the power of his splendid baritone voice with superb renderings of such songs as 'My Yiddishe Momma', 'Dinner For One Please James' and 'The Road To Mandalay'. These songs delighted the members of the club and he was in great demand whenever he appeared there, although he was unfortunately a difficult man to pin down, always in desperate hurry to get away to some urgent business appointment.

He was a confirmed bachelor, partly because of his extreme independence, but also his uneasiness in the company of women; had he been married I believe his wife would have been the permanent grass widow, so rarely was he at home.

George knew the words of so many songs and being an ardent fan of Richard Tauber and Peter Dawson, would sing many of their favourites, such as 'You Are My Heart's Delight' and 'I Travel The Road'. He had a splendid medley that included 'You Will

Remember Vienna' and 'Vienna City Of My Dreams' but the song that I, and all who knew him best for, was 'When The Sergeant Major's On Parade', sung with tremendous gusto plus all the histrionics that go with it.

George had so many friends it was difficult to keep up with them and I, being his 'unofficial' musical director, followed him and his voice around wherever he went. There was his fishing club, angling being one of his hobbies, where their day out was followed by supper at some hostelry or other that had to have a piano on its menu. I would be given supper and George, always needing Dutch Courage in the form of several pints of best bitter, would rise to the occasion with some of his famous arias, accompanied by his MD, on many an indifferent piano. As more of the Barley Mow found its way in into George's glass and thence into George, the songs became more of the 'join me in the chorus' type, although he did do a very fine version of 'Frankie And Johnnie' with some splendid action shots woven into it. I also learned to follow him on the piano with appropriate chords and phrases when he performed 'The Shooting of Dan McGrew' by Robert Servis, a tale of the Yukon Gold Rush.

If it wasn't his fishing club, it was his shooting fraternity or his boxing friends (I don't mean pugilists but those where were ringside seat fans) or horse racing pals or soccer fanatics, but the end result was always the same: a veritable banquet somewhere washed down with gallons of hop mixture with a piano standing somewhere in the room for me to assist with the revelry.

The most outstanding treats with George Armes were the FA Cup Finals at Wembley, where I would accompany him and two or three of his moneyed pals on what would be a complete day's outing. First stop would be a splendid hostelry on the outskirts of London for a spectacular lunch; then on to the match itself, the highlight being the singing before the game, led by Arthur Cager culminating in 'Abide With Me'.

After the football, it was on to another hotel or pub with a room set aside for a private supper, a splendid affair with sumptuous fare and liquid refreshment to match. George, a man with a big frame, huge appetite and an immense capacity for anything wet in a glass would then indicate it was time for the cabaret by directing me to the upright in the corner. Songs would flow, the drinks likewise and I, having consumed enough alcohol to have burst a policeman's little bag (had they been invented) gazed down at my fingers which were performing detached feats on the piano keys as they vainly tried to follow the singing company. I have learned in after years that alcohol does not improve the piano playing and whilst the player may be deluded into believing it does, the listener certainly doesn't.

Until late into the evening those musical soirées would endure, to include all and sundry from the lounge and public bar who bellowed out the songs with King George leading them and the young and totally inebriated Ludwig von Mendelssohn attempting to follow in a vertical sitting position.

Then it was off down the A11 home with the only sober member of George's group driving; a great day out, which always cost me exactly nothing, apart from the splitting head I had next day.

Reg Tyrell, Reg Willis and George Armes were three remarkable gentlemen, who each in his own way, added his special contribution to the cornucopia of my musical world. Sadly, all three have made their exits to go on to a new stage.

CHAPTER 9

'That Old Black Magic'
The Amazing Harry Carson

One of my new colleagues in school was Jean Swain, a Yorkshire lass, splendid teacher and excellent disciplinarian, to whom I took an instant liking. She took me under her wing rather like a big sister would, helping me through those opening weeks of my career.

She told me that she and her husband, whom she called Pat, had been teaching in Egypt until King Farouk was deposed by Colonel Nasser, at which point all British personnel working there were asked to leave within 24 hours or be shot, which Pat and Jean didn't care to do. They had applied for jobs with the Norwich Education Authority and been accepted: well, if they hadn't, I wouldn't be writing this chapter.

Within a short while Jean had gone home and told Pat about me and my musical abilities, with the result that I was invited to their flat in Clarendon Road which they rented from a Miss Elizabeth Cave, a lecturer at Keswick College. Jean had told me that her husband was a magician, an ex-professional and would be continuing his magic act on a semi-professional scale here in Norwich and the county areas, something which excited me and called to mind Colin Dewberry, our 'resident' magician back in college days. Could it be that I would be playing for another magic act and this time an ex-pro?

Pat was to me, on early acquaintance, a complete enigma: I just didn't know what to make of him, his great complexity being difficult to fathom. He was of shortish stature, brown wavy-haired with mischievous grin, twinkly eyes behind the specs and with quicksilver wit and one-liners that left you speechless. I can't exactly remember but I imagine he produced an egg from behind my ear and the Ace of Hearts from my top pocket within two minutes of our meeting, which was the kind of thing that went on all the time.

I learned that his stage name was Harry Carson, that the had been on the variety stage, touring the theatres around Britain, but had called it a day with the decline of variety entertainment and gone to train as a teacher. It was while he was at college he met with Jean, herself a talented ventriloquist and they had conjoined both as entertainers and eventually in matrimonial style. They had lived and worked in Sheerness for a time, in their out of work hours giving magic shows in the area, in the early days under the billing ? Esquire and Jean.

They decided to go and teach in Egypt where their magic act became very popular and their Arabic very fluent, until the change of regime brought them back to England.

Pat had learned his magic craft from some of the best in the world: David Devant, The Great Lyle, Maskelyne, Chung Ling Soo and others, but his one-time hero and mentor was another Yorkshireman called Dick Ritson, who taught Pat so many secrets and routines and of whom he spoke with such reverence and affection. When Dick died, Pat was devastated but much comforted and indeed felt honoured by Dick's widow passing all her late husband's magic property to him, together with a number of extremely valuable books about the art of magic which Pat added to his huge collection. Pat had a thirst for knowledge about his craft and lived and breathed magic as long as I ever knew him.

At our first encounter he showed me his band parts which had been handed to many an MD on a Monday morning band call from Glasgow to Brighton, from Blackpool to Leeds, parts that were beginning to show signs of wear and travel. One of his parts I have even now as a precious souvenir: Irving Berlin's Waltz Medley used during a floral illusion.

He asked me to scan the music to see if I could cope with it, which I said I thought I could and then announced that we had an engagement booked at the village hall, Gillingham near Beccles the week after next.

Pat went through the routine with me, pointing out various stops and pauses, talked about 'tabs' and 'perks' and tried to put me at my ease. I borrowed the piano parts to practise and arrangements were made for pick-up for Gillingham. Neither he nor I possessed a car, so apparently a lady from Gillingham was to come into Norwich and take us to the hall, where we were to give a tea-time show to the populace, followed by tea (well, obviously).

'I would like to present to you Carson the Magician,' said the lady in charge and amidst the applause I sprang into life with 'I'm Just Wild About Harry' which was Pat's signature tune and the signal for his act to being.

Naturally I can't recall the entire sequence of tricks on that occasion, for I played for him so many times it would be impossible to list them with accuracy. I remember his famous bottle and rope trick where the rope went into the bottle, stayed there swinging the bottle while I played Hoagy Carmichael's 'Lazybones'. There was the waiter on board the ship in rough weather, managing not to spill a drop from the glasses on his tray, even when it turned right over to my accompaniment of 'La Mer'. I remember too at one point he had a little lad fire a pistol at a balloon and upon pulling the trigger the lad laughed with the audience as a cloth hung from the weapon which read *'bang'*.

Pat's finale ~ 'Sun And Moon' was a splendid illusion of large red and white tissue sheets being set fire to and changing colours, the routine getting faster and faster as I raced through a number called 'Chinese Twilight', an old piece of sheet music with a photograph on the front of band leader Hal Swain (very distant relation of Pat's). Then it was into 'I'm Just Wild About Harry' and Pat took his 'perks' with the lovely Jean who had been his stage assistant throughout the show, with the audience clapping enthusiastically and Pat indicating to them to direct some applause to me.

He came and said I'd done well and over tea began to talk eagerly about more shows and actually asked me for further music suggestions for his act, which it has to be said was very polished and highly professional. That show at Gillingham was not only the first of a great number to come but the beginning of a partnership and friendship between us which was to last for almost 40 years, during which time I learned a great deal about show business. I also realised how gifted a man Pat was, able to turn his hand to many things requiring this skill in engineering, mechanics, woodcraft and haute cuisine, though I don't think I ever solved the enigma that he was. I suspect only two people got halfway or more to knowing that and they were Jean and Pat himself.

Pat's follow-up to that first show was to get in touch with the local press, the Eastern Evenings News; 'Whiffler' column and at the very next show I was to meet one of the most likeable, delightful journalists ever ~ Steve Amiss ~ who wrote his entertainment articles under the name of Steve James. Pat got him to bring a photographer and a big write-up was born, Steve himself loving every minute of the show and the bonus of a private magic performance afterwards in the dressing room where the rafters rang with his gleeful laughter as Pat deceived him time after time with sleight of hand.

I was to meet Steve many times in my life, one of the nicest men I knew and who was such a friend to so large a number of folk in the entertainment business. As so often, he gave Pat a wonderful spread in the 'EEN' with a splendid picture which of course led to enquiries from many quarters for a magic show, mainly with children in mind.

Pat was a member of the Magic Circle, therefore making me promise as his 'close-up' accompanist never to divulge how many of his illusions and tricks were done, not even to family. Actually, he needn't have bothered, for on stage I never once saw anything passed to Jean, nor did I spot any 'fake', in fact nothing to give me the slightest hint how anything was done. It was only in the privacy of his own home that I learned the innermost secrets but even then wouldn't have had the first idea how to do it myself. You could read a book on magic from cover to cover, learning how to do the tricks and illusions in it but it takes a real magician to perform them properly. Pat would often liken himself to me: 'Lots of people can read a piece of music,' he would say, 'but nobody plays it quite like you.'

Jean had her vent dolly she called Jennie though I never saw her work with her but came across pictures of them together in the 'Carson' scrap albums. Years later, Jean gave Jennie to my great sax player friend Jack Wilkinson, who secretly fancied Jennie ~ for a vent act I hasten to add.

Jean herself at this time, working in Norfolk was perfecting a memory act with Pat as part of their stage show, an act which grew in popularity with our city and county audiences. Pat would announce her to the strains of my piano saying 'Thanks For The

Memory' whereupon I would take a small blackboard and chalk and list 24 items called out by members of the audience, each one against a number. During this time Jean would be blindfolded, mainly to add drama to the thing and Pat would finish off by asking someone to call a six-figure number to put underneath the list of items. This done, he would say to the audience: 'Do you want Jean to call out the first 12 or the second?' Then: 'Forwards or backwards?'

Invariably it was backwards, the audience endeavouring to make things harder for her (they thought!) Jean would then reel off the second 12 followed by the first with Pat then inviting the audience to call out any item from the list, Jean telling them the number against that object. Finally, she would reel off the six-figure number and as she removed her blindfold, received thunderous, well-deserved applause. I'd have left the board and easel to slip back to 'Thanks For The Memory'.

Jean and Pat performed their act, both the memory and the magic in many places in France, for they both spoke fluent French. This was quite a remarkable feat since it would have required some technical word knowledge. Their shows were given great acclaim, return visits being known in advance and posters proclaiming the Great Carson Magic Show with capacity audiences as a result.

The 'Carsons' were truly international and did their part in the 'Entente Cordiale'. Indeed, back in Egypt Jean had performed the memory act in faultless Arabic: formidable! Oh sorry ~ that's French.

All this time I was not only getting used to the magic act and knowing Pat's various nuances and eccentricities but getting to know both of them as very dear friends and would spend hours at their home, discussing future shows and routines over mouth-watering suppers they had prepared. Pat would invite my musical suggestions for various tricks such as 'Pennies From Heaven' and 'Singin' In the Rain' for a trick involving umbrellas and I added 'Chinatown' and 'Limehouse Blues' to his brilliant Chinese Sun and Moon finale.

Pat's stage humour was full of 'one-liners' and he used the two that Colin Dewberry had used at college: 'This is me stick (mystic)' and 'I give them two taps ~ one hot, one cold' which recalled those happy salad days of student life once more. There were many others, terribly corny but a stock-in-trade for magicians I imagine.

'Note,' he would say, 'there is nothing up my sleeves except my two arms and they were a present from my mother.'

And again: 'I learned this trick at my mother's knee ~ or some other low joint.'

And the when the audience roared with laughter: 'How can you look so clean and laugh so dirty?'

As a matter of fact, his mother, a lovely Yorkshire lady who lived to a great age and of whom I was very fond, did a lot for Pat in his lifetime. She had had him learn the violin and paid for dancing lessons which all added to his stagecraft and in later life made many of his 'props' such as the beautiful bag he used for the vanishing egg.

We were doing a lot of children's shows, either at schools, village halls or in private houses and it came as no surprise to me when Pat got himself a rabbit, a white one which was to be part of the Carson show. He taught it to lie down motionless, in fact almost hypnotised it and in the act 'produced' him from a closed saucepan having a ribbon round the neck holding a pocket watch. Earlier in the show Pat had 'borrowed' a watch from a member of the audience, put it in a multicoloured sock and proceeded to smash it apparently with a mallet, to the horror of the owner and the audience. Of course, the delight of seeing the rabbit *and* the 'restored' watch was a sight to behold, particularly on the faces of the children who adored the final 'denouement'.

We did one show at Dowson School where my father was the headmaster which was a great triumph with the children loving every trick and especially the returned watch around the rabbit's neck. Steve James added his weight to the rabbit's appearance in the act with another homely article in the 'EEN', typical of the man who was always so interested in the world of entertainment and magic especially.

As in the dance band business, the venues for shows were very varied and often far-flung. We went out in the depth of winter to give a performance to the sons and daughters of the estate workers at Houghton Hall, in north west Norfolk. After a harrowing journey in which we had to be towed out of a field by a tractor, we were welcomed into a warm stable block at the Hall where the children were having their Christmas party. At the small bar there I asked for a 'Whisky Mac', whereupon the gent behind the counter poured me a glass of Mackeson stout into which he tipped a shot of whisky! Not a concoction for cold weather nor indeed any weather.

The show itself was received with delight, especially when Pat made a snake appear from a basket with the 'correct' playing card in its mouth.

We went to RAF Stations where Pat and Jean did cabaret spots which went down well but I suppose the most unusual gig was at HM Prison in Norwich, where we had to perform to the residents. Various instructions of dos and don'ts were given us by the governor such as no production of cigarettes or alcohol, nor even matches. One prisoner showed us how he made four matches from one using a razor blade to slice it lengthways.

There was something of a disconcerting embarrassment to me to find a couple of ex-pupils among the audience, apparently there for some naughty misdemeanour which I didn't want to know about. However, despite that and the unusual setting for our 'concert' the show was a huge success.

I had the luxury of a grand piano ~ like the curate's egg ~ good in parts and we were given three hearty cheers. With us that day, playing his tenor and soprano sax was Jack Wilkinson who delighted the men with such splendid sounds.

We had one cabaret booking for a dinner dance at Drayton Village Hall where on our arrival were told that the band's pianist had collapsed and died. The organisers asked me if I could 'sit in' with the rest of the band following the magic and memory act to which I at once agreed. The musicians expressed their gratitude to me which was nice of them but unnecessary: there is a great camaraderie among the music fraternity, a bond of friendship to which I have always subscribed. On that night it was my duty to fill the breach, particularly on such a sad and tragic occasion.

Everyone gets asked: Where were you on the night J F Kennedy was assassinated?

Where was I?

With a special show, given by Harry Carson and Company at the Old Folks' Centre on Wroxham Road, Norwich which was at one time run by a splendid gentleman named Tom Higham. Our company that night was talented and assisting Pat, Jean and me were Jack Wilkinson (saxes and mime act), Hilton Tait, a splendid musician singing folk songs to his guitar and George Armes, who had actually found time to come and deliver some of his powerful songs to the packed hall.

Both Pat and George got off to a tremendous start and the quickfire humour had the audience rolling with laughter, so that by the interval we had them 'in the palms of our hands', so delightedly high-spirited were they.

In our dressing room was a radio, which was telling us of the terrible event in Dallas and all of us were naturally shocked, upset and very sombre. With the interval over, Pat went on stage and addressed an expectant audience ~ then entirely ignorant of the tragic news; 'President Kennedy has just been assassinated.'

The reaction was incredible: the entire audience fell about laughing for I suppose they had been treated in the first half to such a bundle of humour, with sherry, coffee and cakes in the interval, that if Pat had gone on and recited 'Mary Had A Little Lamb', the reaction would have been just the same. Not being able to convince them, it was George who strode on and confirmed the dreadful news, emphasising the truth of the matter to the folk that this time we were not joking.

As they say, 'the show had to go on' but the second half naturally lacked the lustre of the first and we were all working under a great strain.

When Alfred Nichols was Lord Mayor of Norwich, he arranged some shows, both in Norwich and the county for the 'Lord Mayor's Fund', though I cannot be sure what the fund was nor exactly why we did the shows. However, I got involved in the entertainment along with Pat and Jean, sometimes Vic Smith and Eric Palmer and others and we went to various village halls, often in remote areas with an occasional appearance of Alfred Nichols himself, a jolly, dapper little man who loved meeting the people.

There were some memorable moments on this 'circuit' such as the Cinema, Briston where Pat and Jean had gone ahead and found the stage filled with tables and chairs and one lamp hanging above the middle or Aylsham Town Hall with a stage made of trestles, one of which slid away revealing a gap down which sank Pat's own table; or the parish hall at Melton Constable where we all changed in a room which served as the kitchen, cloakroom and refreshment counter, as well as our 'green room'.

Pat always referred to the stage as the 'green' which he told me was from the Cockney rhyming slang 'greengage' ~ stage, which naturally made the dressing room of a theatre the green room.

I well remember him severely reprimanding me for whistling in the green room, a terrible thing to do among theatre people, since it was supposed to bring bad luck, especially to the show about to start. I had to be blindfolded, led outside the door, turned round three times and led in backwards. At least, I think that was the order of things but whatever it was or wasn't, it was a reminder to me *never* to whistle in a dressing room again.

Those Alfred Nichols concerts were good fun with a homely and jolly Norfolk audience, hideous pianos and lots of laughter.

One Christmas Eve I had an urgent telephone call from Pat to tell me that his pro magician friend David Berglas was appearing at the Washington Hotel in Norwich and needed help. He had rung Pat and told him that the owner of the hotel, Mr Dashwood had sacked the entire band there and that he, David, was left without anyone to accompany his act. Did Pat know anyone who could come along that evening and play piano for him? Pat did, of course, which is where I came in.

Pat collected me and we went to the Washington, through the front doors, past some heavy looking bouncers and up to David Berglas's room.

He was a broad, hefty man, black curly hair, wide shoulders, twinkling eyes, quite handsome and wearing a black polo neck with trousers to match. He greeted Pat (Harry) like a brother magician would and shook my hand warmly, making me feel very much at home. Sitting on the edge of his bed we went through his 'dots' which seemed fine to me, together with his added instructions and agreed time of arrival, time of cabaret and, of course, pay.

I went along that evening where I was given royal treatment, any drink I wished for with a plate of sandwiches, in fact anything I wanted. The hotel dining room, which was on three sides of the ballroom, was packed and an expectant crowd saw me sit at the piano to wait for the announcement:

'Presenting the world famous magician,
Mr ~ David ~ Berglas!'

Little did they know that my stomach was one mass of butterflies and that I was truly scared stiff. In strode David and his wonderful magic act began, with it has to be said, was simply superb and highly professional and was recognised as such by a most appreciate audience. When he completed his finale to thunderous applause he gave me my perks, clearly appreciated by the audience and off I came.

'Very well done,' he said, paying me most handsomely. 'Is there any chance you could come in tomorrow and Boxing Day?'

I told him that those two days were sacrosanct, that I spent them with my family, a tradition I could not break, which he understood perfectly and like the professional gentleman that he was, did not press the matter further; but it had been a wonderful experience for me.

Something happened to Pat and Jean in 1966 to change their lives completely when Jean, after 18 years of marriage gave birth to a baby girl who was to be Sally, the 'pride of their alley' and of course, the apple of her dad's eye. Very soon, she joined the Carson show for, even as a little girl, she learned her stagecraft well from her talented and devoted parents, coming on to help with the magic, which naturally not only delighted them, but the audiences too. Sally had her own outfit to wear and even her own wand and entered into the act as though she'd been born to it ~ which I suppose she had!

As Sally grew she entered more into the magic and was able to present tricks herself and indeed came on stage at her own school, Notre Dame High when her parents and I were part of a charity show there.

One particular series of shows stands out in my mind at Norwich Castle for Christmas Victorian entertainment for the children, when Pat became Signor Carsoni, assisted by Jean and daughter Sally with music accompaniment by 'Professor Anton', moustached and side-boarded, all reminiscent of college days at the Olde Tyme Music Hall. Pat's mother, just 90 years old, was in the audience that day I remember, enjoying every minute.

Sally herself became a fine singer and musician, playing the clarinet and cello ~ but! ~ not at the same time, with great skill, indeed on occasions like her 'Uncle' Tony using her music to earn her supper. She loved music humour and once directed at me the lovely riddle: 'If you were lost in a jungle, who would you follow to get you out: a pianist who could keep time, a pianist who couldn't keep time or a pink elephant?'

Answer: A pianist who couldn't keep time ~ the other two are figments of the imagination!

When Pat finally decided to finish the magic shows, he took on making 'props' for other magicians both locally and away, for he was extremely gifted in that way too. He had two or three pupils, admirers who listened and learned much, among whom were Peter Fox who rose to become a splendid magician when he was not being a priest ~ or the other way round, David Welch (stage name David Royal) who went on to perform his skills semi-professionally and Keith Dignum who loved magic as a hobby and never aspired for the big time, which is never easy when you're a schoolteacher like Keith. Well, I ought to know.

As well as making, Pat was always mending and with such skill; he once had a tooth filling that kept coming out, despite repeated visits to the dentist, so at last out of sheer exasperation he fixed it with Superglue!

Ann Hornby, a brilliant and well-known violin teacher once took Pat a violin over which she had reversed her car, which hadn't done it much good (the violin, not the car). It wasn't a Strad I hasten to add (the violin, not the car) but it doesn't take much imagination to visualise the state the instrument was in.

'I don't suppose you can do much about it,' said Ann.

That kind of remark always acted like a challenge to Pat, the upshot being that within a matter of days the violin was completely rebuilt and you couldn't see the joins: such was his skill.

His friend John Davenport of the family of Davenports who ran a famous magic store and whose grandfather was a celebrated magician, brought Pat all kinds of very old magic tricks, illusions and automatons to repair. He mended them all of course and John and his wife Ann became close family friends, attending special days at the Swain home when magic conventions were held there.

Included in those gatherings was Paula Baird, first lady magician member of the Magic Circle and a brilliant illusionist in her day.

One of Pat's biggest fans was my dear Aunt Edith who would go to his home with me and delight in his tricks without ever tiring of his magical skill.

I suppose my best memory of Pat is when he was taking his 'practical' exam for the Inner Magic Circle, a coveted title and possessed by an elite few. He told me beforehand that it was very like the time he had an audition with a famous theatrical impresario who sat in the auditorium and watched him come on. No sooner had 'Carson' stepped from the wings than he yelled out; 'Get off! Off! Off!'

This before Pat had opened his mouth. 'Come on again!' he shouted and Pat made his entry.

The same thing happened and the big man barked: 'Call yourself a pro ~ don't you know how to come on? Upstage foot first! Face your audience, man!'

Pat said he never forgot it but it was a hard way to learn.

His 'practical' was seen by Stanley Hammond, a high-up from the Magic Circle with the performance given for children at the old Jenny Lind Hospital on Colman Road in Norwich. I was proud and privileged to be playing piano for him, willing him to do well and with Jean's help and indeed calming influence, he passed with high commendation. In fact, Stanley Hammond was filled with amazement at Pat's skill and could scarcely believe the illusions he was witnessing, totally unaware of any 'examitis' nerves. For here I have to add that before every show Pat was like a caged lion, pacing up and down, worrying about every slight detail, but once on the 'green' was brilliant.

The Carson show closed with its last performance on 9th September 1992 when Pat died of an inoperable tumour, signalling for me the end of a great and lasting friendship both on stage and off and one that holds a pride of place in my life's performance.

I was privileged to write the eulogy to Pat which I read at St Margaret's Church, Old Catton having been preceded by his cremation service at St Faith's. Sally kept a promise to her dad when a tape I had recorded played Carson's final exit ~ 'I'm Just Wild About Harry'.

CHAPTER 10

'Now You Has Jazz'
Brian Green And The Dixielanders

In the Spring of 1955 I bought myself a car, a 1937 Ford 10 which had belonged to a Norwich builder called Westgate and had been locked away in store through the war years (the car, not the builder). It was in excellent condition with very low mileage and was in the saleroom of the Ketteringham brothers in Nelson Street, Norwich, two 'boys' who had been pupils of my father which naturally helped my getting a good deal.

My father taught me to drive and I passed at my second attempt.

The car, which was pale blue, had a sunshine roof, sealed up for some reason, three forward gears, windscreen wipers which worked by air intake and four doors ~ ideal for a gig wagon.

I had saved enough money from gigs to buy the car, having worked 'one-off' engagements with various musicians. I hadn't been able to revive the Maxinas since the members had resorted to other things: Brian Harvey had decided to study for exams at the Norwich Union, preventing him from doing gigs, Richard Brown had gone away, while Roger Vickers had joined another band.

Jack Wilkinson met me in Norwich and we arranged an engagement at Hevingham Fox which I remember was pretty awful and I came across a brilliant but rather eccentric musician called Maurice Stevens, who played among other things, the sax and vibes (vibraphone). I visited his home once where in the lounge were some huge speakers, masses of amplification equipment and one chair, mainly because there was no room for more than one.

I did a few gigs with Maurice, a most likeable fellow but a painfully slow talker and like a proverbial professor having a memory like a sieve.

On one occasion we got to a country venue to play, Maurice due to play vibes but after laboriously setting up the massive steel construction, discovered he had left an essential lead at home which meant a silent vibraphone. Fortunately he had brought his sax with him which saved the day but the dance organisers must have wondered why a huge scaffold-like erection would be standing on the dais apparently not actually making any contribution to the evening.

I lost touch with Maurice who I believed joined a famous circus ~ as bandsman I hasten to add.

The holiday season soon arrived with the prospect of three nights at Potter Heigham with Brian Green and the ever-present Harry Drake running the show in his familiar black outfit reminiscent of an undertaker.

Harry had agreed to a quartet (that is, not counting George Milligan who joined us spasmodically, unpaid) and at my suggestion, Brian enlisted Jack Wilkinson to play sax, since Brian already knew Jack and worked with him before. Both Jack and I were delighted with this because we not only hit it off with his sax playing and my piano, but we shared a love of the same kind of music and I would spend hours at his house ~ number 17 Angel Road, Norwich, listening to his huge record collection.

The season got underway, the holidaymakers came in their droves off the boats, girls made eyes at us (especially Brian) and Harry Drake's wallet made him list on one side. He still gave his 'Oscar' performance with the buckets and thanked 'Brian and his lovely, lovely band which is really a Quartet' at the end of each evening. The fact that George often made it a quintet must have puzzled the dancing public but he was emphasising that he only paid four musicians.

On to the scene arrived a superb bass player, Denis Payne, a friend of Brian's from the past, a member of Jack Andrew's band who had come along to sit in (or rather 'stand in') with no remuneration although we agreed to chip in a little to pay him some petrol money, until such time that Brian could induce Harry to pay for a fifth musician.

Denis came from North Walsham where his parents kept a confectionery/tobacconist shop, helped by Denis and his wife Barbara. He was at that time playing bass with the Ernie Hudson Band, a popular local combo. He was a splendid bass player, purely busking everything since he admitted to being a non-reader and suddenly the rhythm of the band leapt into action. Denis was a great chap to work with, offstage had a tremendous wit and went gliding for a hobby. Little did I realise then what a role he was to play in my musical career.

At the 'Red Lion' in St George's in Norwich musicians used to gather (I suppose being a pub you'd expect that anyway) in an upstairs room where they played a bit of jazz. Brian, Jack, Joe and I went along for curiosity and there we met a couple of young musicians who hailed from Beccles way, who were lodging in Norwich during their working week and going home at weekends. They were Ian Bell, a tall, dark-haired chap studying architecture, who played trombone and Peter Oxborough, a shortish, dark curly-headed lad at Norwich Union who played the clarinet. They were somewhat diffident but said they were anxious to gain experience and would be only too willing to 'sit in' with anyone as long as they played jazz of the trad or Dixieland variety. They both showed extreme promise, although their repertoire was, to begin with, rather limited.

Brian invited them to come over to Potter Heigham which they jumped at, although he was careful to point out that there was no money in it.

Harry Drake was quick to notice two more musicians on stage (he was very sharp in such matters) and to advise Brian he wouldn't be paying them. We were now seven, even if you included George, the small stage became rather crowded and the original band from last year seemed to have grown somewhat.

But the music! It was Dixieland jazz (apart from the occasional waltz) and it flowed from that stage each night, out through the dance hall across the Norfolk Broads, bringing in the boating folk in their dozens.

They loved it, they roared their approval and they roared for more. Each performance got better and better as each night Harry would deliver his thank-you speech to a wildly excited dance set, insisting that the band was really a quartet much to the bewilderment of the customers who could distinctly count seven (sometimes eight) on the stage.

The enthusiasm of the seven of us grew as the sheer brilliance, verve and excitement of the music swept over us. Not George, however, who decided that it wasn't really his scene and quit, for which I felt some sadness for he had been good company in a season and a half and there was as tiny niggling thought: 'Did he leave or was he pushed?'

With the enthusiasm came the question of some payment for Peter and Ian, for after all they were now part of this band that was certainly drawing in the crowds and Harry must have been doing nicely. He agreed to give Brian a bit more cash but kept on reiterating that it was really a quartet, a valid point I suppose since that was what started the season. He was quite a stubborn, difficult man to deal with at times and I suppose had he been a woman, knowing Brian's charm over the fair sex, we could have had an entire symphony orchestra. As it was, the pay was meagre but nonetheless the enthusiasm still ran high.

'What we really need to make the rhythm section swing and sound authentic,' said Brian, 'is a banjo,' to which the others at once agreed.

I recalled that night at the 'Unthank Arms' and a certain Dennis 'Lonnie' Howes and passed on the name to Brian. The upshot was that Brian went into Burton's shop in Norwich and recruited Dennis to come over to Potter Heigham and bring his banjo to sit in with what was now 'Brian Green's Dixielanders'.

The addition of the banjo to the line-up was tremendously exhilarating and the power of the rhythm section was sharp and clear-cut, though it had to be said that Joe Eden had not yet mastered the art of the upbeat and we still had side drum beats on first and third.

Peter and Ian began to complain that the band was 'dragging' which resulted in occasional heated arguments twixt Joe and the front line.

Lonnie's presence crowded the stage even more, of course, although he came gratis, arriving each time leather-clad on his motorbike. A further renewal of a former acquaintance took place when one evening Dick Pearce appeared on the scene.

Gradually the season drew to a close with Harry telling the surprised dancers right up to the end they had been entertained by Brian Green's lovely, lovely quartet, though by then the myth was beginning to wear a bit thin. Brian tried every trick he knew to get more cash out of Harry but to no avail, Harry insisting that he had engaged a four-piece which had somehow become eight and that was that.

Of course, there was mention of next season with Brian declaring he was now an eight-piece Dixieland band and that if Harry wanted the band in 1956 it would be that number for the appropriate fee. No agreement was made, with the result that we closed the season, more or less knowing we wouldn't be back ~ at least not with Mr Drake in command.

Those early days of the birth of Brian Green and the Dixielanders were filled with excitement and anticipation, particularly since there seemed to be a revival of Dixieland and 'Trad' jazz at the time.

We all went to be fitted with band jackets at Alexander's Tailoring in London Street where I believe Brian had a contact; the jackets were green ~ well, what else? ~ with matching ties (not bows) and grey-green flannel trousers. Brian had a green music stand made: there was only the one ~ his ~ since he was the only one who read music, apart from me. The tendency to make everything green to match the name had one rather humorous moment later on when Brian himself had a kidney infection for which he was taking tablets which had the effect of turning his water green. This was noticed by a keen follower of the band (male!) who said: 'This beats everything ~ green name, green uniform, green stand and now . . . green!'

We all attended a photo 'call' at a studio on Price of Wales' Road in Norwich called Raoul's where we had a black and white montage made of the band, showing a portrait of each of us with our instruments under a scroll bearing the band's name. There being no piano in the studio, I was depicted with my hands poised over a sheet of card with black lines representing keys which did look rather amateurish. Several sizes of the composite photo were produced which we used for advertising and display purposes and met our gaze at many a venue in time to come.

A big item at the band's inception was the question of music, a library that is. Brian did not have much of a repertoire of Dixieland jazz which meant that we had to start looking for titles, many of which Peter Oxborough already knew and I had to go and pester Billy Willson and his staff at the music shop for sheet copies.

I went in search of titles like ' Fidgety Feet' by Nick la Rocca of the Original Dixieland Jass Band, 'Jazz Me Blues', 'Royal Garden Blues', 'Shimmy Like My Sister Kate' and many others. Many were not published so I purchased a supply of manuscript paper and coped them off 78rpm records which we borrowed or bought. All it really needed was a melody line for Brian, for brilliant trumpet player though he was, he did not find busking easy, especially with less familiar titles, a few noted chords for me and the rest of the band followed easily.

George Bernard Shaw (not a jazz aficionado by the way) once said there were nine stories by which he meant there were nine basic plots with variations. I don't know about nine set pieces but it's basically the same with jazz, there being variations on a theme or themes with chord sequences following the same or similar patterns. You can see the chords coming which is why when jazz musicians get together for a 'jam session' they gel so well, the chords, phrases and general structure all amalgamating into one harmonic and therefore pleasing sound ~ well, to jazz enthusiasts, anyway. To maiden aunts and retired colonels it can sound like purgatory.

Brian then got a friend to print cards and stationery (in green of course) while I continued to add more numbers to the band library with the help of the exasperated staff at Willson's Music Bazaar or from scratchy recordings of the likes of Jelly Roll Morton, Bunny Berigan, Mugsy Spanier and the Original Dixieland Jass Band.

Practice sessions began at various upper rooms of pubs, probably frequented by music lovers, non-music lovers, the tone deaf or stone deaf or just possibly, jazz enthusiasts. There were just a few of these (jazz enthusiasts) among them another Norwich Union man named Ray Polley, a likeable chap called Jack Stanley who lived at Eaton Street, Tony Coe who was engaged to one of the girls at Willson's Music and my brother David.

So it was that we had a fine band with a good sound, though still lacking the drive in the 'kitchen' department it must be said, with the front line blending well, soloists taking some lovely 'breaks', excellent 'stop' choruses and even solo bars from banjo, bass and piano. In fact we rated ourselves good enough to play along with the best but there was one big question: where would that be? Where were the gigs coming from and who would pay for an eight-piece band?

One idea was to launch our own gig, hiring premises, advertising and trying to get customers. We arranged with the landlord of the 'White Horse' at Horstead, close by Coltishall bridge (it's long since gone ~ not the bridge but the pub) to have a rather grotty room at one side of it to run a dance, hoping to attract both locals and late holidaymakers.

The eight of us set up on a small stage with a fairly ghastly piano, where we were joined by Dick Pearce on unpaid bongos, though why I can't imagine, unless it was for the occasional rush of Latin blood from Brian and band. My mother and father were featured on door as Dick quaintly put it: that is, they were taking entrance money and had come armed with tickets and small change.

For quite some while my parents were the entire audience as we played some passably good jazz and it looked as if the 'White Horse' should have the name 'Dead Duck'. However, gradually people came in, some local, some from Norwich and others from the boats, all to listen or dance or both. The dust from the floor rose in great clouds, choking everybody including us as we received the 'fall out' from those pounding around to 'High Society' and 'Tiger Rag'.

Daylight disappeared, the lights went on and further customers came in, mainly from the 'White Horse' and other local pubs, some intent on trouble (you always get a few who want to cause problems ~ why, I shall never know).

Shortly after my mother and father had left for home, the troublemakers started interfering with the lights, causing the females to scream and Joe Eden to rush from the bandstand intent on 'thumping those responsible'. The lights went up again to reveal Joe, minus jacket, squaring up to a defiant-looking youth who was taunting him and throwing the odd punch with Joe just waiting for his moment to pitch in. What followed was a minor scuffle, the defiant youth receiving at least two very painful blows which made him decide to exit quickly and Joe returning to the stand, somewhat dishevelled with a slightly bloody lip.

On the whole, the 'White Horse' project had not been a very successful one, although the enthusiastic praise of some of the customers had been encouraging. We did try a couple more times but they were both poorly attended and in any case, nobody really cared much for the surroundings, most of all us.

A jazz band concert was arranged by Tony Coe and a few other jazz friends to be held at Cow Hill Hall in Norwich which was to feature the Collegians, a highly popular city trad jazz band and Brian Green's Dixielanders with guest artist George Melly.

I remember that night so well: the place was packed to overflowing and there were great roars from the crowd as the Collegians opened the show with one of their rousing numbers. Their line-up that night was a very familiar one of men who had been together for yonks: led by the eccentric and irrepressible Eric Varnon on drums who always wore odd socks, they were Les Gostling (trumpet), Peter Webb (trombone), Johnny Harrison (clarinet), Charlie Sartain (banjo), John Barker (double bass), Kevin Gill (piano) and Colin Burleigh (vocals).

The crowd, growing in number by the minute, loved it all, for there was no doubt that the Collegians were a fine trad band, playing some superb 'head' arrangements and because of the years they had played together, knew everything perfectly.

'Presenting to you, for their first public performance, Brian Green and the Dixielanders,' said the compere and we swung into 'Washington And Lee Swing' to the crowd's applause. I think I can say without question that the audience was stunned as Brian played some scintillating trumpet, Peter broke into his super clarinet articulation and with Ian driving through with a splendid Turk Murphy style trombone, the hall fairly rocked. When 'Washington And Lee' ended, the crowd erupted with wild delight. We followed it with more of the same to their joy and obvious amazement from the Collegians, who realised they now had some rivalry, which I hasten to add was always friendly.

George Melly, having been summoned from the pub opposite, came on stage next and rampaged and roared his way through some great numbers in his inimitable style up to the interval, during which there was much excited talk and much speculation about the 'new' Dixieland outfit. Apart from perhaps Jack Wilkinson, Brian was fielding a team of unknowns, newcomers with a lot of talent and the crowds were curious and full of praise, particularly older musicians among them.

The second half was even better than the first, each of the bands saving their special numbers for a finale. George Melly, having spent most of the night in the pub across the way, seemed quite incapable of standing, let alone put over his songs, but as soon as he was propelled on to that stage, he presented more of his raunchy, raucous numbers like a sober judge to the great approval of everyone.

The end came with a get-together of musicians blasting out the audience's favourite (and the musicians' least favourite) 'When The Saints Go Marching In'.

At Preservation Hall in New Orleans anyone who wants 'The Saints' has to pay extra for it, otherwise the pensioner band there will not include it in their programme!

Everyone agreed that the Cow Hill concert was an enormous success, including the Press which was to augur well for Brian's band in a very short while.

Two entrepreneurs were quick off the mark to engage the band, two men who were as different as chalk from cheese.

The first was Mr Ashley Thomas, the genial host of 'The Cottage' at Thunder Lane, Norwich where provision was made for dancing on Saturday nights, there being a small dance floor with a low stage near the exit and ~ would you believe ~ a baby grand!

Posters announced the new band's arrival, our portraits prominently displayed with, as far as I remember, a surcharge for dancing.

To say that Mr Thomas had made a shrewd move would be something of an understatement, for that Saturday night saw crowds arriving such as 'The Cottage' had never seen before. By 8 o'clock the place was so full you could hardly move with seats at such a premium that if anyone stood up, their chair was taken and that included those in the band!

One after the other the jazz numbers came, the crowds around the stage almost swamping us, while at the other end of the room Mr Thomas and his staff desperately coped to keep pace with the drinks orders. The fans applauded solos from everybody in true jazz concert fashion, especially when Peter did the famous clarinet solo in 'High

Society' or when Ian imitated the tiger in 'Tiger Rag', followed by Brian's growling trumpet.

I was featured in 'St Louis Blues', starting the minor bit with a Latin pulse which broke into a straight 4/4 on the chorus but the biggest hit of the night was each of us taking a solo in 'Momma Don't Allow No Jazz Band Playing In Here' with the entire band concluding the number, the front line standing. That standing up at the last chorus in most numbers was a great impact on the audience who just roared their approval and demanded more.

Inevitably, the last number was 'The Saints' with the very last chorus all standing, finishing with the familiar 'long ending' ~ saints ~ go ~ marching ~ in. It was scintillating stuff, the crowd loved it, Mr Thomas's takings had shot through the roof and we were booked again under the heading:

Jazz at The Cottage ~ come early to avoid disappointment'

Indeed we were engaged on a fortnightly basis, the other Saturday spot being filled with the Collegians and those crowds kept coming as the word spread with Mr Thomas having to set a capacity limit, turning people away on many nights.

The other enterprising gentleman was Mr Joe Littlewood at the famous Banham Pavilion Dance Hall in South Norfolk where crowds flocked to listen and dance to bands from all over the place, from Suffolk and Cambridgeshire as well as Norfolk.

Joe, a straight-talking North countryman with a garage business in Banham, ran a very profitable 'emporium' (as he called it) with his wife organising the tea and coffee, son Alex assisted by Norwich teacher Marjorie Hey on refreshments and a rather bizarre pair on wines, spirits and beers. I say 'somewhat' bizarre, since the husband seemed very precious and effeminate while the wife wore a man's suit and had her hair plastered with Brylcreem, which I suppose made them the archetypal odd couple, although no-one seemed to notice it much and in any case, they were very pleasant.

The Banham Hall was a large wooden structure, not unlike Harry Drake's place at Potter Heigham, except that the stage was at one end and not in the corner and you could get behind the stage to the kitchens and the ladies' loo.

There were green (yes!) stage curtains, a battery of lights which at times made it very hot indeed, a white baby grand and a vent above the band to give a down-draught when the heat became too much. The seats in the hall were cinema seats for when it was not a dance hall, Joe Littlewood showed films there. Just for once, the seats were not Brian's colour, but maroon!

Joe, a splendid businessman booked us for another fortnightly spot to alternate with 'The Cottage' and a huge following of the Dixielanders was born with an unofficial fan club being run. Photographs of the band were on sale, coach loads of girls flocked to Banham which pleased Joe Littlewood but probably more so Brian and we signed autographs galore during the evening like film stars.

All this time, however, things were not going well for Joe Eden on the drums, who tried so hard to 'get it right' but couldn't and encountered Brian's continuing frustration, as well as Peter and Ian's, even to the extent of Brian himself taking over on drums in the middle of the dancing. That, of course was not very professional of Brian and I recalled how an accordionist named Derek Page, once did it to me in my very early days in dance band work as I struggled to busk the waltz 'The Kiss In Your Eyes'. I remember how embarrassed I felt at the time, conscious of those on the dance floor watching. Derek went on to become a member of George Mitchell's Black And White Minstrels, touring all over the UK.

Joe sought my help, hoping I would be able to show him how to play the upbeats and hold them through the numbers and for a time I thought he had mastered it. However, he kept lapsing, the glares came from the front line with the 'dragging' comments as a piece ended and Joe, half in anger, half in desperate frustration denied he was drumming incorrectly and was certainly not the cause of the 'dragging'. It was evident that Brian wanted a replacement although since Joe Eden was Brian's boss during the working day, it presented him with something of a problem.

In March 1956 Joe had to go on a business course up in Manchester for two weeks which meant that Brian had to find a drummer for the Dixielanders. The obvious choice was Dick Pearce who had followed the band around, occasionally sitting in or playing bongos and often accompanied Denis (Lonnie) Howes when I brought him, together with Jack Wilkinson, to gigs.

With the advent of Dick on drums came a change in the band sound that was a total revolution for his beat lifted the whole outfit, completely transforming the rhythm section. There was now such a tremendous drive that had been so lacking and the numbers now swung into action as never before.

Of course, once we in the band felt the change, so did the customers and as Dick grew more and more confident he really began to 'break loose'. Brian encouraged him to do drum break choruses which the crowds loved as well as the wonderful 'tag' endings at the conclusion of swingers such as '1919 March' or 'At The Jazz Band Ball'.

I think we all knew deep down that Dick was here to stay, that spelled the exit for Joe. It has to be said the Brian was not a terribly strong leader of men which meant in this instance he could not bring himself to tell Joe when he returned that he had been replaced, though I think he feared Joe's fiery temperament.

Brian entreated Denis Payne, forever the band diplomat to break the news to Joe. To say that Joe did not take the matter well might be how a politician might put it, but in fact he was absolutely raging, going round to Jack's (the mildest of men), to Lonnie, to my parents (though why them I really don't know) and then of course to both Dick and Brian.

It was all rather unpleasant and sad, for I felt sorry for Joe who had never really been a drummer in the first place when Brian took him on at Potter Heigham. He teamed up soon afterwards with a pianist named Stan Platten who, between them, did a few gigs but he rather lost heart which was not surprising. As for the shoe shop, I think Brian made his departure from there (rather wisely) and I know that Joe left Norwich to manage a branch in the Midlands.

Both Ashley Thomas at 'The Cottage' and Joe Littlewood at 'Banham Pavilion' saw further than just local talent and decided to attract a big 'name' or two. Of course, here money was a determining factor, Joe having more freedom to spend since it was his own business while Mr Thomas's outlay was governed by the brewery and bar takings. However, we had some solo guest artists at

'The Cottage' and I remember Joe Harriot coming and Ronnie Scott, each bringing their own rhythm section which were big crowd pullers despite not being trad jazz players.

At Banham, Joe brought some big names down but I do remember he pulled out of a contract to have Victor Silvester after he learned that the orchestra required two grand pianos. 'I'm not having that,' he fumed. 'How the . . . ~ . . . does he think I can get two grand pianos; I've got one as it is.'

Truth to tell, Joe's grand was none too grand but to his credit he'd always have it looked at if I found something amiss ~ which was quite often.

Our greatest night at the Pavilion was opposite the Ray Ellington Quartet at the height of their fame with their radio appearances on 'The Goon Show'.

Ray was the leader on drums, occasionally singing a catchy, jazzy or sometimes crazy number, Marion Ryan the girl vocalist, Judd Proctor on guitar, a Canadian bass player whose name eludes me and a marvellous pianist called Dick Katz. They played some great stuff but of course our biggest thrill was to meet them and chat backstage, hearing all about the pro side of the business.

Ray Ellington, a big built West Indian-type man was kind, courteous, all praising of our music and utterly crackers, which he told us came naturally from working with the likes of Peter Sellers and Spike Milligan. He lived in St John's Wood, London, had won £75,000 on the football pools with which he had purchased some property in Park Lane (today you'd probably be able to buy half a one bedroom flat with luck) and was a self-taught drummer.

He invited us to go to a 'Goon Show' rehearsal which he said was ten times more hilarious than the actual broadcast, an invitation which he repeated when we met him and his quartet again at the Samson and Hercules Ballroom in Norwich. It was an invitation we never took up, something I have always regretted for at the time we were all 'Goon Show' fans.

Ray's pianist, Dick Katz, signed my sheet music copy of Hoagy Carmichael's 'Rockin' Chair' with the words:

'To Tony ~ I enjoyed your fine music ~ Dick Katz'

which I have kept treasured ever since.

Not content with going home to rest after a long gig, the band would gather down at 'Bob's Cafe' on Drayton Road in Norwich for sausages, egg and chips with mugs of tea and, above all, a great laugh. Laughter was all prevailing with totally irrational, absurd behaviour such as Dick conducting his 'imaginary' gran around in a wheelchair while Ian blew a toy trombone that eventually took on a bizarre shape. Customers at Bob's (who was a genial man without a surname) began to look forward to our entrance, enjoying the drivel and nonsense and entering into the spirit of the whole crazy and often riotous charade.

Whenever I drive down Drayton Road I see ghosts of Bob, his cafe and my mad youth of yesterday.

There was no doubt that the band needed a base, somewhere permanent. Yes, 'The Cottage' and 'Banham Pavilion' were alternate week residencies but we had to have a regular spot to perform and possibly use as a practice room.

We began hunting for such a place without much luck until Peter and Ian hit on the idea of a jazz club, somewhere the jazz-loving public could come and meet and hear live jazz, not just us but guesting bands or personalities.

Excited by such an idea we intensified our search until we had a big stroke of luck when Dick discovered Herbert Frazer Hall ~ no not an impresario ~ but the social room of the Norwich Labour Club in Bethel Street. Negotiations went on between the club officers and us with an agreement reached whereby they charged us a 'peppercorn' rent for the use of the room on a Monday night and the promise to keep the place in good order.

The room was quite long but narrow with a small stage at one end equipped with a piano (about 6 out of 10) and could be reached by a side door without having to go through the bars of the Labour Club. There was a good supply of chairs with extra available if needed; in fact, a room ideal for the purpose ~ a homely, friendly jazz club for devotees of our kind of music.

We began to make plans for an opening night, the idea that patrons on that night could sign to become members, entitling them to discount entrance on future evenings.

I then designed a large backcloth to go at the rear of the stage on which I sketched a Mississippi River Boat copied from the sleeve of a jazz LP and with help from a couple of the band, painted it in poster colours adding a splash of brightness to the wall.

What's in a name? people say; but it is important and we had to have a name for people to latch on to and remember.

'Brian Green's Jazz Club', 'The Dixieland Club', 'City Jazz Spot', 'Trad Land' were names thrown up and almost immediately thrown out. We asked for ideas from close followers of the band such as my brother David, Jack Stanley and Tony Coe but nothing really seemed to be snappy enough or quick to roll off the tongue, as they say.

It was than that I saw on the doorpost of the Labour Club entrance a number '59'.

'That's it,' I said ~ 'The 59 Jazz Club.'

Everyone looked at each other, then nodded approval.

'Well done,' said Brian, 'and it's been there under our noses all the time.'

So there it was: The 59 Jazz Club was born, posters were put up reading:

'Grand Opening Night of the 59 Jazz Club, Bethel Street,
featuring Brian Green and the Dixielanders with guest band,
the famous Collegians'

and we waited in anticipation for the Monday.

That opening night, with Dick's father, Fred, featured 'on door', exceeded all expectations in every way, with the place packed to overflowing, some standing outside the main room, the larger number of members joining straight away and the sheer enthusiasm and approval shown by all who where there. As for the jazz: it was exciting, thrilling and electric, both bands giving their all and delighting the huge crowd with highly polished performances.

The '59 Jazz Club' was without doubt a highly successful venture at a time when Trad and Dixieland jazz was at its height of popularity with hundreds ~ yes, hundreds of members, both male and female of all ages. It was so good to see the generation gap bridged by what I considered to be such a happy, carefree sound played by highly competent musicians who thoroughly enjoyed ~ nay, loved the music they made and I felt proud and elated to be a part of it.

Each week the crowds came, even in bad weather, with the members asking for their favourite things such as Peter Oxborough's memorable 'Girls Go Crazy About The Way I Walk', the superb harmonies of 'Creole Love Call', my arrangement for the band of 'Great Little Army' and Ian's great trombone spot in 'Ory's Creole Trombone'. They loved too the version of 'I Want a Girl Just Like The Girl That Married Dear Old Dad' with the band singing a chorus of the changed words 'I Want Some Beer Just Like The Beer That Pickled Dear Old Dad'. Our finale was always 'Momma Don't Allow' and of course by sheer demand 'The Saints Go Marching In' with Dick hammering out drum breaks until we thought he'd burst; often his sticks would go flying but he always carried a spare pair while the first set was retrieved.

We invited a few 'names' via our agent Ray Polley which included the great veteran trumpet player Nat Gonella who was such a charming man and wonderful character, Les Hague, the Norwich-born guitarist who delighted all with his dextrous playing, Norwich girl Beryl Bryden and other guest bands were brought to Norwich but the 59 Jazz Club was not big enough to accommodate the huge numbers of people which was why Laurie Singer at the Gala Ballroom in St Stephen's allowed the concerts to be held there. I remember the splendid Cy Laurie band and the Terry Lightfoot Jazzmen filling the Gala to capacity crowds with the able backing of the Dixielanders.

My brother borrowed a trumpet which he taught himself to play and was allowed to sit in for one or two numbers at the Club, much to the delight of his own fan club, one of his favourite numbers being 'Just a Closer Walk With Thee' which began in slow hymn style and then went wallop into a brisk stomp.

Some of my happiest jazz memories are of that 59 Jazz Club where people came together to enjoy and 'lap up' the music they loved, both performers and listeners alike, a club that has long since gone but is wistfully recalled by many who were a part of it.

My music life would be incomplete without the mention of Ann (or Anna) of the 'Jolly Butchers' in Ber Street in Norwich, known by some as 'Black Anna' on account of her raven black hair braided on the top of her head and her black clothes which she always wore.

She was Ann Hanant, neé Carrara of Italian origins who kept the 'Jolly Butchers' which became renowned for Ann's jazz voice with jazz nights there regularly, many fine musicians doing 'jam sessions' at will.

Ann's singing was of the Blues variety with the style and panache of Sophie Tucker, Ma Rainey, Billie Holliday and others all rolled into one, both raucous and raunchy which the customers adored.

Members of our band would go there often, either for a chat at a quiet time or when the pub was bulging at the seams with folk hardly able to breathe, let alone sink a pint.

Ann would say, 'The young people ask me to sing some of my dirty songs but tell them I don't sing dirty: it's only what's in your mind.

Some of her titles I recall were 'Let Your Linen Hang Low' and 'You've Got the Right Key But The Wrong Keyhole' ~ admittedly all suggestive blues numbers which she put over in her rather saucy way but she was most certainly a lady and highly professional as an entertainer. I played for her a few times with Brian and the others 'backing' but often the place was too crowded for musicians to have room to breathe and it was left to the piano to be her accompaniment, the bar being of such bijou proportions.

Her regular piano player was the highly accomplished Derek Warne who later went on to become Ted Heath's pianist and arranger.

Ann would occasionally leave her beloved 'Jolly Butchers' to sing with the Dixielanders at a private function or at the 59 Jazz Club but she was never very willing, often highly nervous and as a result her performances lacked the verve she achieved in her own surroundings.

She was a wonderful artiste, having a tremendous repertoire of songs which she put over in great style, delighting hundreds of her unofficial fan club who came from far and wide to see her.

Alas, she is long gone and so too has her beloved public house, just like the great jazz era she and I knew and loved.

In 1956 Brian and the Dixielanders went up to London on a two-fold mission: first, to make a 'demo' recording and second, for an audition with BBC Radio.

Ashley Thomas of 'The Cottage' drove us to the smoke in his minibus where we headed for Aeolian Hall to meet Graham Muir, producer of 'In Town Tonight' and Eric Maschwitz, who wrote the song 'Room Five Hundred And Four' and 'These Foolish Things', head of Light Entertainment.

It was quite early in the morning, everyone was nervous as we played a couple of numbers carefully rehearsed which were 'Washington And Lee Swing' and 'When My Dreamboat Comes Home' but we did not play well.

It reminds me of the story that went around of when impresario Larry Parnes was hearing a group play 'Telstar' and said, 'No, no boys, I don't like it. Take it up a crotchet.'

Mr Maschwitz asked us to do a couple more which they recorded, after which we went along to the canteen for something to eat and drink.

Whilst we waited for some decisions we met John Barry and the John Barry Seven who had been recording for audition in similar vein.

To everyone's delight and amazement we were booked to appear on 'In Town Tonight' in a week's time to broadcast 'live' and with that exciting thought we made our way over to a street just off Soho where we met my brother David who was already in London and seemed willing to play unpaid agent for the band.

We crowded into a recording studio and cut two sides, the first numbers we had played for the BBC audition earlier. Whilst we were waiting for the record to be produced, my brother conducted us to a Chinese restaurant he knew and we all ate a good lunch.

Everyone agreed the disc was a great success and we all came away with a copy each which was a 45rpm Extended Play to then make our journey home to Norwich.

It is not my intention in this book to defame anyone living or dead but it is sufficient to say that the BBC broadcast never took place, much to the disappointment of the BBC and certainly us, all down to reasons which are best unrevealed. I can only sit and reflect on what might have been, for unlike the John Barry Seven who went on to find fame and fortune at national level, Brian Green's Dixielanders did not.

Seven of the Dixielanders took a week's holiday at Butlin's, Skegness that same year, Denis Payne unable to get away from his father's shop in North Walsham. We all took our instruments, although I'm not included here, since pianos were rather hefty to carry around and I just had to hope that pianos on the camp were high out of 10.

The talent competition was held on the second day starting at 8.30 in the morning ~ with us!

We staggered from breakfast into the theatre and I remember a redcoat asking me if I could see the music, the stage being dimly lit, to which I replied I could hardly see the piano, let alone the music!

Anyway, we played a couple of numbers which seemed to please the redcoat and we left for the 'Pig And Whistle', the camp pub.

Brian had a word with someone behind the bar which led to our playing impromptu jazz there at lunch time to great crowds of enthusiastic campers.

Now you musn't do that sort of thing, it seemed, for after a while through the cheering, happy crowd came two uniformed gentlemen to inform us that we couldn't play there as it wasn't allowed, which certainly didn't please us or the people around.

We went off to the Empress Ballroom to listen to the Don Black Orchestra and whilst we were there, some official gentlemen came and asked us if we would like to play each morning in the Empress Ballroom. We agreed straight away and next morning we appeared there from 10.30 to midday playing Dixieland jazz to large numbers of campers and would you believe ~ wanting autographs and photos! We also played a jazz concert to around 5,000 campers.

And then it started to rain without stopping for the rest of the week, with some folk considering building an ark while others actually left for home. Duckboards had to be put along routes to chalets (or billets, as Ian Bell kept insisting on calling them) folk got drenched going from chalet to breakfast or restaurant to ballroom and I believe songs around the camp fire fizzled out.

We enjoyed evenings in the other dance hall where Joe Daniels and his band played, making friends with the musicians and also becoming friendly with a redcoat named Dave Allen, later to become a well-known TV personality. Dave had worked at Butlin's as a redcoat with another friend of ours ~ Joe Dade who has to keep turning up in my musical life from time to time.

At the end of the week with the rain lashing down harder than ever, we were miserably packing our cases when an excited lady who had some difficulty in sounding her esses, rushed through the puddles shouting to us, 'You musht come. You've won shum prishes. You've won shum walletsch!'

We followed this lady who kept reassuring us, 'Yesh, yesh, you've won shum walletsch' into the Empress Ballroom to the cheers of the crowd.

There, after an announcement that Brian Green and the Dixielanders, who had delighted everyone with their jazz each morning, were to come forward and receive a 'thank you' gift from Billy Butlin (well, not him personally).

It was like the team going up for medals at Wembley as we received our gifts and a Butlin badge with the now familiar lady guide standing by repeating her favourite word ~ 'Walletsch'.

It was a consolation to a week which had been very wet but a happy experience to remember.

Back at Norwich the band played on with the Lord Mayor's concert at the old Hippodrome Theatre in aid of Hungarian relief, an event we shared with other bands, including of course, the Collegians.

We played the first half of a jazz concert at Saint Andrew's Hall, the second half being held by the great Sidney Bechet and Humphrey Lyttleton and there was a trip to London to play at a jazz club where Acker Bilk was starring but not a great one to relate since we got stuck in horrendous London traffic, making us extremely late at the club.

The Dixielanders and I parted company early in 1957 and Roy Copping took my place at the piano.

It had been a tremendous experience, the music had been of a very high standard and the band had enjoyed a huge success everywhere, which I had been privileged to share.

Not long after my departure, the Brian Green Dixielanders broke up, the members each going their own ways and the jazz public ruing their loss.

As for me, I was thinking about putting a quartet together to cater for a dancing public and ideas began to form in my mind, until one day I knew just what I wanted.

Brian Green and the Dixielanders at the 59 Jazz Club

Dick Pearce in a drumming stint at the jazz club

The Dixielanders at the ballroom, West Runton Pavilion

The Rémon Quartet taken at the studio of Alex Forbes Wright
Circa 1958

The Signor Carsoni entertainers at Norwich Castle 1981

A scene from 'Let's Ask The Teacher'

The opening chorus from 'Double Dutch'

A scene from 'The Prince and Gipsy'

The Dance of the Tartars from 'The Willow Pattern'

The members of the school jazz band

CHAPTER 11

Seven Years Of Plenty ~ The Rémon Quartet 1957-64

PART ONE
'The Stately Homes Of England'

Just two weeks after leaving the Dixielanders I had a letter from a trumpet player called Johnny Playle who lived at Apple Tree Cottage at Aldeby, near Beccles asking me to play piano with his band at ~ guess where? The Dance Hall, Potter Heigham no less, Harry Drake and all!

Well, I was free, so why not?

The season started with me on the same old piano, Johnny himself on trumpet, doubling guitar, Brian Crane from Beccles on tenor sax and clarinet and Neville Brown on drums with the same old Harry on front of house.

The outfit hadn't changed, neither had the brevity of conversation with any mention of Brian Green giving a response 'Silly boy, silly boy.'

I got on well with the others in the band, enjoyed the music and renewed acquaintances with several holidaymakers who quite naturally asked after Brian and the others.

The season was uneventful, Harry was as grumpy as ever but at least it was a regular gig twice ~ sometimes three times a week and all the time plans buzzed around in my head.

Towards the end of that summer I went to see Jack Wilkinson who was now out of work and outlined my plans for a quartet to him, who in turn mentioned it all to Dick Pearce and Denis Payne.

When the Broads gig closed in September with my farewells to the three musicians and Harry Drake, I went to see Dick and Denis to ask them to join me as drummer and bass player, along with Jack Wilkinson on tenor and soprano saxes.

They had been convinced that I would want reading musicians since they knew I read music, probably expecting me to use published 'orks' which would have been 'out' for them, being non-readers. However, I knew what I wanted: good men who knew the business well, knew scores of buskers and were ready to embark on a venture with me into the highly cut-throat business of gig work.

I wanted my quartet to be the best, to play the best and to aim for the best. I recalled my student adventure to Bagshot 'Pantiles' with the glam and glitter, the Rolls and the Caviar. We would break into that world of the landed gentry and the stately homes and in our small corner of England be like Tommy Kinsman, Jack Barker or even Paul Adam, all the 'Deb's Delights' and darlings of the Upper set. Whether or not I thought that if I should bleed, the colour would be blue or perhaps I just had ideas of illusions of grandeur, I don't know.

If we were to aim high, we wanted to look good with a really special distinctive feature, apart from just our handsome profiles and who better to ask about band jackets but our own Dick Pearce at Burton's Tailoring. As luck would have it, Burton's had been commissioned to make the new outfit for the Cromer Town Crier from some wonderful crimson material especially ordered and Dick enquired of his manager, the genial Mr Bert Harvey, if there would be sufficient left to make four band jackets for us.

Apparently there was and the four of us were measured for an outfit of heavy barathea/wool mix by Dick and his colleagues with the promise of a generous discount. As a matter of fact, Dick, whilst working at Burton's would always slip one of our band cards into a customer's new jacket or suit, with his usual eye to business, something of which Montague Burton would have been proud!

The finished band jackets were superb, officially in 'hunting pink' as was pointed out to us many times in months to follow but they looked bright red to us, both elegant and smart.

Now we needed a title for ourselves, completely rejecting ideas such as Tony Ireland and his Band or the Tony Ireland Quartet but wanting a special word as distinctive as our jackets and one that people could retain.

The Maxinas had been a simple name but it was out of my past and out of the past long before that, an old dance of vintage years. Still at a loss for inspiration, I duly perused some music of my brother's ~ hand-written music for the jazz trumpet of some Creole tunes and other things from Martinique and the French influenced parts of New Orleans.

Among the many bits of manuscript was one bearing the title Rémon ~ just one word, nothing more and I knew in that instant I had a name: The Rémon Quartet. It looked classy, it looked intelligent and it looked different and distinctive, though I hadn't the least idea what it meant.

Strangely enough, in the seven years' life of my quartet I was hardly ever asked about the name or its origin.

A school friend of mine, John Bacon (later to become an Anglia Television newscaster) had joined in partnership with Terry Read (later to become a distinguished horticulturist) in a printing business by Blackfriars' Hall in Norwich. John and Terry designed and printed me some cards and embossed notepaper in red and blue which looked very attractive.

At the same time I went to a shop in Magdalen Street and set us up with an amplifier, mike and mike stand, a 'toy kit' when put alongside the vast collection of ear-splitting paraphernalia used today.

Jack Wilkinson and I compared our busking lists which showed we had more than enough quicks, slows, waltzes and Latins to call on, together with the necessary Olde Tyme and novelty dances.

I remember that one such novelty dance then was the 'Hokey Cokey' which, according to a retired band leader named Jerry Hooey, was his own invention called after him 'The Hooey Cooey', something which he would relate to his customers at 'The Arcade Stores' in Norwich and later the 'Woodside' at Thorpe.

Although Denis and I had cars, we really needed transport of a larger nature to take us around or in other words, a 'band wagon' and we renewed acquaintance with one of the Dixielanders' followers, Jack Stanley. Jack had a van, one of indeterminate age that shook, rattled, let in draughts, had extremely uncomfortable seats, needed various bits of repair and looked from the outside as though it might be carrying something up to Covent Garden.

However, it had engine, brakes, four wheels and a spare with a few other essentials and what was most important ~ room for drums, double bass, amplifier and four musicians, but sadly not a piano.

Jack readily agreed to be our transport manager, willing to drive us to our various venues in return for payment (naturally) and a few drum lessons from Dick.

There's a great story told about a sax player with the Count Basie orchestra that used to tour the USA by luxury coach, sometimes covering many hundreds of miles between gigs. The musicians would sleep on the journey, with this particular sax player going 'all the way' and changing into pyjamas.

On one particular trip, the coach stopped at a highway café and our saxophonist, feeling a call of nature, went to the washroom. Imagine his horror at finding the coach gone, so with no alternative began to hitch a lift to the nearest police station.

Imagine too the conversation with a highly suspicious police sergeant, suddenly being confronted with a pyjama-clad, probably unshaven character in the early hours.

Police Sergeant: 'How can I help you sir?'

Sax P: 'I'm afraid I lost my 'bus.'

PS: 'Oh yes sir and who might you be?'

Sax P: 'I'm the lead tenor with the Count Basie Band.'

I rather think the officer's reply or comment can be filled in by the reader.

With our new jackets, music, stationery, instruments, amplification and transport, we were 'ready to roll' ~ but where to start?

I had already sketched out a one-page brochure about us, actually in rhyme since I thought it sounded better and in any case, fancied myself as a poet.

On my father's italic typewriter I produced a master copy with I took to a printer who ran off one thousand for me and then purchased the telephone directories for the Cambridge area and the Colchester area. I already possessed the Norwich area, of course, but the other two had bits of Norfolk included in them and we were prepared to cover England's fourth largest county and possibly beyond.

We then sifted through the directories, listing anyone who lived at a Hall, a Manor, a Grange or even a Castle, in particular noting those with titles like Sir, Lord, Earl, Lady and in one case princess.

To all these people we sent our rhyming circular, not really knowing which of them would have need of a quartet for dancing and I had secretly amusing visions of old retired ladies and gentlemen reading an invitation to have the Rémon Quartet play for their next dance as they sat in their bathchairs in the baronial hall.

Incidentally, it was extraordinary how many people lived at a 'Frog's Hall' which I didn't think sounded a particularly attractive address.

Advertising pays or so it's said but ours cost a lot with the printing and posting of somewhere around one thousand letters with the hope that something would come of it.

To my delight, I had a reply ~ yes, one but it was enough as I was later to realise. The letter was headed Tacolneston Hall from Mr Jocelyn Gurney of the well-known Norfolk family asking if we would be able to play at his home for his daughters' Christmas Party Dance.

I wrote back at once to confirm the booking subject to price agreement to which Mr Gurney agreed but pointed out a major snag in that he didn't own a piano!

This was 1957 ~ long before portable keyboards and our band was reliant on the venue being equipped with a piano. Mr Gurney said that he was ready to rent or even buy for the party but had no idea where to find one and could I help?

It so happened that my dear Aunt Violet and Uncle Godfrey wanted to sell their 'Amyl' upright and without further ado I put Mr Gurney in touch with them.

Within hours, the piano I had known since childhood had left Buxton Road, Norwich and was now in the grand surroundings of Tacolneston Hall just waiting for me to play.

I had a major setback just before the date of the dance when Dick went down with chronic flu, leaving me without a drummer. On Dick's recommendation I called on a friend for help in the person of Colin Copeman who willingly agreed to 'dep' and was also about Dick's build to fit the band jacket.

We arrived in plenty of time to set up in a room of old timbers and beams, a blazing log fire and some very pretty young ladies ready for the special party.

We looked smart, we played some good music, I tried to say the right thing and were admirably looked after by the Gurney family and their staff.

The youngsters had a wonderful evening, Mr Gurney was clearly delighted and we had made our mark, despite not having Dick with us, Colin deputising admirably. When Mr Gurney paid me, he asked if there was anything he could do for me for he was highly appreciative of our efforts of the evening as well as my arranging the piano (which he had bought, incidentally).

I gave him a dozen or so of our cards and asked him if he would circulate them to his friends which he said he was only too happy to do, although I think the seeds of our eventual success had already been sown by our performance, the young people being the ones who would pass the word on to their friends.

Whether it was them or Mr and Mrs Gurney I shall never know but that engagement at Tacolneston Hall set the ball rolling for us and I shall always be grateful to the Gurneys for launching the Rémon Quartet into the world of the aristocracy to become the 'in band' to book.

I have often wondered about my aunt's piano and if it's still at Tacolneston Hall, our first 'stately home' which holds a special place in my heart.

In no time at all the enquiries came for the 'band with the red coats' as we became known in the society set, first from the Barclays and the Birkbecks whom I found were related to the Gurneys.

In the beginning, not surprisingly, the parties and dances were for the young people, some of them barely into teenage and having their first social event, clearly excited by it all with eyes aglow and so eager to make a good impression. Some of the young lads were at either Eton or Harrow which meant that at some time during the evening they demanded the 'Eton Boating Song' or 'Forty Years On', the former being easy for me, the latter not and hardly known to me.

We were obviously becoming firm favourites with these youngsters who loved Dick's drumming and zany humour, our readiness to play anything they wanted, our ability to play in the dark to let them canoodle and above all their instant recognition of the red jackets on arrival. You could hear the conversations that went on:

'Are you going to . . .'s party? So am I; they're having the red coats! We're having them for ours in March' and so on.

It was literally music to our ears!

My dear mother, bless her, became my booking secretary, a job she loved, enjoying many a friendly chat over the telephone with ladies or gentlemen from some hall or other. I know full well that she secured many an engagement for us with her lovely telephone manner, for I would often be told by her ladyship, 'I had such a pleasant conversation with your charming mother' which made me glow with pleasure and realise what a wonderful PA she was.

I couldn't possibly list all the grand and beautiful houses we played at but it is sufficient to say that we were treated with the utmost courtesy at all times and during the time that Jack Stanley was our 'chauffeur' he was always dined royally along with the other drivers who had brought young guests (though in rather better looking vehicles than our van!)

In the main, the dance parties for the younger set had a supper interval in which we were given the best of fare, very often in a room to ourselves, though occasionally invited to select from the buffet table and have the odd word with some of the teenagers.

Among outstanding engagements in my musical memory was that at the beautiful Lexham Hall, near Litcham, the home of the Foster family where we played for a superb Christmas party. By the staircase stood the tallest tree I have ever seen while below ground level was a ballroom with red flock wallpaper where we were to play for some delightful young people all in fancy dress and I remember one of the sons was in the guise of a doctor.

Then there was the impressive Heydon Grange, the home of the Bulwer-Longs where we arrived in darkness and making our way round the marquee were suddenly confronted by the Brigadier himself who asked: 'Who the devil are you?'

'We're the band, sir.'

'Band? I thought you were the AA. Know anything about lamps, what?'

'Er, no.'

We had learned that one trait of the upper set was to add the suffix 'What' to all questions, something which I'd heard in Ealing comedies but was now experiencing 'live'.

We returned to Heydon less than a year later, not this time to the Grange but the palatial Heydon Hall, then home of Sir Frederick Rawlinson.

We were engaged to play for a glittering charity ball in aid of the Red Cross and it was there that I met Mr Fred Barnard, an old teaching friend of my father's and a tireless worker for the Red Cross.

It was a superb occasion with so many well-known Norfolk personalities present, sumptuous food of course, endless supplies of liquid refreshment including the inevitable champagne and the music going on until well after midnight.

We had met Sir Frederick's' son known as 'Puddy' many times and at the end of the evening mentioned the fact to His Lordship.

'Oh Lord,' he replied, diving his hand into his wallet, 'how much does he owe you?'

We must have pleased a lot of people at that ball, for we were booked again for the next one which was held at the lovely Wolterton Hall, owned by the celebrated Walpole family.

At Barton Hall, where the Peels were giving a party for their son Jonathan, Lady Peel warned us that we might encounter their pet ghost, the grey lady of Barton Broad, a nun who had been bricked up in the house at one time and now walked the grounds and on the water of the Broad itself.

Lady Peel said she had seen her many times and often passed her on the stairs and in the corridor, something which clearly disturbed Jack Wilkinson who keep looking fearfully about him all evening!

Another of the Gurney family, Mr Richard Gurney, at one time Lord Mayor of Norwich, booked us to play for a huge family event at Keswick Old Hall.

The party was to be in two places, the adults in a vast marquee dancing to the music of Jack Barker and his Orchestra while we were in the more intimate surroundings of a converted cellar playing for all the youngsters.

I remember it was a very hot night with us booked to start at 10pm playing through 'til the early hours ~ or until such time as the dancers (or we) dropped. At sun up, the last few stragglers left while we went outside into the bright, clear morning to be greeted by Mr Gurney himself bearing champagne for us and inviting us into the house.

There, in the big kitchen he donned an apron and cooked us a lovely breakfast of bacon, egg, sausage, mushrooms, tomatoes and fried bread while he chatted to us about the events of the night and tales of his mayoral experiences. Certainly a night to remember.

Another of his extensive family living at Heggatt Hall near Coltishall gave a party for his children and the reason I remember that engagement is because we were conducted to a room by two liveried gentlemen, carrying all our equipment where there was a huge table set out, groaning with food and two buckets of champagne. This was our 'band room' and all the sumptuous fare was ours!

Between our band room and the main room for dancing was a swimming pool into which, during the course of the evening several young ladies and gentlemen plunged, many omitting to cast off any clothing which was all very hilarious. We had ideas of throwing Jack and his sax in but he declined our invitation owing to his dislike of Handel's 'Water Music'.

It was during this period I began to learn about 'U' and 'Non U', an expression coined around 1954 by Professor Alan Ross about the English usage of the Upper Classes, a theory scorned by many and refuted by others including the aristos themselves.

However, there were dos and don'ts that I was careful to note such as young ladies referred to dresses as frocks and a mirror was a glass and you always wrote 15th June and not June 15th. Toilets were loos ~ the first time I had come across the word in the late fifties.

Such things may have been trivial but it was important to do them correctly which included us.

Two very important things we learned on our 'stately homes' tour were:

> *1. Never mention money, especially if his lordship or more likely, her ladyship approached at 2am and*

requested another hour. 'Certainly' would be the
reply and the invoice sent later would include the
extra hour.

2 *The top people wanted non-stop music known as*
   segue (pronounced 'segway' by musicians)

Here I was fortunate in that Denis Payne could play the piano and Jack could play the drums, which meant we took our breaks in twos, either to have a meal or a drink or a smoke. The idea worked well with the dancers happy to have something going on from the band all the time.

The late Benny Green told a wonderful story about a quartet doing 'segway'.

Two of them were left on stage, pianist and drummer but the pianist felt a call of nature and disappeared, leaving the drummer playing solo. A bright young thing, dancing around by the bandstand called out the drummer: 'I say, could you play 'Just One Of Those Things'?' to which he replied, 'What the hell do you think I'm playing?'

Before I leave the story of our high life with the other half of society, I have to relate what happened at Fundenhall Grange on the occasion of Robert Bothway's 21st birthday in 1958.

On that day, a Friday, I had taken a train load of children from school, along with other staff for an outing to London, visiting Regent's Park Zoo, the Tower and other landmarks. It meant being at Thorpe Station, Norwich at 7am and knowing I had to be at Fundenhall for a 10pm start for dancing, I asked permission to return home from London by myself on an earlier train.

There were three huge marquees, one for drinks, the second for food and the third set out as a ballroom.

Dancing went on well, a lot of young men proceeded to climb the thick tent poles to the cheers of the crowd, while others scaled the marquee from the outside and slid down to the ground in the coming dawn.

Indeed, Robert's father Mr Henry Bothway, not to be outdone by the youth around him, made is own ascent of the pole to the delight of the watching dancers. As he waved in triumph he let go his hold making a very rapid descent to which his good lady said, 'Don't do that, dear,' ~ but he already had!

Now whether or not my tiredness caught up on me or whether somebody 'laced' my drink with a 'Micky Finn' I shall never know but suddenly everything went black and I found myself in one of the bedrooms being dosed with black coffee with the lady of the house asking me how I felt.

In the meantime, Denis, now on piano was asked if he could play anything from 'My Fair Lady', the 'in' show of the day and for attempting sixteen bars of 'On The Street Where You Live' had a tenner thrust into his hand! Had I been 'compos mentis' I could have played the entire selection!

I was asked to quote for the Staff Christmas Dance at Sandringham House but received a polite letter of rejection from Buckingham Palace, something of a disappointment, although I did learn later from an informed source that I had greatly underquoted!

There always has to be one engagement that stands above the others and we would all have reason to remember the young people's party at the moated Mannington Hall, near Aylsham, then the home of Mr and Mrs Rex Carter, whose son Nick came to me for a time for tuition in 'lounge piano' style.

The evening started well with the family in the usual way welcoming us, seeing to our every need and always giving us plenty of time to set up and begin the dancing, but there seemed to be a special kind of excitement among the young guests like an air of expectancy I couldn't define.

About halfway through the dancing there was commotion near the door and cries of 'He's here' and into the room came a handsome young man accompanied by Mr Carter, who introduced him to me as Prince William of Gloucester. I was momentarily taken aback and stammered, 'Good evening, your Highness' to which he replied, 'Please ~ no ~ call me Willy.'

So Willy it was for the rest of the evening, as he danced and jived and smooched with all the rest until it was time for him to go. He came across to me and said, 'You're bloody marvellous. Your band is the best, old man. I'm going to have you play for my 21st in

London ~ the Dorchester or maybe the Ritz. Will you say you'll come?'

I readily agreed and we shook hands: in fact he shook hands with each of us and made his exit.

The sadness was that he never made his 21st birthday for that vivacious, handsome and very gracious young man met his death not two years later at an air display.

We never forgot that night at Mannington and how we had met Prince William of Gloucester who had been so effusive about our quartet to the extent of promising to have us play for his coming of age.

I suppose our 'graduation' from young people's parties and dances to those of their elders was really inevitable, since many parents came to collect their offspring long before the evening was spent and so heard our music, with the result that many cards were asked for. It seemed that there was a great circle of families who went to each other's party-dances and we were breaking into that circle, just as indeed I had hoped would happen. It was not surprising, therefore when my mother began to get bookings for the Rémon Quartet (those with the pink coats!) from many quarters, particularly from the western side of the county and into neighbouring Cambridgeshire.

We went to some grand houses at Elm and Emneth right on the county border and to Fring Hall where there was the most beautiful grand piano, to Holme Hale, to Hillington . . . the list goes on.

The furthest journeys we made were to Chatteris, Stamford (Lincs) and Peterborough which in those days had its own 'soke', although long distances were extremely tiring and during the week meant late nights and up for work next day.

By this time Jack Stanley had bade his farewells and Denis Payne had bought a Martin Walter Dormobile which had plenty of room, sliding doors, a front 'bench' seat and benches comfortable enough for sleeping. Denis himself was the driver which sometimes meant an enormous round trip for him, since he had to make his way home to North Walsham after a gig which resulted on a couple of occasions him falling asleep at the wheel!

The 'top' engagements grew more and more in number, with dances at Sloley Lodge for the young Kerrison family, followed by another at Burgh Hall, Aylsham for their delightful parents.

We went to Harpley Hall, Hoe, Guist Hall where I met another superb grand piano owned by Lady Cook and Sheringham Hall with the kindly Mr Upcher and his family.

We had some wonderful evenings with a horse racing gentleman called Tim Finch at Hapton Hall who laid on a superb barbecue and suppers with champagne by the bucketload, a man who loved life's enjoyments to the full.

King's Lynn's St George's Guildhall must be among the grandest places we played at for a dance given by Mr Paul Hawkins, later to be an MP, for his daughter's birthday. The setting was magnificent with glittering chandeliers and all the guests in their finery, with many gentlemen sporting cummerbunds.

The stage for us was quite high, rather on the small side and made it somewhat cramped for playing, particularly as Mr Hawkins had requested a six-piece to include a trumpet player who as far as I remember was Brian Green. Suffice to say that the evening was a great success, with our cards being distributed like confetti and Mr and Mrs Hawkins praising our efforts.

Whilst the 'Debs' scene had almost reached its demise, the Hunt Ball was alive and kicking, as we were to find out. Actually I never did discover the difference between a ball and a dance, never finding anyone who did know and could only assume one was grander than the other.

Into our lives stepped a bubbly, busy and delightful lady called Monica English who engaged us for charitable events like Hunt Balls, held all over the place such as at Swaffham Town Hall, where I took a great sax dep (Jack was ill at the time) named Ray Nabarro who also doubled on swing fiddle. Ray was an exceptionally gifted musician and a wonderful personality, loved and respected by many fellow musicians.

The outstanding venue for such events was 'The Rose And Crown' hotel at Wisbech where we played many times for the fund raisers of Monica English.

On one particular occasion they auctioned a live pig which escaped from its owners and ran amok on the highly polished dance floor. I'm not sure who was more alarmed ~ the manager or the pig.

Two other hotels stand out in my mind: one was Ingoldisthorpe Manor near Sandringham where we played for a Christmas party and dance in surrounds of Old World England with oak beams and a roaring log fire.

The other was at Newmarket, though the actual name of the hotel escapes me, where we had to play for a gentleman's birthday party. He had been somewhere to hear us play, subsequently booked us for his 'do' with the strictest instructions to only play 'three tunes per dance' ~ no more, no less.

Of course, as so often happens, the dancers at one point shouted for more, a demand we at once met ~ well, quite naturally as was our wont.

You would have thought I had committed a serious offence such was the sheer rage of the host who reminded me of his instructions which I had flagrantly disobeyed, that he was in charge and incidentally paying us.

Quite right ~ he was and I conceded such but he was really responsible for 'putting a damper' on his own party since after that the cries of 'more' or 'encore' went unheeded by us and the evening fizzled out.

Bill Sims-Adams was a man who loved and lived life to the full and became one of our great friends, as well as employer.

He lived at the beautiful Brancaster Hall, close to the sea and was the grandson of a maker of toilets and urinals from Scotswood upon Tyne in Northumberland. I immediately connected the name 'Adamsez' which I always believed to be French but Mr Adams corrected my mistake when he told us it was simply the way the said toilets had been designed and built by his family ~ the Adams's (spelt Adamsez).

Bill Sims-Adams was tall, handsome, the very double of Terry Thomas, with a lovely wife and the happiest crowd of friends you could wish to meet including ~ yes, Monica English!

He had a manservant called Turner who used to bring us trays of champagne and other drinks, get completely sloshed himself and pull faces at us while we played. Bill, who was ecstatic about our music, said to Turner: 'I say, Turner, what do you think of the band? Aren't they bloody marvellous, what?'

'I think they're bloody awful, sir,' replied the half-cut flunky.

'Oh Turner, you can't mean that, what?'

Turner gave a huge grin which made his guv'nor roar with laughter and tell him to bring the band whatever they wanted.

Bill was obviously very fond of Turner, who in turn was devoted to him, despite his strange ways, one of which was poking his finger through a hole in his trousers pocket and directing it through his flies much to the amusement of some guests and the consternation of others, especially females.

Those parties at Brancaster Hall were one glorious romp, in summer months going on until sun-up, whereupon all the guests, led by Mr Adams would leave us to dash down to the sea for an early swim, some of them 'skinny dipping'. On their return they would be treated to a superb breakfast of bacon and egg washed down with champagne, to which we were also invited.

On one occasion Bill's daughter asked Dick to 'test' drive her Nash Metropolitan sports car round the estate, since he had one himself and presumably knew lots about them. Mr Sims-Adams's eyes nearly popped out of his head when he saw Dick driving his daughter's car but as always, he found the whole thing a huge laugh, his lovely laugh being something I can hear even now.

We met Bill Sims-Adams on many other occasions at other places, including a charity dance at Brancaster Village Hall run by Monica English where Bill told us that Turner had had to go into a home, though we didn't enquire why.

Later on, at another function we learned the sad news that Bill had been badly smashed up in a car accident and was confined to a wheelchair, something which shocked us all. He was a lovely, happy, lively and great personality, a delight to know.

A final word about Brancaster.

My brother and I had stayed with my uncle, an RAF officer and his wife (my aunt) at Staithe House, Brancaster Staithe around 1948, then the home of Mrs Lake.

They had rented part of the house and David and I spent a wonderful holiday there.

Around twelve years later, I made a nostalgic return to the house with the Rémon Quartet to play for a dance there, taking in past memories as I looked around and actually renewed acquaintance with the aged gardener who remembered me and my brother!

The experience of playing for the aristocracy was unforgettable, a fulfilled dream and I look back with pleasure at what we did and the very 'gentle' folk we met, who treated us with the courtesy that was part of their very nature and upbringing.

PART TWO
'Come Fly With Me'
The RAF Stations And USAF Bases Scene

East Anglia was dotted with RAF Stations and USAF Bases in the late fifties and I sent our letter of introduction to all of them, Officers, Sergeants and NCOs alike.

The first engagement was a disaster.

Halfway to RAF Stradishall's Officers' Mess, Jack Stanley's rickety van got a puncture but with the aid of a torchlight we put on the spare.

Now behind schedule, we pressed on, never expecting lightning to strike twice ~ but it did, when about five miles further on we got another puncture, as luck would have it by a garage and a phone box. Whilst I telephoned Stradishall, Jack was buying a new tyre and everybody was getting very fed up.

We arrived at the Officers' Mess to rather ironic cheers and clapping from a bunch of young officers and their wives or girlfriends, none of whom probably had ever had a puncture in their lives, let alone two!

We volunteered to play longer into the night, which we did, although the officer in charge, not best pleased with us, wanted to cut our money ~ quite justifiably of course.

It has to be said we did not play well that evening, partly due to our weariness and frustration and partly to a clear hostility from some of our guests. It was a gig best forgotten except for one thing; that it made Denis decide to buy a reliable, more up-to-date gig wagon!

However, bookings came in from other RAF Stations including Officers' Mess balls at Honington, Watton, Coltishall and West Raynham.

The last named had one memorable night for us when I was asked to augment the band for a particular big occasion and I took Peter Oxborough on clarinet and Dick Le Grice on vibes. We launched into what was virtually the Benny Goodman, Lionel Hampton sound with the large crowd applauding and cheering everything, stopping dancing to stand three or four deep around the bandstand.

138

They wouldn't let us go with the music going on far into the night and I'm not sure who enjoyed it more ~ the customers or us, especially a wonderful 'hammed' version of 'Sing Sing Sing' straight from Carnegie Hall.

Swanton Morley was a favourite station of ours where we played for the Sergeants and NCOs, as well as the Officers ~ and always got well looked after at both.

I remember breaking a rule at the Sergeants' Mess there of never letting someone come and sing, since I'd learned my lesson in the past (or thought I had!)

A group of NCOs kidded me on to let a girl sing, saying how good she was, that everyone loved her voice and I wouldn't regret it. Very reluctantly I agreed and asked the young lady what she would sing.

She said, 'Lady Is A Tramp'.

I said, 'What key?' to which she replied, 'I think it's C.'

We duly did an intro in C and she launched into 'I get too hungry for dinner at eight' with all her 'fan club' clustered around the stage, grins spread across their faces. And no wonder!

She was terrible, absolutely terrible, mainly because she had no sense of pitch and was singing (if you could call it that) 'in the cracks', the notes bearing no relation to anything we were playing.

She had said 'I think it's C' and now I know why she had her doubts!

She also hadn't the faintest idea of timing, missing beats, rests and even whole bars along the way. The biggest problem, however, was getting her off, since not only did she think she was marvellous but her 'fans' seemed to think so too, yelling for encore after encore.

I knew it was a caper, that I wished I'd never agreed to it but I didn't know how to finish it and the dance looked doomed with some obviously irritated dancers out there.

Two sergeants saved the evening, persuading the young lady to stop and leave the stage, despite mock howls of protest from the group of NCOs around the stand.

When the officer in charge came to pay me he said, 'Your band is very good and we shall certainly book you again, but please, next time do not include your girl vocalist ~ she's awful.'

My girl vocalist! I must have been too flabbergasted to answer and he strode off into the night. This time I had learned a lesson the hard way, one never to be forgotten.

The Officers' Mess at Swanton Morley was one of the friendliest we ever went to , where we got to know staff who always made sure we had food and drink and officers and wives who treated us royally. Into the sixties they clearly booked other bands of the day as well as us and one night we arrived to find a new entertainments officer who said, 'Do you know how to play a waltz?'

'Certainly,' I replied, 'we were teethed on waltzes.'

'Thank God for that,' he said. 'We had a bloody twang gang here last time and when I asked them to play a waltz, they didn't know what the bloody hell I was talking about!'

We all gave wry grins at that one, loving the expression 'twang gang'.

A great deal of the fun was had at Swanton Morley when the dancing was finished, for while the young officers and their ladies sat around, we gave an impromptu cabaret which seemed to give them all great amusement.

Dick brought out his imaginary deaf 'gran' and proceeded to do a 'double act', Jack did bits of his mime routine while Denis, putting his shirt on back to front performed a screamingly funny act as a vicar giving out notices and banns of marriage.

He had all the corny old patter, such as, 'We are having a font built at the east end of the church so that babies can be baptised at both ends' and 'The Young Mothers' Group meets in the vestry on Wednesdays. Any young lady wishing to become a young mother, see me after church in the vicarage.'

Somehow, the whole thing stuck and the entertainments officer would always ask if we could stay afterwards and do 'the cabaret'. This entertainment, unpaid of course, but rewarded with pints of bitter or tots of whisky, would go on quite late and we would make our return journey to Norwich at some ungodly hour of the morning. Dick had a megaphone from which he would blare at sleepy villages and hamlets 'Attention, attention! Water will be turned off . . .' and we would be gone, though I doubt very much if anyone was ever awakened by these unofficial water board announcements.

RAF Marham has to be my favourite Officers' Mess, mainly because of the fancy dress balls we played for there, besides the ordinary mess functions.

We must have done four New Years' Eves at Marham, each time being asked to dress up and join in the fun along with the guests, some of whom had the most fantastic costumes.

I remember we went as the Black and White Minstrels once but the heat from the lights made our black make-up run and we all had filthy shirts!

One particular night there stands out above all others.

As usual, we had donned costume and make-up before leaving home, Denis as a commando with khaki outfit with branches and twigs in his helmet, Jack as the Auguste clown, Dick as a policeman and I as an Egyptian with gown and fez.

The first laugh came when we all trooped into the local pub at Wendling which was on our way, to the amused looks of those in the bar. With my olive brown face I turned to a chap wearing a red and white striped waistcoat and asked him what he was going as. I think he took exception to my question since he wasn't actually wearing fancy dress and we made a wisely hasty departure from the said hostelry with animosity about to begin. Our route to Marham in those days took us through Swaffham Town and on this occasion we arrived at the main traffic lights behind a considerable queue of traffic waiting for the green.

The red continued to show without change, causing quite a build-up of vehicles behind us, which prompted Dick in the front seat to leave us and wander up to the front of the line.

You will recall that he wore a policeman's uniform, borrowed from a friend on the Norwich force (apart from the helmet badge which was not allowed) and that he had replaced with a metal oval one cut from an Ovaltine tin.

'What seems to be the trouble?' Dick inquired of the driver in the leading car.

'The . . . lights have stuck.'

'Oh.'

'Well, aren't you going to do something about it?'

'Who, me?'

'Yes, you. Well, you're a . . . policeman aren't you?'

'Well, er . . .'

Since the drivers behind the leader looked somewhat grim and threatening, Dick, quickly weighing up the situation, decided something did have to be done and without further ado, strode into the middle of Swaffham High Street and waved on dozens of stranded cars (ours included) against the red lights.

Just across the way near the library we spotted a real bobby who had clearly witnessed in a somewhat bemused fashion the whole incident and must have wondered to this day which member of what constabulary had carried out the whole thing. It would have come as something of a surprise to him, particularly since the 'officer' in question sported an Ovaltine badge on his helmet!

However, Dick had his reward, along with the rest of us, for we were presented that night with prizes for our fancy dress efforts.

The United States Air Bases were quite different in almost all respects but in any case, the majority of our US engagements were for the NCOs.

We did the odd one at Lakenheath, Scunthorpe and Bentwaters which brought no returns but we had a regular spot at other bases which were each in their own way so different.

When we arrived the first time at Sutton Heath near Woodbridge, a middle-aged lady sat by the entrance of the NCO club who said, 'Gee, it's always so great to see you boys back here again.'

I quickly explained that is was our first visit to which she replied, 'Gee, that's my big mouth ~ there I go, blabbin' in my beer again.'

The sergeant in charge explained to me that she had DTs to which I said, 'Oh' with, I hoped, an inflection indicating I knew just what that was, although I really hadn't any idea. It was only later that I learned the term 'delirium tremens' and its connotations.

There was one very strange man at the NCO Club who kept 'barking' like a seal and was forever requesting 'How High The Moon' with his voice climbing high on the word 'moon'.

The requests came thick and fast, just like the drinks which littered the top of the piano and they had there what we supposed was an American custom, that each time we played a request, money was put on the piano.

We seemed to collect good bonuses at Sutton Heath which was a strange but pleasant place, albeit rather a long journey for us.

At USAF Tuddenham they would break the dancing with cabaret and we saw there a fine artiste and impressionist called Johnny Silver. The sergeant in charge told me they were desperately short of girls (to dance with) and would I organise a coachload from Norwich which he would pay for (well, not he personally) and we could come on the coach with them.

I agreed and got in touch with the personnel officers at Harmers, Colmans and Caleys, each of whom quite rightly wanted to know every details, that things were 'above board' and so on. The result was that we and about two dozen young ladies boarded a hired coach from Norwich and went off to spend an enjoyable evening at Tuddenham among surprised and pleased men from the United States ~ and it didn't cost the girls a penny. We did this several times, but as the numbers of girls fell off, the idea became financially unsound and had to be dropped.

Master Sergeant MacWilliams at USAF North Pickenham was probably the most gentle American I ever met, speaking softly, never getting aroused and always so courteous to me and the rest of the band. The parties there were always so full of fun and I particularly remember a wonderful Thanksgiving Night when we were included in the meal of pumpkin pie and 'Southern Fried'.

Sgt MacWilliams liked me to take a vocalist, preferably female so we used two in the time we were at North Pickenham.

Sheila Moore came a couple of times and on other occasions we had Diane Bramble, both of them popular with the US guys.

One night, Dick Pearce, not at all well, came to Pickenham against his better judgement, having dosed himself with anti-fever/malaria/beri beri tablets which he proceeded to wash down with liberal quantities of Schlitz/Becks/Buddweiser.

His drum solos were always in demand, Pickenham being no exception and he therefore let rip with the sweat running from him in torrents, grimly determined to reach his finale where the sticks would go flying. They did, with Dick beaming his triumph and with no pre-warning he promptly collapsed.

Whilst he was being revived, his place was taken by Jack Stanley, at that time transport chief and the dance went on. However, I do remember that Dick was off sick for a couple of weeks after.

'Take your partners for the Gay Gordons,' I announced ~ no, not at a typically English dance but at a USAF NCO Club at Shepherd's Grove near Bury St Edmunds where we played regularly to a packed floor.

The place was run by a lady officer who insisted on the American personnel learning to dance properly all the English and Scottish dances which they were taught during the week. On Sunday nights they put their newly-learned steps into practice, from fox-trot to tango, from Valeta to Cha Cha Cha and we were able to provide the music she wanted, which is why I suppose we were booked again and again.

Our favourite USAF Base was without doubt Mildenhall and although we did some occasional weekday or Saturday gigs there, we were booked for months on end to play at the NCO Club for most of Sunday.

We shared weeks with other bands such as Ken Stevens from Cambridge, Paul Chris from West Norfolk and the Teddy Taylor Trio from London but they also had one or two big names like the Kirchen Band and Eric Delaney.

Our Sundays began with a pick-up from Norwich around 12 noon and off down the A11 to Thetford where we would stop for a pint and a chat with the jovial Neville Bishop at the 'Anchor Hotel'. Neville was a great personality, retired from the band business where he had been best known as 'Uncle Neville' at the Great Yarmouth Marina with his wonderful showband.

The Anchor was filled with photographs of all the stars he had known, many signed and dedicated to him and it was a veritable treasure trove of memorabilia out of his illustrious career. I wonder what became of it all?

Then it was off down to Mildenhall to be playing at the NCO Club where we would often walk out of brilliant sunshine into a dark room with curtains drawn and dim lighting.

We started at 2.00pm which was 'Happy Hour' meaning one particular drink, usually vodka or Tom Collins would be at a 'silly' price and we'd have them lined up along the front of the stage which was quite a high one.

A few couples would dance to one of three basic tempos: quick (jive), Latin (cha cha cha or bossa nova) or slow (smooch) in semi-darkness with a glittering ball twirling and coloured lights moving in the ceiling.

There were, of course, many characters such as a coloured guy known as 'Moon' who was somewhat slow but egged on by others in the club to sing. Invariably he would choose 'Blue Moon' taking the mike down to floor level for rarely would he come up on stage ~ I can only suppose for lack of confidence.

You could hardly describe what Moon did as singing, for it can best be called whining at a high pitch with no actual reference to words or melody. However, he was always wildly applauded with cries of more, although he never once obliged, keeping to the one number (mercifully). He would call me 'Brubeck' which caught on with other NCOs and he did have a rather annoying habit of tugging at the trouser legs of Jack and David, our vocalist when he sought their attention, sometimes in the middle of a sax solo or a song.

Another character we knew was called 'Dutch' (we never knew his other name) who would ask to come on stage with his trumpet and join us for a couple of numbers. He became a good friend with a host of sayings which we got to know and repeat such as 'We don't make much money but we have a hell of a good time.'

He brought us a lot of 'goodies' from the PX including, I remember some powerful Bourbon called 'Old Grandad' and such a good pal was he that we all felt 'full up' the night he had to say farewell and leave for the States.

The chef there at the club would always shout, 'Hey Dick! Give us 'Big Noise'!'

This meant the number 'Big Noise From Winnetka' where Dick would start with playing on Denis's bass strings with his sticks, then breaking into a furious drum solo which brought the house down and thick T-bone steaks for all of us at 5 o'clock.

While we dined in splendour, many older NCOs would come and talk to us, some clearly fantasising about clubs or bars they owned back in the States, in New York or Chicago and offering us work

145

there when their National Service was over. Of course, we took it all with huge pinches of salt, but humoured them nevertheless.

After our meal we would take all the gear over to the Airmen's Mess where there was to be dancing interspersed with cabaret. The cabaret acts were a 'package' show provided by the Alf Preager Organisation from London, often comprising as many as four artistes, though more in number if there were two or three strippers included.

When we first encountered the cabaret I was 'told' by the presenter he would need my drummer and bass player which meant, of course, no actual break for either of them with no mention of payment.

I soon had a word with 'Dusty' Miller, the civvy in charge of it all and was told to put the extra session on the bill and after the cabaret, Dick and Denis could take a short break while Jack and I played for some dancing.

We met a few 'names' in the Preager set-up such as the singer Malcolm Vaughan, Billy 'Uke' Scott, the singing group The Southlanders, a comedian called Frank Berry, a clever magician named Gogia Pasha and a dance duo Dorita e Pepe, who were as cockney as jellied eels.

Another comedian, George Williams ~ 'I'm not well' ~ died the death but our biggest surprise was ~ Dave Allen, who took one look at us and said, 'Skegness ~ 1956!'

Some memory and some act: the Americans loved him.

Again, in the Airmen's Mess which was invariably rowdy, there were some 'oddballs' like the one who asked us what we wanted to drink, who when we said 'no thanks' said, 'Me Apache. When I say you drink, you drink. Otherwise . . .'

And he drew his hand in cut-throat fashion under his chin. Naturally, we changed our minds about having the drink and during the course of the evening when he looked in our direction to indicate he was offering us a drink, we all nodded firmly in the 'Yes' position!

Sometimes I would be asked to augment the band at Mildenhall, something I was never very happy about but we did have some good sessions with Lew Day, a fine guitarist and Peter Oxborough on clarinet. Brian Green came on a couple of occasions, also bringing with him his own drum kit as well as the trumpet and he and Dick brought the house down with a 'drum battle' that lasted fully twenty minutes!

The session would finish at 10pm and it was time to pack up and off home to Norwich, after bidding farewell to the two sergeants in charge, one a very fat guy and the other the tallest man I've met (6ft 8in) ~ from Florida who told me that his daddy was 7ft tall! We had been there from 2 until 10, working hard, giving enjoyment to the men and women from Stateside, making some good friends and of course getting well paid for our trouble.

The RAF and USAF part of our dance band career was exciting, very different and highly memorable, one we would all treasure for years to come. Like the world of the upper classes, it was another side of life which, but for our musical abilities and prowess, we would never have experienced.

PART THREE

'Dance In The Old-Fashioned Way'

Our third 'circuit' was under the heading of miscellaneous with dance engagements in the public and private sectors which I suppose was the 'bread and butter' work of the dance band business. Some of the gigs were in Norwich, while others, so familiar to many bands, were at village halls dotted around the county and in the small towns at Town Halls or Corn Exchanges.

It was at two of these functions that we came across young men who were to join the band in separate eras as vocalists, an inclusion often required by people booking us.

Of course, the great Nat King Cole began as a fine jazz pianist with his trio, with legend having it that when his vocalist went sick, took on the role of singer himself and look how he rose to fame.

In my case I did not attempt to emulate Nat (whom I greatly admire, by the way, as both pianist and vocalist) since I had not been blessed with his dulcet tones and such efforts on my part could well have damaged our band's reputation.

It was at Dereham Memorial Hall in December 1957 that we met David Valentine (real name David Blyth) who had just won a talent contest and was appearing as guest at the hall where we were playing for a dance. He was with his manager, Billy Clarke and was using the stage name of Valentine after his singing idol Dickie Valentine with his own voice not unlike that of his hero.

After the dance I fought my way through the hordes of girls surrounding David and asked him if he would like to join the Rémon Quartet, that is with the consent of his manager, which he seemed delighted to do.

For the following two years he sang with us at various venues, including the American bases, gradually learning a lot of points about the business, especially four bar intros to numbers and picking up at the middle eight bars second time through. He learned well, became popular, in fact popular enough to have his own fan club. Such was his admiration for Dickie Valentine that he married his lovely wife Josie on Valentine's Day and I know he was devastated when his idol died in a motor accident.

David sang and learned (and earned) a lot in that time and became a personal friend. He gave that personal touch to his singing, delivering his words so clearly to the couples on the dance floor and in a style not unlike Dickie Valentine or Pat Boone.

He described my quartet as 'simply the best', a fine tribute that I hold dear. When he left us he became a talent scout for up and coming artists in the entertainment world such as magician Ronnie Hill who, as Ronnie Kane went on a world cruise entertaining passengers and Patrina Johnson who as Patrina Johns went on to star in West End shows.

I was to catch up with David in later years as I shall relate in a later chapter.

When the quartet was engaged to play for Brisley Cricket Club Dance, I wasn't to know that we would be meeting our next vocalist, the talented Hilton Tait. Always having misgivings about letting 'singers' invade the bandstand, I was doubtful about being persuaded by a host of young people to let Hilton sing.

However, they were the paying public who were demanding a song from him, assuring me how good he was. I succumbed and Hilton mounted the dais to huge cheers from his many fans. A few bars into his first number, we had no doubts of his ability: it was style, it was class and it was us and I had no hesitation in asking him to join us as vocalist on future gigs. He had no second thoughts on the matter and sang with the Rémon Quartet over the next three years whenever he was asked, becoming a favourite with the dancers and a good friend of ours.

He lived at Brisley where his father and mother farmed along with Colin, Hilton's brother. Later, Hilton married the pretty Daphne Bugg at Hillington and they settled in Colkirk village near Fakenham, she running a hairdressing business and he working for an animal feed firm.

His heart was always in music, however and he became the owner of a music shop in Dereham, an organ and keyboard tutor and a prominent member of Dereham Operatic Society.

Hilton had a swinging style of singing with us, in the mould of Frank Sinatra or Matt Munro and although he was a Norfolk man 'bred and born' with a rich accent of his county, displayed none of it in his performance. He did a lovely version of the Matt Munro song 'My Kind Of Girl' in which he would sing the line 'She even cooks like an angel cooks' slipping in the words (spoken) 'Angel cakes' which typified his lovely sense of humour.

Village hall gigs, on the whole, were good fun with many a laugh all round.

At Carbrooke I didn't find it half as funny as the others when I attempted to plug into a giant electrical circuit at the side of the stage and got shot fifteen feet across the floor almost electrifying myself.

Amazingly enough, I gave a repeat performance about a year later at the Saint Raphael Club in Norwich which got a similar reception from my musicians.

At Great Moulton's ancient village hall, the dances were very popular with a delightful old gentleman in charge called Mr Mouncer who would gleefully tell us that all the Norwich City footballers would be coming over. They were often there, probably drawn by the magnetism of our playing or possibly the female village population, though I never knew which.

The rival village, Aslacton, would run a dance on the same evening which put both our band and the one appearing there on our mettle, since people would go from one to the other, the villages being so close.

There was Great Ryburgh where all the young men would sit along one side of the hall with the girls on the other ~ for a good hour, despite our desperate efforts to make them dance.

At Heacham, a gentleman named Basil Smith who called himself Basil Leroy, ran dances to which people came from miles around to shuffle along to their favourite bands and when they were not dancing, sit out on old maroon coloured cinema seats. We went there a few times but the most popular band from Norwich was Harry Sunderland's with John Garwood (piano), Jimmy Beaumont (Guitar), Joe Dade (accordion), Basil Coleman (saxes) and Harry himself on drums.

At all the village hops (I couldn't name them all), spot prizes were always popular, an excellent inducement to people to get on the floor. There were the old ones, tried and tested over the years:

'A prize to the couple underneath the glittering ball'

(or balloon if there wasn't a ball)

'Jack will walk down the hall . . . twelve paces . . . turn left . . . two paces forward . . . put out your right hand . . . nearest couple on your left!'

'First couple to bring me a picture of the queen'
(Pound note or postage stamp)

'First gent to bring me a pair of green (k)nickers'
(Two pound notes)

One or two were a bit more subtle which set the crowd thinking:

'First gentleman wearing a rose-coloured shirt'

Someone with a higher IQ would rush up to me wearing a white shirt to claim his prize to indignant cries from the floor: 'His shirt is white!'
'Never heard of a white rose?'

'First gent to bring me his partner's nylons over his arm'

This one would have over-enthusiastic girls trying to remove their stockings while others were taking great exception to their partner asking them to do any such thing until of course another with above average intelligence would not make his girl go through all that rigmarole but simply pick her up and bring her to the stand with her legs over his arm!

'The next prize is two guineas'

~ a fair sum then to get folk on the dance floor. When the music stopped, the MC would come forward with a tray bearing two 'Guinness' bottles to the groans of the crowd.

'First couple to bring me a set of black teeth'

Up would come someone with a black comb.

'First couple to bring me two coins to the value of fourpence, one of which must not be a threepenny bit

Great consternation.

Our bright boy brings up a threepenny bit and a penny.

'Yes sir! Two coins to the value of fourpence: one must not be a threepenny bit ~ but the other one can!'

Further groans of dismay from the floor.

There was the catch question type when the music stopped:

> *'What was the largest island in the world before Greenland was discovered?'*

Such excited discussion.

Then our 'mensa' type: 'Greenland, because it was always there, discovered or not.'

'Quite right sir. Your brains have won you a prize!'

> *'What was the Prime Minister's name in 1930?'*

More rapid discussion.

Another bright lad: 'Harold Macmillan ~ it was his name then ~ same as it is now.'

'Brilliant, sir. Have a box of chocolates.'

You had to vary the dances with Gents' Excuse Me, Ladies Excuse Me, General Excuse Me and Ladies' Choice. In the early days we had the 'Paul Jones' where the girls made one circle, the gents another round them and to the tune 'Here We Come Gathering Nuts In May', they went round in opposite directions until the music stopped. At this point the man faced a new partner and they would dance for a short while to a fox-trot, waltz or quickstep until 'Nuts In May' signalled another gallivanting circle. The 'Paul Jones' rather died out, although the 'Stately Homes' folk invariably requested it, oddly enough. I think it was replaced by the 'Snowball' where one couple would be asked to start until the music stopped when each would take a new partner and so on until the floor was full. Then the MC could tell everyone 'All change' which was where Irving Berlin got his inspiration for the song 'Change Partners'.

At what was called 'Party Time' we would play the 'Palais Glide' in which everyone would link arms and do a forward and backward step dance to tunes like 'Poor Little Angeline', 'Ten Pretty Girls' and 'Horsey Horsey'.

This would be followed by the 'Hokey Cokey' ~ 'You put your right arm in, . . . and shake it all about' which would end at high speed with 'Your whole self in' and into 'Knees Up Mother Brown' for those left with any energy.

Occasionally we would launch into the 'St Bernard's Waltz' with the floor-stamping sequence and 'Hands, Knees And Boomps-a-Daisy' a novelty dance composed by Annette Mills of Muffin the Mule fame and who was sister of John Mills, the film star. In the dance couples would bump rears together on the boomps-a-daisy bit which varied from a gentle cheek to cheek to a violet biff such as you would often see at a Young Farmers' Dance.

One great favourite at the end of the night was undoubtedly the 'Conga' when everybody made a chain following a leader all around the room. If he should be a leader with lots of imagination, the chain could go out of the room to often we knew not where (on summer nights outside!) leaving us to play 'I Came, I Saw, I Conga'd' to ourselves until they eventually returned.

At private houses I've even known it to go upstairs. At the end the music would get much faster until the whole chain would collapse, exhausted.

Mention of the young farmers reminds me of one particular gig we did at a barn down in deepest Suffolk where, when we arrived, I jokingly said the young chap in charge as we drove up: 'Hope the piano's in tune.'

'Piano?' he said, 'What piano? We ha'n't got a piano.'

I thought it was a YF joke but no, they hadn't got one which momentarily presented a problem.

With the Young Farmers problems are there to be solved and soon I joined them as they trooped in a body down the village street to a small house where we all marched in straight through the sitting room where an entire family sat staring at a small TV set. None of them averted their gaze as we bodily removed the piano from the room, not one word or surprise or question being uttered. They never noticed what we were taking which could have been the family silver!

Out into the sunlit street we went, all pushing the giant instrument to trundle down to the barn where we put it in place. Any piano tuner would have had apoplexy.

The barn was filled with straw bales on which were perched all manner of domestic fowl which remained present for the entire evening, accompanying the music with squawks, quacks, cackles and crowing. Every so often a cockerel would fly up on to the piano which in itself was somewhat disconcerting but it was when it decided to use its alighting point as a loo that I decided it should be discouraged and crap elsewhere. As if responding to my wishful thinking, he flew up on to a rafter, letting a fresh lot fall into the bell of Jack's tenor to which the normally placid sax player uttered a couple of expletives.

It reminds me of a classic Thomas Beecham story when he was conducting a rehearsal in the USA of a particularly awful production of 'Aida'.

The scenery was tawdry, the costumes threadbare, the singing and acting around fifth rate, in fact everything was diabolical.

On to the stage trooped a variety of animals: horses, camels, bullocks, goats and elephants, one of which suddenly deposited a massive excrement in its wake at which Sir Thomas turned to the orchestra and said, 'There, ladies and gentlemen, you have a most discerning animal.'

We had some very interesting country gigs, one of our regular spots being the Oaks Ballroom at North Walsham, Denis Payne's homeground where Saturday night dances were run by a Mrs Cutting.

I remember the very fine refreshments she laid on there, catering for a large number of personnel from nearby RAF Coltishall who came along in the hope of meeting young ladies from the surrounding area.

A friend and neighbour of mine later on in life, Phyl Flatman (née Wright) met David, her husband at the Oaks where I knew many a match was made. Indeed, Dick Pearce himself with the help of David Valentine, our vocalist, got introduced to Denise Smith of North Walsham who not long afterwards became his wife. I always maintained that she was the double of Mai Zetterling, the film actress, though much prettier.

Another North Walsham venue was the 'King's Arms' run by Tom Beckenham and his son Jack who gave us a lot of private work there, where they had quite a nice ballroom upstairs as I remember, filled with large mirrors all the way round. The stairs were noisy and breakneck but it wasn't a bad place to play and Jack Beckenham always looked after us well, particularly as Denis was a good friend.

We did a couple of gigs for Westwick Fruit Farms since Barbara Payne, Denis's wife, was Mr Alexander's secretary there.

We also did a few nights at Scarborough Hill Country Club at North Walsham while six miles north of there we played for a good few dances at Bacton Village Hall. I remember one evening there where Pat Swain (Harry Carson, the magician) came to do his act and one young 'gentleman' in the audience protesting that Pat had robbed him of a ten shilling note in a trick, threatened to 'do him in'.

Of course Pat had done nothing of the sort and when I informed the lout, much 'in his cups' that Pat was Black Belt in Judo, he slunk away into the night. Pat and his wife and assistant Jean, however, taking no chances left almost directly in case the young man should return with an armed escort.

On the north Norfolk coast line we played for dancing at Cromer Links where there was a lovely large ballroom and stage but was generally very poorly patronised, though we could never understand why. The manager, whose name I can't recall tried everything he knew, with my help to attract people but in the end had to give up.

There was one lady, a regular with an American drawl, who clearly well-oiled would come and say quite loudly, 'Give us some jazz boys ~ like they do on Easy Street' and then proceed to do an impromptu cabaret in the centre of the floor to the amused delight of the dancers. Her final 'curtain' was to whirl round on one leg in crouch position (like ice skaters do), going faster and faster until she collapsed in a heap and had to be carried out semi-conscious.

Much further round the coast we got to know Hunstanton well, playing some 'class' gigs at the Le Strange Arms hotel and also at Hunstanton Hotel and Country Club on the cliff front owned by a young man called Peter Lewis Green, a devotee of jazz.

His club was quite small but managed to have the Paul Chris Big Band play there, alternating with our quartet adapting our style to jazz which was a refreshing change.

We went over there one night to hear Paul Chris and his music, a very find sound led by a very likeable and energetic drummer from East Rudham, who sadly died all too young.

I remember one night at the club, Peter Lewis Green took us for drinks to his apartment where we listened to a 'voice' on record singing 'You Keep Me Swinging' which sounded for all the world like Frank Sinatra. It was, in fact Matt Munro on the opening track of the Peter Sellers' LP 'Songs For Swinging Sellers' and as we downed a few beers, we listened to the talented Mr Sellers doing all kinds of sketches making us rock with laughter. That introduction to the LP made me a fan of the man and I went out next day to buy the record for myself which I treasure to this day.

The other venue at Hunstanton was the Kit Kat Ballroom by the pier owned by a gentleman called Mr Colisanti who may have been Italian, Greek or Cypriot, though I was never sure.

He was a tall, heavily built man of a Mediterranean appearance, nervous, shy and extremely soft-spoken to the extent that I did not always catch what he said.

We seemed to be very popular with the dancing public there, though with Mr Colisanti himself I could never be sure and at times he almost seemed afraid of me for some reason.

In my musical career I have never made a 'double booking' ~ not wittingly, that is. It is where someone has arranged to appear in two places at the same time ~ live. Nor have I ever missed an engagement through my own mismanagement, so imagine our amazement when Dick, sitting quietly at home reading, deeply absorbed in his copy of the 'Spotwelders Monthly' received a call from Mr Colisanti at the Kit Kat asking where our band had got to.

Apparently he had a ballroom full of people expecting dancing to begin in a few minutes to the Rémon Quartet! None of us had the fixture in our diaries and I rather fancy that Mr Colisanti realising he had forgotten to engage a band for the occasion, panicked into ringing any one of his regulars to pretend that they had slipped up and not he. I don't remember what happened, save that we didn't belt over to Hunstanton and if there was a black mark for us, it didn't show since we still continued to play at the Kit Kat for some time after that.

We had connections with the sailing fraternities in the area where I knew Jimmy Tillett, the Norwich jeweller who happened to have been at Norwich School and also happened to be commodore of Wroxham Sailing Club.

We played for some of their socials at the club house which led to one or two private engagements, the most memorable being for the wedding anniversary of Mr Bentall, the Norwich surgeon.

The party went on pretty late, after which Mr Bentall invited us aboard his yacht for more merrymaking with drinks and nibbles.

I remember the precarious walk from the bank to the yacht along a narrow plank with was even worse on the return trip after the several drinks we had downed. It had been a lovely summer evening with much laughter and fun, Mr Bentall being a great host and perfect gentleman.

Further south, it was the call of the sea that drew us to the Royal Norfolk and Suffolk Yacht Club at Lowestoft where we played for the lavish parties held regularly there, although Dick didn't find it funny when he was asked to leave the bar, the commodore telling the steward he had 'actually seen a member of the band in the bar' ~ an unheard of event.

One night after the dance was over, I stacked some chairs very high behind the floor-to-ceiling curtains and the window and climbing to the top, poked my head out which gave the appearance I was about fifteen feet tall. Everyone was highly amused but unfortunately one of the chairs in the tower slipped and I crashed to the ballroom floor where I gave vent to some loud moans and groans, fancying I had broken every bone in my body!

On another occasion we wore bright yellow papier maché sombreros purchased from Strivens' shop in Norwich to look just the part in the Latin American medleys. Jack sat at the front of the small stage with we three behind him and Dick, ever the practical joker, set light to Jack's hat. Very soon flames began to rise from the top of Jack's head and he kept repeating, 'I can smell burning ~ I'm sure I can smell burning.'

Of course, the highly amused dancers were pointing at him which puzzled him greatly and he kept asking, 'What are you looking at? What's the matter?'

When Jack eventually realised his hat was well and truly alight, he leapt up, threw it to the floor and jumped on it, amidst laughter all round. In less than a moment he too saw the funny side of it, laughing with the rest, never surprised at things Dick might do.

Seaside places reminds me of West Runton where there was a very fine ballroom called the Pavilion to which many famous bands came. The bands, both locally and nationally were booked by Joe Tuck whose family and he ran the post office at West Runton. Joe, a fine drummer led his own band too, being resident at the Pavilion for many years.

We played there several times where on one occasion we were opposite Sid Philips and his Band. I took with me my LP of the Sid Philips Band, who autographed the inner sleeve for me. We began by calling him Mr Philips but he would have none of it, insisting that he was 'Sid'.

He also congratulated Denis and me for our 'double piano' spot which we often did in Sid Philips fashion and which he asked us to do a couple of years later when we met up again at Dereham Memorial Hall.

Sid was a fine musician on the clarinet as well as a classical composer and arranger and a perfect gentleman too.

In Norwich we played at the Samson and Hercules Ballroom which in the early days was owned by Geoffrey Watling assisted by his booking manager, Rose Ecker. As well as bookings in the main ballroom, we appeared at the Dell which was in Waggon and Horses Lane and more often at the Flixton Rooms above the main building ~ all for private functions.

The Flixton Rooms engagements all followed a similar pattern: I would play piano throughout dinner, after which came speeches followed by dancing, sometimes interspersed with cabaret.

I was often asked to provide cabaret which was the opportunity for Jack Wilkinson to perform his clever mime act to records by Spike Jones, Danny Kaye, Elvis Presley, Jerry Colonna and others. He was a very talented entertainer with perfect timing and did particularly well with the Danny Kaye numbers such as 'Hello 'Frisco Goodbye' and 'The Peony Bush' but my favourite was Jerry Colonna's 'It Might As Well Be Spring'.

Of course, Pat Swain and Jean would often be the main attraction and the Flixton Rooms was an ideal spot for both cabaret and dancing where the patrons could relax while 'Carson' performed his delightful magic and then dance in very pleasant, romantic surroundings.

I do remember one gentleman I included in a cabaret who went under the name of Tony Pelaw, a name he took from a Co-op tin of boot polish, would you believe. He did impressions or more correctly, impersonations, pretending to be Count Dracula or Charlie Chaplin, among others. He would enter in dramatic fashion with black cloak and fedora crying, 'Come with me to my castle in the mountains,' imitating the voice of Bela Lugosi perfectly.

Tony ~ I don't recall him by his real name ~ used to plan his new routines all the time and I remember him stopping Jack and me in the back of the inns in Norwich to demonstrate his latest one in full view of all the girls working there in a lingerie shop much to their amusement and our embarrassment!

Geoffrey Watling sold the Samson and Hercules to Mecca who also bought the Lido on Aylsham Road where the great Billy Duncan had played for many years to an admiring Norwich crowd. Mecca called it the Norwood Rooms, and the popular and likeable Chic Aplin became resident, although we did the occasional function there, mainly in the smaller room upstairs.

The Samson Mecca had Jan Ralfini and his Orchestra resident while we were asked to be 'relief band' playing at the side of the main bandstand while Jan and his men took their breaks. The Mecca people were very strict about many things with everyone inspected by the management before a function to see that they were clean, tidy and properly dressed.

We had to 'follow on' from Jan's men in the same key and tempo while they left discreetly for the band room and the same thing in reverse when it was their turn to start again.

Between dances Mecca insisted on only nine seconds' wait so as never to let the dancers' interest flag and presumably make us earn our crust!

We learned a lot from Mecca who in the heyday of ballroom dancing led the field in the halls, the staff, the bands and the slick efficiency for both private and public functions.

It was working at the Samson that brought me face to face with the Norwich Union once more, who it seemed were ever determined to put me in charge of their Dancing Department.

Actually, it was through a great friend of mine, Robert (Bob) Laurie, an ex-Norwich School pupil who seemed to wield great influence on the entertainment/dance committee at NU, assuring them all that the Rémon Quartet, perhaps augmented, would be ideal for the NU Social.

Indeed Robert appeared to be a man of much importance in the company's set-up (probably one step away from General Manager I should think) since they put him in entire charge of the Union dances, organising the cabaret, compèring the whole evening and I daresay running the tombola too!

He was a great MC and we got on so well with him in charge.

One of his reassurances to the dancers when a fox-trot was announced (always the most difficult one) was, 'If you can't do the fox-trot, do the quickstep slowly!'

Bob was a good dancer himself and would lead on the floor, encouraging others to follow just as he did when we played for the International Friendship League Dances at the Chantry Hall in Norwich which were always good fun with folk from all parts of the globe dancing with each other.

Other Norwich venues were the Gala run by Laurie Singer, husband of Eileen Page who had vainly taught me to dance as a teenager, the Royal Hotel (Norwich's finest, no longer there) where I foolishly sold my piano stool to Major Mace, a furniture dealer and the Grove in Arlington Lane owned by a self-made man Paul Dendy, a very laid back entrepreneur.

Actually, we were very popular at the Grove and had a quite a fan club following, including a few ex-public school lads.

Of course, being in the teaching profession, I was contacted by the NUT Secretary (I mean for Norwich ~ not nationally) to play for the NUT Ball at the Assembly Rooms, a sort of hallowed hall of Norwich where one had to mind one's ps and qs.

It followed that there were quite a few of the City Hall hierarchy there and I was soon spotted by one particular lady who came swiftly towards me, presumably to tell me I was to 'see her in her office first thing in the morning'.

I feared this because another Norwich teacher who like me ran a dance orchestra had been summoned to see the Director of Education to explain how it was that he dared to be a teacher by day and a musician by night.

He had been told that he was employed by the LEA for 24 hours a day and would have to make up his mind whether he wished to follow a teaching career or that of a musician. It was as clear as that.

However, the lady who had advanced towards me did not have any such rash threats for me, but wished to engage us for a private party. Yes, really! How wrong could I be?

It was a jolly good evening, spoiled only by a grumpy caretaker at the end who wanted us to pack up our gear faster than the speed of light so that he could get home. It is not my intention in this book to vilify all caretakers, since we did meet one or two pleasant ones, but generally speaking I found one of their CV qualifications was to be as grumpy as possible and/or totally unco-operative.

The mention of NUT reminds me that when they had a ball at the Norwood Rooms in Norwich, they engaged the resident band there, who I believe at the time could have been Lionel Black, the pianist being David Denny, Physical Education Adviser for Norwich Education Authority.

Dave just had to disguise himself, since the might of the City Hall top brass would be there and it would hardly do for a semi-high up like Mr Denny to be seen in the orchestra, now would it?

David's band colleagues set him up with bushy beard, moustache and glasses so that he would be playing 'incognito' not to be recognised by the director et al.

They hadn't been playing for more than five minutes when Sir Arthur South, then Education Chairman sidled up to the bandstand and said quite audibly, 'Hullo Dave ~ like the new beard.'

So much for the disguise!

My teaching profession also got us the regular dance spots at the Teachers' Training College at Keswick where we played to a packed ballroom floor with young men being invited by members of the all female college (as it was then) to very enjoyable evenings which ended around 10.30pm.

We had some engagements at the Grosvenor Rooms on Prince of Wales' Road in Norwich, owned and run by a Mr Blackman, a Jewish gentleman who true to the manner of his race, had a good eye for business.

Some engagements were of his own making with the ballroom open to the public but more often than not we were booked for private dances, one I remember well being the Norfolk and Norwich Amateur Operatic Society. It was organised by Mrs Ivy Oxley, a delightful lady who with her husband Lewis, were in fact the N&NAOS and booked us for the party following their production of 'Oklahoma'.

The MD for that production was the splendid Fred Firth, a musical genius and hero of mine, who on that occasion persuaded us to play a selection from 'Oklahoma' which proved quite difficult music.

Mr Blackman was undoubtedly a Jew as I have said but I don't think he was a practising one for I never saw him at the Jewish socials for which we played on a great number of occasions.

They were held on a Sunday evening at the hall adjoining the synagogue on Earlham Road and were attended in the late fifties by a large Hebrew community of which Barry Leveton was organising secretary.

I had known Barry from Norwich School days so I supposed the 'old school tie' had something to do with my getting the bookings. They were happy evenings with mainly conventional Western dances but the occasional Hebrew one was added and we had to play for a Jewish hymn or two.

162

When we first played there, we were not allowed in until after the supper and I well remember the old rabbi saying to us, 'You boys would like a drink, yes?'

'Oh yes, we would please.'

He replied, 'Vell, the Tree Tuns is just up the road.'

Two or three years later when it seemed that policy changed we were allowed in and actually had supper though policy had not changed as far as having pork on the menu!

Then there was the Jewish wedding.

We were booked for the party after the marriage but I was asked to play in the synagogue for the actual ceremony to be officiated by Rabbi Larner who I believe went to work in Canada later.

I arrived early about the same time as a gentleman who could have stepped out of a production of 'Fiddler On The Roof', dressed all in black with homberg, long curly black beard and pince-nez specs. He was looking intently at the Hebrew inscription above the synagogue entrance. He turned to me: 'Please ~ vot is it saying?'

'What?'

'Vot is it saying up there?'

I don't even have a smattering of Hebrew and told him I didn't know although I did find it surprising that a Jew should be asking a gentile to translate what was presumably his own language!

We went into the synagogue where he turned to me again: 'Please ~ vere do I sit?'

'I'm sorry?'

'Is it left side or right?'

I burbled something to the effect that in the Church of England those with the bride sit on the left and those with the groom sit on the right ~ or was it the other way round?

Clearly I wasn't being much help, he being more confused than ever until another gentleman came to both our rescues, directing my 'Fiddler' friend to a pew and me to the organ, having first given me a black paper skull cap to wear.

The organ was an American organ or harmonium which has to be said had seen better days. I think it was suffering from chronic emphysema by the way it wheezed horribly and I found great difficulty in actually managing a semblance of a tune from it.

The pews began to fill up with extremely noisy wedding guests who called continuously to each other while others took flash pictures of family and friends, the crescendo of noise making it impossible for me or anyone to enjoy the odd sounds emanating from the wheezing organ.

When the bride entered, followed by Rabbi Larner, I attempted to reproduce Wagner's Bridal March as instructed but the few sounds coughed up from the bowels of the harmonium hardly bore resemblance to what I had on the music copy. I hissed to the rabbi, 'I can't make it play.'

'Pump the bloody thing,' he hissed back.

Several of the congregation looked surprised but I took it they knew of the vagaries of the harmonium. I pumped harder as he had suggested with the result that the wheezings were definitely a lot better and a lot louder which seemed to satisfy everyone ~ except me.

At a special evening at the Norwich City Supporters' Club on Rosary Road, we went to accompany the infant prodigy, one Laurie London with his 'hit' of the day 'He's Got The Whole World In His Hands'. We attended a rehearsal in the late afternoon when we met the aforementioned young man who was Jewish, extremely polite, immaculately dressed and with a lively personality. He was accompanied by his father and manager (one and the same) who was equally pleasant and the whole thing went off smoothly as did the actual performance in front of a large audience of admiring fans.

One other elegant place we went to was the Norfolk Club in Norwich where we played for a young people's party dance organised by Mr Desmond Longe who was a high-up in both the Norwich Union and farming fraternity. We performed in beautiful surroundings and I remember we were served supper by a couple of very formally dressed gentlemen in tailcoats and white gloves.

We were persuaded to join the musicians' Union for 'promotion of work and our own protection' and presumably, we thought, they would help in problems that might arise.

So it was that we attended meetings on Sunday mornings at Keir Hardy Hall to hear the various grievances that I decided to make out a case for blacklisting village halls which had inadequate pianos (my polite word for bloody awful).

After my brief but succinct proposal, the 'committee' went into deep discussion on the matter, after which it was announced that no such list could be made, that unfortunate as it was sometimes, bands would have to 'make the best of it'.

I am not one to get involved in deep argument and I simply stated that if the MU were not prepared to take steps to help in what we considered a most important matter, then we would secede from the union, since there seemed little point in continuing membership.

By the reaction you would have thought I had issued a declaration of war and I was given a stern warning that dire consequences would follow, such as our band being banned from 'all village halls and other venues'.

It was a remarkable thing that we could be banned, but with halls having atrocious pianos, they couldn't. Something was definitely cockeyed somewhere, I felt.

I expect there were other threats like putting sand in Jack's tenor or filling Dick's bass drum with cement but the upshot was that we left the Union to make our way through the musical world, alone and unsupported, something which we seemed to manage quite well, really.

It always amused me when afterwards we would arrive at a venue and be greed with the question: 'Are you the band?' which I immediately thought of as being spelled b-a-n-n-e-d ~ and give a wry grin.

We took our music seriously of course, but we had hilarious moments along the way and life then was one great laugh.

We would announce the most corny things such as song titles that had play-on-word twists.

'The Big Horse Song (Because) 'The Dog Song' (Trees) 'The Wheel Song' (We'll Meet Again) 'The Dentist's Song' (I Saw You Last Night And Got That Gold Filling) 'The Forty Winks Song' (Oh Forty Winks Of A Dove) and 'The Pimple Song' (I've Got You Under My Skin).

We made commercial announcements such as, after the dance dine at Wong Fu's Restaurant, The High Street, Peking.

I made a fictitious washing powder packet called 'Stuft' and we would announce, 'If your whites don't wash really white, then get Stuft' showing the packet to our audience. All harmless nonsense and a lot of fun.

In my childhood I was always being told that 'all good things must come to an end' ~ why, I don't know but it seems that they do.

In 1964 I decided to play the last bars of the Rémon Quartet and call it a day informing Jack, Dick and Denis of my decision, after much soul-searching.

The reasons were basically twofold: one was the style of music and indeed dancing had changed with the three chord guitar merchants bashing out a deafening noise that had no connection with music but seemed to send young people into paroxysms and elderly folk into hiding. It was something alien to my music and I had no wish to compete with it.

I remember a gig at Horning Swan in that year where a youth had come up and asked if we could play a stomp, which bewildered me slightly, since it was a term I had known in my Dixieland jazz days and we remembered things like 'King Porter Stomp' (Jelly Roll Morton) and 'Mahogany Hall Stomp' (made famous by Louis Armstrong and others).

With our line-up such numbers might have been possible but would have sounded ridiculous.

However, always willing to oblige, we struck up some kind of a stomp, as we remembered it, but clearly this was not what the north country adenoid wanted: he was referring to the latest sound emanating from the Liverpool Cavern, though even to an untrained eye one could tell we were minus three guitars for one thing which put us at a disadvantage.

At one of the last gigs together, some rather unpleasant youth came up to me and said: 'Can't you play somfin' by the Stoones?'

When I answered in the negative he commented, 'You want to get with it, mate.'

I wasn't sure what 'it' was I was supposed to get with but I dislike the term 'mate' anyway and was sorely tempted to invite him to try a packet of our own washing powder, but desisted.

I think I knew then that this was the beginning of the end when good music was being replaced with what Benny Green described as 'the stuff from the sump' and it was time to make a graceful exit.

The second reason I had for ending our seven years together was that I was to be married to Jane Palmer in August of that year.

I knew about 'Orchestra Wives' and that dance musicians, so often out on gigs, left their women to while away evenings alone and sometimes grow very lonely. I intended to set up home with Jane, putting aside thoughts of gigs as unselfishly as I knew.

Of course, it could be argued I was being selfish to three musicians who had been my close friends for all that time, one of whom (Jack) depended on his band work for a living and I was certainly not without guilt feelings in all this.

Looking back at those 'seven years of plenty' which were both joyous and financially rewarding, I can say without doubt they were my greatest years in the dance band profession and that the three of them ~ Jack, Denis and Dick were the best musician pals I ever knew and was proud to be associated with.

As for the Rémon Quartet, now faded into history, it was, as David Blyth said 'simply the best'.

CHAPTER 12

'I'd Like To Put On Record'
Alex Forbes Wright And Friends

The Rémon Quartet needed to be on record which meant finding someone who had the proper equipment as well as the studio and I began to ask all round for such a person.
I forget who told me about Alex Forbes Wright but I learned that he was just the chap to see and that by day he was to be found at Kenning's Motors on Prince of Wales' Road in Norwich where he was chief sales executive.

One afternoon I duly made my way to seek him out, slightly apprehensive of the man, his high reputation and his double-barrelled name!

I needn't have had any qualms about meeting him, for he was the merriest of men with a mischievous smile, a great sense of humour and an infectious laugh. I explained what I wanted which seemed to please him no end and we arranged for the four of us to go over to his home at 'Trees' on the main Norwich road at Salhouse to make a record or 'cut a disc'.

It was an attractive bungalow set in a large plot which led to farmland at the back and which contained a large soundproof lounge, a baby grand piano and a mass of impressive looking recording equipment. Alex was there to greet us with such enthusiasm and charm, obviously delighted to be making a record of a dance band which was something of an innovation for him, having been used to choirs and soloists mainly in the classical field.

He was being assisted by the laconic Ben, a gruff but amiable man who did a lot of garden work and other jobs for Alex as well.

The recording got underway with all the technical trappings + headphones, mixers, reel to reel and yards of wires and cable. As we were, in essence, using the recording to display our strict tempo dancing ability, we played a set of quicksteps headed 'Strictly For Dancers' which included 'You're Dancing On My Heart', 'White Christmas', 'Button Up Your Overcoat', 'At Sundown' and 'Calling All Workers'.

The slow fox-trot for Side Two was 'Moonlight In Vermont'.

Several times we went through the taping, until Alex was happy with the sound but insisted on it being 'right' for us which I always found a mark of his professionalism.

By the end of the evening we were exhausted and were glad to sip coffee, chatting about the recording, listening to Alex describing how he intended to make a ten-in. 78rpm and generally sharing our love of music with him. We had made a recording and a new friend.

Alex Wright was a Lincolnshire man, the son of a farmer who moved south into Norfolk in the twenties. To start with, Alex worked for his father but hated it, knowing that his heart was not in farming but rather with anything to do with motorised wheels, whether two or four. Thus it was that he was a long number of years with Kennings and very early in his career bought 'Trees' at Salhouse where he lived the contented bachelor life, having had a couple of 'near misses' (pardon the pun) with the opposite sex and finding them not to his liking.

It happened that a near neighbour was a Mr A Wright which often meant a mix-up in postal delivery and Alex decided to do something positive about it.

He added his Scottish mother's name to his own, thus making him Alex Forbes Wright and distinguishable from the other gentleman. So he wasn't really double-barrelled after all but nevertheless, not only did it make him distinguishable but very distinguished with everyone, knowing him by the surname 'Forbes Wright' (no hyphen).

Alex was a great thespian too with an excellent singing voice and had taken leading parts in many Gilbert and Sullivan operas over the years, including 'Gondoliers' and 'Mikado'.

He had been associated with Norfolk Operatic Players for many years and was a long time friend of Bob and Audrey Yates and of Ivy Oxley of the Norfolk and Norwich Amateurs.

In the splendid surroundings of Alex's lounge we had our photographs take in colour, grouped around his grand piano with the standard lamp behind. The pictures were very impressive with our red (sorry, pink) jackets looking just great, setting off well the four handsome guys we were.

The photographer was one of the partners at the Norwich Camera Centre in White Lion Street who told us that he and others were in the process of making a movie film for a festival to be held the following year.

He asked me if I could compose the music and then have the quartet play the soundtrack, although the movie itself would be silent.

Naturally this excited us and we agreed to attend a showing of the film at the other partner's house.

We all went, including Alex and Ben to a farmhouse way out in the wilds of Norfolk, so far from anywhere that I really wondered if we would ever get back to civilisation, as it were!

As we watched the film, shot first in black and white for the opening scenes, I made notes about the music, decided the mood, tempo and changes of style suitable.

The story was simple enough: a young man (Played by Lynn Wardle) is sitting on a bench in Great Yarmouth in dull, drizzly November looking utterly fed up when suddenly a pretty girl approaches (played by Lyn Ashton) in coat and pink chiffon scarf. As he looks up to see her, the film scene changes to a beautiful blue sky, sunshine and holidaymakers all around, transforming the setting to high summer.

They immediately hold hands and go off round Great Yarmouth on a horse-drawn Landau which takes them to the Venetian Waterways, the Funfair, the seafront and along the Golden Mile ~ all very romantic with the same excellent film sequences.

They finally return to the bench where they sit for a while and he turns from her momentarily, at which point the film returns to bleak November and he finds she has gone. It's clears he thinks it has all been a dream but what is this? Lying on the bench beside him is the pink chiffon scarf at which point he walks disconsolately away and the film ends.

I set to work on the music score and it was arranged to make the soundtrack at Alex's in three weeks' time which was cutting things rather fine.

However, the recording went well, the film-makers seemingly please with everything and the movie was entered for the festival under the title 'Winter Fantasy'.

We watched the finished production at Norwich's Noverre Cinema and were delighted not only with the result but also to learn that it had won several prizes.

At the beginning came the captions: there it all was:

'Music composed and arranged by Tony Ireland'
'Played by the Rémon Quartet'

We felt proud and rightly so and as the picture progressed we listened to the music ~ us playing and lending the right colour and atmosphere to the film.

That was many years ago and I lost track of the film and its makers but since beginning this story of my musical life I have been fortunate enough to find the film through Mr Eric Brown who is connected with the Norwich Film Society. He it was who kindly showed Denis Payne and me the film through after all those years and then had a video made for each of us.

Lt Colonel R E S Ingram-Johnson turned up at Alex's with an absolutely spiffing idea which would involve the quartet.

He had written a brand new song for Carrow Road (yes, another!) at Norwich City FC to 'replace that dirge On The Ball City'.

It's quite remarkable how many songs have come and gone to replace the 100-year-old dirge and 'Inky' Johnson's effort was, needless to say, one of them.

The punch-line of the song is about all I can remember:

'The object of the exercise is Bang it in the Net.'

The tune, it has to be said wasn't bad, having been composed by 'himself' as well as the words and we duly recorded the whole thing in one evening session at Alex's, 'vocal refrain by Colonel Ingram-Johnson'.

He was a dear man who meant so well as an ardent City supporter and remember he was our patron so I really hadn't the heart to tell him my true opinion of the song. It was simply awful.

It was given pre-match hype in the local press and on the day of the match 'Inky' stood at a microphone in the main stand to introduce the new Battle Cry 'Bang It In The Net' to the Carrow Road faithful, who had the words printed in their programme.

171

He delivered the whole package in typical Colonel of the Regiment style which culminated in the playing of the record, 'Inky' superimposing his voice over the top, exhorting the crowed to join in.

At first there was a half-hearted response with the colonel doing his utmost to rouse the enthusiasm among the ranks but even as we listened, utterly embarrassed, we knew it was doomed to fail before it even started.

The comments and language around us do not bear repeating, suffice to say that the epithets directed at both 'Inky' and the song were colourful but hardly complimentary.

The biggest insult of the afternoon came when a huge section of the crowd took up the stains of 'On The Ball City' drowning out the colonels' pathetic pleas to 'Bang It In the Net'.

Finally, amidst catcalls and insults from all directions, he kept his cool thanking everyone for their marvellous vocal support and hoping that they would make the song their new anthem.

We went to Alex's for a conference about it all with ideas put forward (mainly from 'Inky') how it could be improved with Dick, I recall, suggesting (out of earshot) that an adjective be inserted before the word 'net' which propriety prevents me from writing . . . Needles to say, the ripping idea died the death with 'Bang It In The Net', like so many others before and since ending up in the waste paper basket.

Alex came with us one Saturday to USAF Mildenhall, where in the NCO Club he made us a two-hour recording of the Rémon Quartet plus David Valentine playing for dancing to a packed house.

I have been lucky enough to trace the reel to reel tape which was made on a Grundig machine and have listened to music made by us with splendid vocal numbers from forty-odd years ago.

It comes over to me as slightly eerie with my own piano playing, Denis's splendid bass work, Dicks' impeccable tempos but above all Jacks' mellifluous tenor being played by a delightful man who left us all too soon but now such a long time ago.

The reel to reel is now on cassette being saved from extinction and in a small way the music of my fine quartet is preserved, as they say for posterity.

When the quartet finished in 1964 I regrettably lost touch with Alex for almost twenty-five years which was very remiss of me I must admit. However, our paths crossed again when he recorded my playing cocktail lounge music, then later a programme of violin and piano with a new-found violinist named Jimmy Skene (of whom I shall speak in a later chapter) and then a complete cassette of Jimmy and me accompanying the singing of Miriam Batterbee, who was later to become my second wife. The three of us attended a musical party at Alex's where everyone did a partypiece.

I had been to parties at Alex's before where everyone's name went into a hat and were picked out at random to perform a song, piano solo, organ solo or even a duet to entertain everyone else.

Among the talented guests were Martin and Heather Wyatt, Brian Ellum, Pip Jenkinson and Chris Speake which made a musical evening of such high quality.

An organ club also met fairly regularly at 'Trees' for a musical get-together which was sometimes preceded by a garden party with stalls, competitions and games, followed by excellent food and drink with music afterwards.

I was privileged to be at Alex's 90th birthday celebrations at Saint Gregory's Church in Norwich, mainly organised by Martin Wyatt to which many distinguished Norfolk singers and musicians were invited.

I played the grand piano during the reception to Alex's delight after which many musical tributes were given to Alex by some very talented ladies and gentlemen. Alex's speech was excellent and so full of humility with hardly a quaver in his voice in such an emotional moment.

It was unfortunate that Alex's eyesight and hearing deteriorated rapidly until he became blind and deaf, something which he found so frustrating, having to give up his beloved recording and sell his equipment.

How many recordings made by Alex Forbes Wright are in so many homes all over the country, I wonder?

Complete operas, concerts, musicals, orchestras, bands, choirs, soloists and so on all from the skilful hand of a man who became a local legend in his own lifetime: Alex Forbes Wright ~ a man for all seasons and one of life's perfect gentlemen.

CHAPTER 13

'An Apple For The Teacher'

1. The Operetta Years

So far in the story of my musical life I have barely touched on my profession as a teacher, allegedly my full-time career for which I had been trained and become fully qualified.

It has to be said that from a financial viewpoint I was earning considerably more in my early days from dance band gigs that I was as a teacher, which certainly said something about government attitudes to evaluation of those employed to shape the future of Britain's children.

Since I am writing about the music in my life I shall not dwell much upon my general classroom work except to say that I taught a class of 45 children at Thorpe Hamlet School in Norwich, all (or nearly all) eager to learn, bright-eyed and bushy-tailed.

In my first classroom stood an ancient rickety piano, put there one would assume because I was to take the singing for all the other teachers whilst they would take my class for something else of an artistic nature ~ crochet, tapestry, petit-point or such.

One day I made the mistake of moving the piano which tipped, pinning me underneath, causing deep concern to the class, some of whom rushed to the adjoining room, dramatically crying that Mr Ireland was 'underneath the piano'. I think they were convinced I had been flattened at the very least. As it was, I never attempted to move it again.

The then headmaster, Mr Stan Sinclair had a couple of remarkable incidents with school pianos: he was renowned for his considerable strength and one day was attempting to wheel a large upright through a doorway when for some reason the instrument stuck. Not bothering to see why, he put all his brute force behind it and with a great splintering of wood, the giant beast lurched through, leaving a shattered door lintel and the piano locking key (the reason for the jam) sheered in two.

One morning I came into school to discover the upright in the assembly hall lying on its back.

On enquiry I learned that our muscular headmaster had attempted to retrieve a pupil's bracelet from inside the piano, going in with his arm via the top with all his weight on the instrument.

The result was that the piano had tipped over, Mr Sinclair rapidly withdrawing his arm first, leaving the ancient upright face upwards on the floor. Such was the force of the fall that the keyboard bore the bizarre resemblance of a rollercoaster which necessitated sending for the expert help of Mr Arthur Cooke, who when he arrived had a few words to say on the matter and declared he had never seen anything like it before ~ or words to that effect.

In my second year of teaching at Thorpe Hamlet it was decided to put on an operetta called 'The Pierette Princess', a published work, written especially for children.

It featured what seemed like a cast of thousands with me as the entire orchestra on a Kemble white wood piano, so beloved by education authorities and RAF NAAFIs and NCO clubs.

The producer was one of my new-found colleagues and friends, Mrs Cathy Restieaux who knocked the whole thing into shape, with coaxing, cajoling, advising and sometimes threatening to make what turned out to be a resounding success, highly acclaimed by parents, staff and the press.

With such a brilliant production giving the school a high reputation, Mr Sinclair called for another in 1956 but although Mrs Restieaux searched far and wide, perusing many published school operettas, she could find nothing which really grabbed her imagination.

As the Christmas holidays approached, she asked me if I might try writing a play with music, perhaps putting words to popular tunes, an idea which had its appeal, although I have to say I was not feeling too confident.

First of all I needed a story around which to weave songs and dances, but as any composers of operas or operettas will tell you, finding a good plot isn't easy and it has to be said that the storylines in some of them are pretty thin or pretty awful.

I had hopes as I scanned books in the children's section of the city library with folk around me no doubt thinking I had reverted to second childhood. Nothing seemed to jump off the pages until in an old volume of stories I found what I was looking for: it was the story of King John and the Abbot of Canterbury, where a poor shepherd disguised himself as the latter to deceive the king.

I simply changed the characters, though not the plot, making the Abbot a wicked wizard who whisked away the princess whilst she was walking in the palace gardens. He would return the king's daughter only when he could answer three questions: can you show me something I have not seen, tell me something I cannot do and finally, tell me what I am thinking.

My excitement grew as I hit upon the idea of changing the shepherd to a 'poor, common schoolteacher' who would meet the wizard face to face disguised as the king. I felt that the introduction of the schoolteacher together with his class would add a definite interest to the whole scenario and would give scope for some comedy.

I set the story in Rainbow Land with a girl chorus dressed in all the seven colours of the spectrum who would open the operetta with a happy song with a good lilt.

An idea began to take shape as I worked on a Viennese waltz song in the key of G with the opening line:

> *'Come with me to Rainbow Land'* which went on
> ... *'To the land where people understand*
> *What it means to be so gay all day*
> *Who laugh and sing their cares away ~*
> *So come where skies are always blue*
> *To the land where you can spend*
> *A life of joy, both girl and boy*
> *In the Land of Rainbow's End.'*

After the opening chorus, the plot began to unfold and my entire Christmas holiday was spent in putting together the book, the music and the lyrics, my excitement growing more and more as songs and script began to fit into place.

One song in particular was destined to become a huge favourite which was sung by the schoolchildren about their teacher, Mr Freddie Potter of the Rainbow School:

> *'If you want to ask a question, ask a teacher*
> *For you will get the answer straight away*

*To how and why and when just ask a teacher
It's what you want to know without delay.'*

By the beginning of the spring term I suppose I'd completed about two thirds of the operetta which was enough to let Cathy Restieaux hear, together with the synopsis of the entire thing. She was delighted with what she read and heard, at once planning costumes, dance sequences and auditions for the leading parts.

Within a month I had completed the book, the music and the lyrics and after Mrs Restieaux had done her casting, rehearsals got underway. As the whole play began to take shape, children became excited and for me there was the thrill of hearing my own words and music coming over the footlights.

Cathy was indefatigable, encouraging the young actors and actresses to double their efforts to get lines and songs across to the audience without the aid of any microphones. She was a superb producer, ably backed by members of staff with make-up, etc and parents helping to make costumes. My first teaching colleague and great friend Rex Hancy, made many of the 'props' and helped me to paint the scenery.

The operetta ran for three nights in July 1956 to packed houses of enthusiastic parents and friends, my own parents among them on the final night, the Saturday. It was a resounding success with the 'Eastern Daily Press' giving an excellent write-up, the journalist comparing me with professionals and suggesting that with more experience, I could make it as a writer of musicals.

The children performed and sang magnificently, especially on the final night with many VIPs present. At the end there were speeches, bouquets and presentations with the whole evening bathed in glamour in the age-old tradition of the theatre.

With two successful operettas under our belts, we had set a precedent with everyone looking to me to write and compose another to be produced in 1958.

Mrs Restieaux was keen to carry on the tradition, Mr Sinclair gave us every encouragement and I was determined in report form terms 'to do better'.

Again there was the problem of the story but I had an idea in the back of my mind to set a story in a European country, although I had no fixed place as yet. At the time, I belonged to the International Friendship League, a group of people in Norwich who came from all parts of the globe and who met together weekly for social events and 'special' evenings.

We would have a party with a Danish theme or a French theme and one night we went to a 'Dutch' theme party organised by our friends from Holland who were in the IFL.

It was from this party that I hit on the idea of setting the new operetta in Holland, with all the colour and costumes of that country coming into it.

A simple plot began to take shape in my sketchings to include a couple of English tourists having trouble with the Dutch language, two quarrelsome shoemakers, one having a daughter, the other a son attracted to one another, along the lines of Romeo and Juliet. George Bernard Shaw did once state there were only nine stories with variations on each.

I added an ineffectual policeman and a mysterious magical lady to complete the whole thing with the rather obvious title of 'Double Dutch' and a new operetta was born.

I set to work on the songs, unable to change my habit of a 3/4 opening chorus entitled 'Come Join The Dance', a simulated clog dance which got the play off to a good start.

In the comical sketch involving a timid English tourist with his harridan of an aunt, I introduced a song 'Don't You Think It Would Be Better If We All Spoke The Same?' and I flatter myself that Messrs Lerner and Loewe used the same idea in 'My Fair Lady' with 'Why Can't The English . . . Learn To Speak?'

Once again the parents and staff worked wonders with costumes, Rex Hancy helped with the scenery: Dutch canal, houses and, of course, windmills, one of which had sails that went round and Cathy Restieaux slaved away at getting the children animated and singing and speaking with perfect enunciation.

I had the joy of watching my words and music come alive, playing the part of rehearsal pianist and on the performance nights once again being the orchestra.

My delightful journalist friend Steve James was there on the first
night to give us a splendid crit next day in the morning and evening
papers which caused a sudden rush in tickets demand.

All the performances were packed to the doors with a rapturous
reception ending with speeches and bouquets and presentations on
the last night, once more attended by my parents. Mrs Restieaux had
been the tireless producer making 'Double Dutch' a resounding
success and leaving me with the thought: 'Yes ~ I'm quite pleased
with it, the songs, the words and so on, but I know I can achieve
something better if I put my mind to it.'

As it turned out, I had four years to work on something better, since
it was decided to give operettas a rest for a while and produce a new
one in 1962.

Various ideas came and went, many of them too complicated or
ambitious or not really 'me'.

I needed clarity of thought and decided to take a holiday in the Lake
District in the summer of 1960, going for a ten-day spell with two
friends in Eskdale close to Scafell and not far from the sea at
Seascale and Drigg.

We climbed (no walked up) Scafell, walked for miles through
Langdale and Borrowdale, went high into deserted places and rested
by the peaceful tarns. The altitude and the clean air cleared my brain
and with the beautiful mountainous country all around me, I began
to form an idea for my third operetta.

I would set it somewhere in Eastern Europe, in a mountainous region
with valleys, lakes and forests, involving gypsies, princes and
archdukes plus of course a love story. Original? No. Straight out of
Romberg or Lehar? Well, maybe the ingredients would be the same
but it was going to be my story, my music, my words and the more I
thought about it, the more excited I became.

In Keswick a bought a notebook and some sheets of manuscript
since I knew I had to get all my ideas that were flooding my mind,
down on paper. I seemed to be inspired by the beautiful countryside,
for I had never experienced such lucidity of thought and words and
music simply tumbled from my brain on to paper.

Unfortunately the hotel had no piano with the result that I had to rely on my mental powers to create new melodies that would lend themselves to the ideas I had in my mind.

One of my ideas was certainly not original for I based my opening scene at the 'Bower House Inn' where we were staying, calling it 'The Happiness Inn' which of course Stolz and Benatsky had used with 'White Horse Inn', a musical I had actually seen though knew the music well from my parents' record collection.

Thus, the operetta 'The Prince And The Gypsy' had its beginnings in Lakeland but I could hardly wait to return home and start putting the pieces together. I worked very hard on researching Eastern Europe, costumes, names, dances, music, folk songs and traditions, all of which I found with the great help of some extremely kind people in Norwich library. I knew as I worked I had started on what I knew was my best yet, for the story seemed to flow, the songs with tunes and words just fell into place and I could hardly bear to leave my work.

My parents went away on holiday, my student brother was off somewhere earning money which left me alone with my piano and my brain a-whirl with the operetta. I found ideas came to me late at night and similarly at early morning with word-rhyming certainly easier after a night's rest.

Waltz songs and gypsy melodies took pride of place in this musical which I had set in the make-believe country of Waldenstein, somewhere in Europe at midsummer. Indeed, the opening chorus by village folk was 'Midsummertime In Waldenstein' which featured a folk dance outside the Happiness Inn.

A show always seems to carry one particular song that has everyone singing it which was the case with 'Prince And The Gypsy'. The song was called 'Dance Little Gypsy' which was soon being sung and danced by dozens of children in the playground at break and lunchtime and indeed, as we were told, by hordes of very young children down at Thorpe Hamlet Infants' School who had been taught it by their elder brothers and sisters!

Cathy Restieaux loved the story, the characters, the setting and most of all the songs and found a great joy in casting the main characters, particularly a dark-haired beauty called Karen Fogarty playing the role of Katrina, the gypsy girl.

There was an archduke, a prince (of course), a wicked brother (well, naturally), two evil ones employed by the wicked brother, the fairies led by Maritza, their queen and Puk, a mischievous elf (by kind permission of Mr W Shakespeare and others).

We decided to be more ambitious, veering towards the professional and have an orchestra, a strong quartet to provide the music accompaniment alongside me at the piano.

I went to see Mr Fred Firth, then music adviser for Norwich Education Authority who was kindness itself and extremely interested. He and I went to see one of his music students who was studying orchestration, highly recommended by Mr Firth and who would be able to take on part of the scoring.

We all met over a pint at The Bell Hotel in Norwich where the music was passed around with the ideas gradually taking shape and my excitement intensifying by the moment.

It was decided that as one batch of music was scored it would be passed to me and I would write out the parts for first and second violin, viola and cello.

All went according to plan, or nearly since some of the orchestrations came very late and we were running dangerously close to deadline.

Mr Firth himself played first violin, Miss Ann Hornby second, Miss Coyle played viola and Mr Ivan Cane played cello with the orchestra getting together for final rehearsals. Naturally there were difficulties and stoppings with a few alterations here and there but gradually it all came together and harmony began to set in.

It was at this time that I met my friend John Bacon, ex-Norwich School, one time printer and now television newsreader who also had connections with a small recording company called Spire Films.

When he suggested the operetta should be put on Long-playing record, I jumped at the idea and immediately persuaded Stan Sinclair to get it organised.

The work behind the scenes for 'The Prince And The Gypsy' was phenomenal. A little man called Sidney Hastings on our staff planned and built the sets with the help of Rex Hancy while I set to and painted the mountainous background with forest and lake at the front.

The gable of the inn was covered with paper roses, all made by the children supervised by the skilful Jean Swain. The costumes had been designed entire by one person ~ a pretty young member of staff named Jennifer Shelley, who drew patterns for the parents to follow and chose all the material herself from Butchers' in Norwich.

The results were stunning with yards of pink and blue net, sequins and sashes, jackets and skirts and the most delightful head-dresses imaginable. She really was very gifted, so clever at design and needlecraft and so willing to help make it all very colourful and professional looking. She had two very able assistants in Irene Marriott and Marion Fitt, both members of staff.

Came the show, with dozens of excited youngsters anxious to please their proud parents and their producer too.

The orchestra took its place, the recording equipment stood ready and the front row filled with VIPs, including the Sheriff of Norwich and, of course, Steve James.

That evening and the three that followed were something I shall never forget with the sheer magic of it all, the delightful presentation by the young cast, the touch of the orchestra behind it all, the wonderfully appreciative audience and, above all, my personal thrill at witnessing what I had composed and written, spring into being.

Backstage, staff worked like Trojans getting children on and off and there was one amusing incident involved the wicked brother, Rudolf, played by David Edwards.

In the story he had been dumped in the pond and should have come on stage covered in weed.

From one end of the long dressing room Mrs Restieaux called out to another member of staff: 'Rudolf's weed! Rudolf's weed!' which was completely misinterpreted as though he had 'spent a penny' causing a moment of great consternation since he was just about to go on.

Steve James gave the show a wonderful write-up with pictures. The school telephone was hot next day with people wanting tickets, some of whom wanted to come again and the whole place seethed with excitement. On the ensuing nights Mr Sinclair announced that an LP record would be available for sale as soon as possible which produced vast orders beyond expectation.

The final night (the Saturday) was absolutely stunning: a huge audience, more VIPs including my family, the best the children had yet performed and speeches, bouquets and presentations with a finale repeated twice over by sheer demand all made it such a memorable evening that would live with me forever.

My own emotions spilled over at home afterwards and I remember shedding a few tears, knowing that it was over.

The long-playing record was very good considering it was a 'live' one with a certain amount of 'background' from the audience, a disc that has gone all over the country since, indeed abroad too ~ a permanent reminder of one of the happiest times of my musical life.

In the audience on one of the nights was a friend, Ina Bullen, then head of music at Costessey High School who approached me afterwards and asked me if she could put on 'Prince And The Gypsy' at her school. I felt flattered, agreeing at once not only to allow such a performance but accepting her invitation to be the accompanist each evening.

It was produced by Ina herself in her own individual way and presented to the school's parents on three nights in 1963. It was interesting to see how the children a few years older interpreted the operetta, having more sophistication and stage presence.

It was hinted to me that Cathy Resieaux was intending to retire from full-time teaching and would like to make her exit in a blaze of triumph, which of course meant one final operetta.

In the theatre there is the well-known saying 'Follow that if you can' and it was up to me to do just that, though just what the story would be I didn't know then. Rainbow Land, Holland and Waldenstein had been lovely settings, but where next?

Sometimes ideas come by pure chance which is exactly what happened with me.

I was out playing for a dinner at a private house and in my break for speeches, went to the large kitchen for tea and bun. A huge Welsh dresser stood at one side of the room filled with plates of all sizes in the 'Willow Pattern' design.

As I sat there looking at this wonderful display I suddenly knew my setting, my plot, my characters, my music ~ everything in one inspirational moment. I remembered from my own boyhood the story of the Willow Pattern Plate: the two lovers, the little bridge, the boat, the mandarin and the doves ~ the perfect tale for what I intended to be my best ever piece of work.

My search had ended in that kitchen.

I set to work next day, planning everything, but to make a few adjustments to the story, making the hero Chang a teacher instead of a fisherman and bringing into the plot the British Ambassador and a Tartar chieftain with his host of Tartar warriors.

Having sketched the story, I set to work on the libretto, creating the girl as Li Ming Tsu, the mandarin (her father) as How Now and the rather pompous British Consulate as Sir Wilfred Court-Napping from Little Snoring in Norfolk.

Even as the book began to take shape, I knew if it was going to be a winner, then I would need good, witty, sophisticated songs with lots of tuneful melodies and I began to work very hard at it.

I attempted this time to use harmony parts for chorus and also two-part lines for duets, trying all the time to give a Chinese 'feel' to each composition.

The summer holiday of 1963 arrived with my mother and father going away for two weeks, leaving the house to me during which time I pressed on with 'The Willow Pattern' in feverish excitement as the ideas fell into place in rapid succession.

Sometimes I worked late into the night, while at others I would get up early with a fresh mind to write more.

I remember coming up against a musical problem of chord sequence in the fiery 'Tartar Dance' and decided to telephone Fred Firth who put me right straight away. His musical skill and knowledge was wonderful and he is someone I have admired for much of my musical career.

I created an opening chorus (not in 3/4 time!) sung by ladies of the mandarin's court: 'Very Lovely Is Our Li Ming Tsu', Chang's song to Li Ming Tsu: 'Little Petal Of The Blossom', the school children with Chang singing 'Confucius Say', and my best song ever 'Some Day I'll Take Your Hand' which was the love duet.

Before the August break had ended, I had completed the operetta, prompting me to tell Mrs Restieaux. However, she happened to be in hospital so without further ado I delivered book, songs and lyrics, together with a synopsis to her hospital ward, giving her the chance to read it all while she recuperated.

Within 48 hours she had written me the loveliest of letters in which she expressed her congratulations on a superb operetta, her joy at reading every line and how she was already planning costumes, casting various children in her mind and couldn't wait to get started. Imagine my feelings then, knowing the musical had approval and deep within me feeling I had really pulled out all the stops to make it the best I'd done.

Without further ado I went to see Mr Firth, who at once agreed to write the score for four strings and a clarinet to add the oriental flavour. He elected to play first violin (again!) and chose Ann Hornby for second, Denis Johnson for viola, Ivan Cane for cello and Les Fereday for clarinet.

When the term began in September Cathy started work, selecting those pupils who would fit perfectly into the parts. For Li Ming Tsu she chose a beautiful raven-haired girl called Anne Hunt, while Chang was to be played by Andrew Bennett, a lad with a lovely singing voice. A big, strapping lad named Stephen Read was to be the Lord of the Tartars and she picked the comical John Chilton as the British Ambassador who was to bring the house down with his Gilbert and Sullivan-type song 'I'm The Master Of Diplomacy'.

We were lucky to have Jennifer Shelley (now married and called Simpson) with us and Irene Marriott who took our costume design and picked materials for all the major roles as well as chorus.

There were, in addition, the flower fairies ~ Wisteria, Camellia, Lotus and so on for whom Jennie designed such exquisite costumes and I know how much Cathy valued her skills.

In the 'Willow Pattern' there are a great number of dancing scenes and here Mrs Restieaux was lucky enough to have the help of a friend called Norah Bradfield who was highly skilled and imaginative in choreography.

She devised the graceful Chinese girls' dance and also the dramatic Tartar dance, full of fire and fury, which was to be one of the highlights of the play.

Norah worked tirelessly, coming in day after day to take groups for their special steps, always seeming to enjoy what she did and always seeking Cathy's opinion or mine of what she was doing.

There were props to be made and here we had the help of my great friend Pat Swain who produced some wonderful Tartar sabres and spears painted gold and bejewelled with wine gums!

The fur and leather fabric for the Tartar costumes was supplied by another good friend, Colin MacLaren of 'Mac' Handbags of Mousehold Lane.

For my part, I persuaded John Bacon and his team to make another LP, although this time John thought it best to make the recording without an audience and arrangements were made to do this on a Saturday in the school hall, orchestra included. John was good to us, in that he used his influence to arrange for local television to come along and film part of the production which was given about three minutes viewing in the items of local interest.

I worked with my friend Rex Hancy once more on the scenery, the backcloth being a mountainous terrain in Chinese painting style and the house of the mandarin as a separate unit at the fore.

It was with the latter that I had an interesting and rather amusing incident.

I wanted the words 'House Of The Great Mandarin' written above the doorway in Chinese writing and having no success with Chinese-English dictionaries at the library and my Mandarin not being too hot, went down to the Great Wall Chinese Restaurant on Prince of Wales' Road where I consulted a somewhat puzzled waiter.

He disappeared into the kitchen, re-emerging minutes later to beckon me through the red swing door. When I turned I was taken aback by the sight of a large, fearsome-looking oriental wielding a meat cleaver. In a voice that matched his appearance, he spoke harshly to the waiter in presumably his native tongue and there followed a lengthy conversation with occasionally grimacing looks and gesticulations in my direction, like a sketch ideally suited for 'The Two Ronnies'. It always seems to me that when two Chinese are talking to each other they are venting their anger by the very tone of their voice, but I am told this is not so and that they always speak so.

The protracted conversation didn't seem to be producing much fruit but eventually, the waiter, taking my notebook and pen, wrote down (or rather, drew) some quaint-looking hieroglyphics, while trying to explain in his pidgin English what he had put.

Ghengiz Khan, still sporting his meat cleaver, then interrupted with some ferocious sounding words which seemed to lead to a lengthy, heated discussion on the correctness of the wording for 'House Of The Great Mandarin'.

All I could do was stand in awe of all of this, trying to smile, nod and appear highly intelligent until such time that the two of them had agreed on the perfect form of the five words.

Finally, agreement seemed to be reached, the waiter handed me the notebook, I proffered my thanks in my very best Chinese and the awesome gentleman with the meat clever roared his farewell as he smashed it down on the counter.

I beat a hasty retreat, clutching my notebook and feeling like James Bond getting away from some fiendish oriental den.

On the set I carefully drew the Chinese writing, fondly believing I had printed 'House Of The Great Mandarin'.

Rehearsals got underway, songs were taught to entire classes, not just cast, mothers, aunts, neighbours, friends, sketched costumes of all descriptions, orchestrations of numbers kept coming to me to copy up the individual parts and the entire school got caught up in the fever of it all.

Nearer to the opening in July 1964 art classes designed programme covers and posters, tickets were printed and letters went to parents asking how many seats were required and for which performance.

About a week before opening, dear Steve James appeared with a photographer to do a big write-up for the 'Whiffler' Column in the Eastern Evening News and interviewed Mr Sinclair, Cathy Restieaux and me for a 'background' story.

Great excitement followed when the articles and photograph were given a big spread two days later and demand for tickets exceeded all expectations, so much so that it was decided to run four nights instead of three.

I suppose 1964 was something of a 'vintage' year for me, not only with the final operetta Willow Pattern' but the fact that in the March I had become engaged to Jane and that I was to be married almost as soon as term had finished. You can imagine that life was rather hectic with my feet barely touching the ground.

The evening performances, held in warm balmy July were quite breathtaking. I thought that 'Prince And The Gypsy' was magical enough but the 'Willow Pattern' quite different in its way, was outstanding and from a musical viewpoint the best I'd ever hoped for.

Again, Steve gave us wonderful coverage with pictures, each night was a complete sell-out, the LPs sold like hot cakes and the children themselves were magnificent.

The amusing follow up to the Chinese restaurant incident occurred on the second night when two ladies from Hong Kong were present. After the performance they came up to me and informed me that the inscription on the 'House Of The Great Mandarin' was utter gibberish!

On the final night my parents were there, Jane and my future in-laws and dozens of friends to witness the glamour of it all: the speeches, the bouquets to Cathy, Jennie, Norah and Ann Hornby, the presentations of bottles of wine to the orchestra players and to me and the rapturous applause from an audience that had been transported to another time, another place, a world of make-believe.

For me it was a personal triumph with the double act of Ireland and Restieaux going out on the highest possible note, I to be wed and she to retire.

On the last day of that summer term in 1964 I was presented on stage with masses of wedding gifts but the most emotional moment for me was when Cathy had the members of the cast of 'Willow Pattern' sing from the back of the hall 'Some Day I'll Take Your Hand'. I endeavoured to hold back tears and attempted to make the speech expected from me but I was so highly emotionally charged I found it almost impossible.

I knew there would be no more operettas, for there was never a producer like Cathy Restieaux for she had produced five in less than a decade, four of them mine, a remarkable achievement from a remarkable lady.

This is a verbatim account of Mrs Restieaux's association with me and the operettas from her own letter to me dated 22nd July 1997 in her 88th year:

> *'It has been one of the permanent pleasures of my life to have produced those wonderful operettas. All the time, however, I believe I was quite unbearable.'*
>
> *Rex Hancy said, 'As soon as she approached us with that determined look, we leaped to attention and became a slave to her requirements.'*
>
> *The children chosen to perform were so amenable and word-perfect with no prompting that my dealings with them was a joy.*
>
> *It is not easy to pick out anything outstanding as they were all so perfect. After our first success, several parents rang the school to ask was there a chance for their child to be included in any other production.*
>
> *As the operettas included a 'lover', the handsome 11-year-old approached me saying, 'Mrs Restieaux, I feel I can't do this part.' It involved his putting an arm round the heroine's waist. I replied, 'My boy, when you are 16, you will be only too happy to do this.'*
>
> *Whether an anticipatory thought sounded alluring or not, the poor boy gave in gracefully and became quite ardent!*
>
> *My most difficult task was to show the children in the classroom scene to be really naughty. They had a strict but kind teacher who expected best behaviour and they always gave it. In time they 'cottoned on' and succeeded extremely well.*
>
> *In the Prince And The Gypsy I was lucky to have found two boys who were natural comics and they were so funny that at all performances that had everyone in fits*

of laughter. This applied to the reporter whom I understand was doubled up!

One hitch personally! When they came to my house for a rehearsal, my carpet wore thin!

The costumes were professional. Mothers gave loving attention to what their children would wear.

I was fortunate to enlist Mr Butcher of Butcher's large store. Coloured net was required and he served me well. He became so interested in the operetta that he accepted tickets for a performance and seemed quite spellbound by it all.

My last wonderful chance came after I had retired. Tony asked if a performance could be arranged to celebrate Mr Sinclair's retirement. I accepted with enthusiasm and between us we selected the general favourites.

We practised every Friday morning and soon found the children as enthusiastic as in former days.

We began with a great favourite ~ 'Come With Me To Rainbow Land' and at the end of the first scene and curtain closed, the boys said, 'Mrs Restieaux, Mr Sinclair is crying.' Exactly as I had hoped. In fact he told me he sobbed.

What wonderful days they were. How clever is Tony. Although all his operettas included a love match, the children performed with a sweet simplicity which I found very touching.

These operettas must be revived. I couldn't repeat producing but there must be many teachers who would be proud to take it on.'

So the term ended and on 8th August Jane and I were married at St John's Lakenham by the lovely Canon John Webdell, the organ played by Gertrude Allen (who opened with Bach's 'Sleepers Wake' and closed with Walton's 'Crown Imperial') and attended by a great many musical people.

Included were the other three members of my quartet, my vocalists, John Bacon and his wife Angela, many school colleagues and of course my family with my brother David as my best man.

Unofficial cameraman was Pat Swain on a 8mm movie camera.

My life had taken a great change: I was now married, the operetta years had ended, the Rémon Quartet was no more and I was to settle down to a quiet married life at number 4, Valley Side Road, Norwich with no telephone!

Had the music in my life come to an end?

CHAPTER 14

'The Sound Of Music'
The Great Thorpe Hamlet Music Dept 1965~1989

Music at the school prior to 1959 could be described as lukewarm, that is to say, from an orchestral point of view. There was a splendid choir under their conductor Cathy Restieaux which enthralled audiences at different times and indeed went to entertain at old folks' homes and the nearby infant schools.

The orchestra, as such was somewhat 'thin' with an assortment of recorders, some inconsistent violins, a lone cello and a couple of uncertain clarinets.

I wrote out a few scores for this combination, but without training or experience in this particular musical field, I was feeling my way with the result that the overall sound struck the ear as both strange and lop-sided.

I bought myself a book in the Teach Yourself series called 'Orchestration' by King Palmer which I suppose helped a bit and indeed I had to admit that sounds did become less strange and less lop-sided. We had some charming peripatetic music teachers at the school who visited each week on their given days to give instruction in their various skills.

For the few violinists we had Ann Hornby who had been a professional in her time, playing with many orchestras and now so good as a teacher. The children achieved such excellent progress under her guidance for she was strict but kind, the essence of good teaching. Ann Hornby was a delightful lady who later on had the tragic loss of her brother and his family in a terrible road accident, something she never really got over.

Ivan Cane came to the school to teach the cello, in the beginning to two pupils sharing one instrument. Very soon we procured another cello and I as able to use two girls in the orchestra, such as it was.

Throughout my career as head of music I invariably found girls more attracted to string instruments, at least I had more female violinists, viola players and cellists than male. Even when we came to have double bass players later, they were girls.

Ivan was a gentleman in every sense: he had taken up the cello in adult life and had become a very fine player, being a leading light in the Academy of St Thomas in Norwich. Like Ann Hornby, he was a strict teacher standing no nonsense but his love of the cello came across in his teaching and he had absolute respect from his pupils.

We had a couple of clarinets that had seen better days but with some wonderful repair work by Derek Spinks (about whom I shall relate later) we were able to have some tuition time from Eric Unwin, himself a sax and clarinet man and Musicians' Union secretary at Great Yarmouth.

As with the strings, I found more girls taking to woodwind than boys which may indicate that those instruments are perhaps more 'feminine'.

I found myself writing orchestrations for recorders in variety, violins in tune for some of the time, two cellos with restricted range and two clarinets which I found were pitched in Bb ~ highly technical.

The resultant sound was quaint, often bizarre and certainly very different. We had not reached the era of music publications suitable for schools from people like the Hal Lennard Corporation in America or the American company of Belwin-Mills based at Croydon who produced exciting music for school orchestras.

The British firms of Boosey and Hawkes, Chappell, Schott and others could only offer the most uninteresting stuff imaginable, being still in the previous century with their musical publications, which was why I made the effort to do some arrangements of my own. I was inexperienced and could only try out my tentative attempts on my guinea pigs, the young musicians in my charge. Lots of them went into the waste paper basket (the scores, not the pupils) but others began to sound slightly musical and harmonious as I read more, experienced more and worked at something completely new to me.

At the beginning of this chapter I spoke of the year 1959. Why was it such a significant year for me, for Norwich and for music in my life? It was the year the Norwich Education Authority appointed Mr Frederick Firth as Music Adviser to the city, undoubtedly one of the finest appointments ever made, for Mr Firth brought with him a 'new beginning', a 'fresh start' that would literally revolutionise the musical culture of Norwich's young people from infant age to late teens.

I soon got to know him and his charming wife Erin and I have already mentioned his excellent contribution to two of our school operettas.

Fred Firth was from Morecambe in Lancashire and was a remarkably skilful musician, being proficient at the violin and piano and with a wealth of experience behind him, having done 'the lot' ~ classical orchestras, theatre pit work, dance band and jazz. He also had perfect pitch, a wonderfully useful gift and an ability I have tried to master over the years ~ though not very successfully.

Fred wanted to reach out to all the schools in Norwich and one of his first tasks was to visit each one to meet the heads and heads of music with a view to discussing their particular needs and problems.

With all this in mind, he began to spend money on pianos, instruments and music stands as well as to gather around him a team of peripatetics, old and tried as well as new.

I remember the first time he came to Thorpe Hamlet to watch a singing lesson of mine.

After a while he asked if he could take over, beginning with some little musical 'tricks' which delighted the children and then asked them their favourite song they had learned that term with Mr Ireland. As one, they chorused 'Nymphs And Shepherds' of which I am reminded so often when I hear the 'Common Entrance' sketch on Peter Sellers' record. On that particular track 'Miss Pringle' was the pianist; in my classroom it was Fred Firth with no music and suggesting different keys to try in order to suit the young voices.

He was quite superb, so friendly, making the children laugh and getting such response from them which to a young teacher like me was a splendid example of what good teaching was all about.

Fred Firth and I became good friends, always having time for a chat over a cup of coffee in Norwich if we met and he would come to Thorpe Hamlet staffroom many a time on the dot of 10.30, knowing he would get a coffee and just to chat to me about some music topic or other.

Fred couldn't abide 'sham' musicians and dreaded facing 'commissioned works' at festivals, written (if that is the correct term) by some weirdo or other who hadn't ever learned to differentiate between harmony and discord.

After one such rehearsal for a big concert, I met Fred, who had quite a string of uncomplimentary things to say about the bright boy whose commissioned work he had just been unravelling. He said when they started, he thought the orchestra was simply tuning up, such was the cacophony. My brother tells me the same thing happens in Canada where, in the early days audiences used to wince visibly; now they simply smile or even laugh out loud.

During his reign Mr Firth brought in some fine peripatetic teachers, three of them through my own recommendation.

There was the brilliant Angus Honeyman, Norfolk's 'Mr Percussion', who must have taught many hundreds of young drum enthusiasts from all parts. He came to our school and he and I had such a good rapport, for he would relate hilarious musical stories ending with his lovely laugh which I recall to this day.

'How are you this week, Angus?' I would say, to which he'd reply, 'Well, I've scanned the obituaries and my name's not there, so I suppose I'm all right.'

Angus was a perfectionist, taking such pains to get everything correct, spending ages before a concert with tuning timps to correct pitch.

He travelled all over the county doing far too much mileage and teaching at far too many schools, especially in his latter years. He wasn't well paid but supplemented his income working with a trio at a couple of pubs.

Wherever you meet drummers, you always hear them speak reverently about Angus, a splendid musician who died in 1997 long before his time. There must be hundreds of young percussionists working in all sorts of spheres who owe their skills to the teaching of Angus Honeyman, a much underrated man and one who was never fully appreciated at County Hall.

One piece of his droll humour comes to mind.

I had at one time two very young drummers being taught by Angus at the school. One afternoon he came in to find them practising their paradiddles (it's quite legal) looking the picture of innocence, expectancy and eagerness, looks which changed to disbelief and dropped jaws as Angus said, 'Aren't you lads into heavy metal yet?' We had an array of string teachers.

Ann Hornby I have already mentioned, who wanted me to get some violas, which before we became a middle school taking pupils up to 12 years old, were too big.

I set about restringing four violins as violas which didn't sound perfect but filled the alto place in the orchestra. The problems with violas are firstly convincing children of their lovely sound, their usefulness in the orchestral set-up and encouraging them to keep on with an instrument which doesn't give an awful lot of inspiration in the early stage.

The alto clef was no problem to them but to me, so used to treble clef and finding scoring them into orchestrations at first something of a nightmare.

After Ann Hornby's retirement we had Beryl Starling who stayed with us for a long time despite an assortment of pupils, some of whom would never make violinists. Beryl rarely complained, showing the patience of Job (or Mrs Job I suppose).

In the early seventies the school music began to be a tour de force with Mr Firth giving me all the peripatetic help I asked for.

Maureen Elvidge came to teach violas, shedding some of the work from Beryl.

The school bought a half-size double bass and on to the scene came a splendid teacher named Colin Boulter who taught part-time at the Blyth-Jex school, supplementing his income as a peripatetic bass teacher. He had been a pro with the Bournemouth Symphony Orchestra under Charles Groves but one day decided he didn't want to spend the rest of his life scraping a living (sorry about this old gag) and promptly left.

At Thorpe Hamlet he had some very bright pupils who responded well under his teaching.

When Eric Unwin died after a short illness, Fred Firth appointed Eric's son Russell to be a woodwind teacher. Russell had been to music college but had gigged in and around London with all sorts of bands, although in his early days his father used to worry about him a great deal.

There was an interim period between Eric's death and Russell's appointment when Fred Firth allowed me to employ Lionel Black to teach the clarinets during time he 'took off' from his insurance company to pop into school.

Lionel played a simple system clarinet, yet was teaching children the Carl Bohm fingering, something that amused him greatly and something that was never detected!

In 1974 we became a middle school which meant pupils staying on until 12 and heads of music were pushed up a scale (another musical pun ~ sorry!) Mr Firth visited the school to persuade Stan Sinclair to make me head of music minus class, something which he agreed to, knowing the success the music in Thorpe Hamlet had already enjoyed. I could now work towards building a splendid orchestra, a windband and who knows what else?

There was a grant to go with the new post plus a generous cheque from the parent teacher association to buy instruments. However, the price of new instruments was high which made me realise that with the cash I could probably manage three, possible four new ones. This was no good if I were to buy a large number, so what was I to do?

I decided to advertise, not just locally but nationally and with the consent of Stan Sinclair I placed an ad in the 'Exchange And Mart' music section for a three-week run, asking for help to build a school orchestra.

As well as this, I wrote to Charlie Chester on 'Sunday Soap Box' with a similar plea.

The response was overwhelming, each day the postman bringing letters offering instruments of all sorts, either for nothing except the cost of postage or at very low prices. We had parcels coming from all parts of England and Scotland that contained musical instruments, usually in need of repair but sometimes in excellent condition.

There was a matching pair of military band metal clarinets, an old Boosey and Hawkes trombone with a handle for 'pedal' notes, an ancient accordion, three C Melody saxophones, several well-worn flutes and clarinets and a large variety of violins, some in cases with bows and in one case, riddled with woodworm!

Accompanying these instruments were charming letters from people who had lovingly looked after them and who wished to give the chance to young people to learn. Some of the letters told of sadness, of departed loved ones, of a father, a mother, uncle or aunt who used to play, whose violin or whatever had been in the attic for years, long forgotten and now never played.

Enclosed with some were piles of old music with dates of many years ago written by the owner's name and I spent many a nostalgic hour going through a myriad of correspondence together with many bags of sheet music.

As well as this, I heard from two schools that were closing down and selling instruments cheaply: one was in Cheshire and the other in Midhurst, West Sussex. From the school in Cheshire I bought an oboe for £30 with some music stands thrown in, while the Midhurst school sold me a pair of timpani, fetched by a local old boy of Thorpe Hamlet School, David Shailer with his small carrying service.

What happened after all this in fact, was that we became a mini Exchange and Mart ourselves. Some of the instruments that reached us were of little use to the school but of value to collectors with the result that I raised more money for the music department selling them privately or to antique dealers.

Those instruments that were in need of repair I kept to take to the men I had already got to know well who were craftsmen when it came to making old instruments look like new. Well, not quite but near enough.

There was the reliable and very patient Derek Spinks living at Heartsease, so very near to the school and who worked in a shed behind his house mending trumpets, trombones, clarinets, horns ~ in fact anything that made a musical sound. He beat a regular trail from his home to the school for many years repairing things that had been well-used, ill-treated or even smashed to pieces, sometimes repairing repairs, solder welded on to solder!

He would look at an instrument sometimes with sardonic face, shake his head in disbelief, drive away with the bits in his car to return the following week with the broken plumbing ready to face further rigours.

Derek was a drummer himself, playing with the Cawston band and also leading a dance quartet called the Galvanos, instantly recognised by their frilly Latin American shirts. Before he retired to take up school instrument repair, Derek had worked for many years for the Willson family at Willson's Music Bazaar by the steps nearly opposite Norwich's Bell Hotel.

Part of his job had been repair work for Billy Willson, so it was an almost automatic step from the shop to our school as well as many others.

Then there was Reg Cadywould, a skilful repairer and rebuilder of violins, violas, cellos and his own instrument, the double bass.

Reg lived on Eaton Road in a house with walls festooned with violins and bows, where there was a workroom above the garage and an ever-pervading smell of glue about the place. He spent a great deal of time rehairing bows with the horse hair which came from Russian or Poland, as well as setting bridges perfectly for the height of the violin strings.

The one skill he had for which I personally envied him was that of setting a fallen sound post just under where the bridge stood: they have to be free standing, just like the bridge itself and whereas I used to find getting them to stay in place a nightmare, Reg could do it in minutes. Indeed, Ann Hornby could too, although she simply used a piece of string.

The mention of free standing bridges reminds me of how Ivan Cane told me had visited one of his schools where there had been an accident with a cello with the bridge collapsing.

'Not to worry, Mr Cane,' said the headmaster, 'Our woodwork master fixed it with Superglue.'

Ivan said he spent hours with knife and hacksaw trying to put right the damage!

Reg Cadywould had worked at City Hall engineers department for most of his career, following a part-time musical life, playing the double bass (seriously, as they say!) in the Norwich Philharmonic and Mozart orchestras and not so seriously in the Bert Galey dance orchestra.

In his retirement from City Hall, Reg had gone in for repairing string instruments and also visiting various auction and sale rooms with his friend Eric Williams to snap up bargains in violins and other string instruments.

I would send many a promising pupil to Reg with a view to buying a decent violin ~ or at least their parents!

I also had a friendly repair man called Mr Daines who lived in Aerodrome Crescent, again not far from the school, a retired engineer with Heatrae, having a wealth of tools and machinery to help take some of the burden of work from Derek Spinks. Mr Daines had an engineering mind, seeing immediately what was wanted and promising me a repaired trumpet or horn in 'a day or two'. He became interested in the school's music and he and his wife came to a concert there.

Another engineering mind was that of my magician friend Pat Swain, who had been an apprentice engineer in his youth and did many a repair job for me including a bent trombone slide that had to be perfectly straightened. Trombone players know that a bent slide is nasty, difficult to cope with and even more difficult to correct but Pat managed it ~ as I knew he would.

Of course, with all these instruments in the school, I needed more peripatetic help so I simply asked for it. If you don't ask, then you won't get because no-one is going to guess your needs.

I asked Fred Firth personally, who sent two woodwind men along, whom I had recommended to him anyway: the quiet, soft-spoken and brilliant Joe McKenna who had been a pro dance man with Lou Preager and others and the impish, loveable sax and clarinet man of so much talent, the late Ray Nabarro.

Both these turned out to be excellent tutors, very popular with the children who gained much musicality and inspiration from them. In short spells we also had John Last teaching the flute and Stan Lyon, another sax/clarinet man and a personal friend of mine.

Then of course, there was the brass ~ no, not money but trumpets, trombones, French horns, a baritone, a euphonium and would you believe ~ a tuba!

Mr Firth sent along an ex-pro named Bobby Auld who had played with many leading dance bands and was a fine trumpet player. His Scottish accent was a problem, nay a drawback with the children, for unlike Joe McKenna, he gabbled his words making it difficult for pupils to know what he was saying, although he found a kindred spirit in Stan Sinclair, himself from Motherwell.

Bobby didn't stay with us long, returning to his native land for a similar post there, which meant I was temporarily without a brass teacher. Fred Firth asked me if I knew anyone who would fill in until a permanent man arrived and I asked David Buchan, a friend and local dance trumpet player if he would come. He agreed and Fred paid up with David coming along on a temporary basis to take lessons in what was called the 'Railway Carriage' on account of its long and narrow shape. The room was well away from the rest of the school teaching rooms, adjoining the kitchens and on one occasion when the fire alarm rang with the entire population of the school filing out into the playground, Eric Unwin continued teaching two pupils in there, totally oblivious of anything amiss. The simple reason was that the fire alarm could not be heard in the Railway Carriage and as Eric said at the time: 'We could have gone up in smoke with no-one knowing' ~ a little exaggerated, perhaps but he did have a point.

Eventually Fred Firth appointed a marvellous brass teacher, Barry Mason, another ex-pro dance man who had played with many bands including those in 'Geraldo's Navy' ~ on the Queen Mary, playing between Southampton and New York in the last days of the luxury cruises.

Barry originally hailed from Cambridge, was a former pupil at the Perse School and whose father owned FitzBillies Bakery and Patisserie in Fitzwilliam Street. Barry had married Christine Grint whom I already knew and had worked with for two summer seasons at Great Yarmouth, so it wasn't any wonder we became good friends.

With all the visiting music teachers finding odd corners to take pupils which included, on occasions, cupboards, it was clear that we needed a music room. The school PTA formed a special working party and in due time a collection of muscular parents (probably just fathers) put up a music room adjoining a sports room, both made entirely of cardboard ~ or so it looked.

The music room was in two parts: one for lessons with the other for storing instruments and music.

Cupboards were put in both, a roll of blue carpet installed, my wife Jane made curtains for the windows, an upright piano went into the lesson room, I found some splendid posters to adorn the walls and the place began to look civilised. I also put some self-adhesive mirror tiles onto one wall to enable musicians to watch their stance at practice or lessons and I completed the decor with a cork noticeboard for various announcements as well as lists of practice and lesson times.

Naturally enough, the visiting teacher crew were well pleased, especially with the privacy being out of range of other classrooms.

There were a few changes to personnel: Colin Boulter, the bass teacher left Norwich with Andrew Durban taking his place for a while, followed by Gill Alexander, a marvellous jazz musician who commuted from Suffolk and who had a lot of personal problems.

Russell Unwin became our full-time woodwind teacher, while Barry Mason's hours were increased to all day on a Thursday. He and I would have our packed lunch in the music room each week, discussing many aspects of music ~ well, what else?

With all this wonderful help from the music teachers, the repair gang, the PTA, other members of staff, I went ahead with some ambitious plans. I established a school orchestra of strings, woodwind, brass and percussion which included violas, a second double bass which I bought myself from Dick Le Grice, alto saxes and a C Melody sax.

We rehearsed on Friday afternoons from 1.30 in the school hall, giving concerts to parents and friends in the summer and occasionally to outside bodies such as the nearby Crome Companions. One of their number, a Mr Harry Mayall volunteered to help with the percussion, since he had been a drummer in his day. Now retired, he would come along each week to guide and encourage my young percussionists, even working behind them at concerts.

Harry was a very dear man, hailing from the north of England, a 'no nonsense' man who sadly had to quit the music scene when his eyesight began to fail, but I will always remember his kindness and the invaluable help he gave to the school.

With the free hand I had at the inception of the middle school, I built up a windband or military band minus the uniforms, which used to practise after school every week becoming quite proficient at Sousa marches, popular themes of the day and even short selections.

By now the Americans were flooding the music market with some splendid scores, delighting the children with things like 'Tijuana Taxi', the 'Muppet Theme', showstoppers and Glenn Miller numbers. The practices and hard work paid off because the band took bookings for summer fetes and also played in the city at Christmas for carol singing, once at Anglia Square and several times at Hay Hill.

I remember one Christmas at Hay Hill, it was so bitterly cold with youngsters having freezing fingers on trumpet valves or flutes and clarinet keys that they kept dodging in C&As for warmth!

We were allowed a one-hour spot by the authorities which was long enough for the children, long enough for the public, but long enough to collect around £100 for charity.

It was about this time that I bought myself a clarinet from Billy Willson, a Boosey and Hawkes' 8-10, determined to play with a view to teaching and also 'fronting' a windband. I took lessons with Joe McKenna at his tall house in Cardiff Road, going each Sunday afternoon for a one-hour stint, enjoying Joe's tuition, the music, the instrument as well as his wealth of stories about the music business. These lessons with Joe went on for about eighteen months, by which time I could play reasonably well and was able to do what I had set out to do: lead and conduct the windband at outdoor events and help with the clarinet teaching in school.

My interest in jazz made me wonder if it would be possible for a jazz band with youngsters of 9, 10 and 11 and whether they would be able to reach my level of sophistication, whether they would have the 'feel' for it and whether or not improvisation would be possible. Well, there was only one way to find out: give it a try.

I ran off some blues and quicker jazz standards and launched the first practice with me leading from the piano. The resultant overall sound was much better than I had expected, certainly a Dixieland/Trad effect, although thoroughly imbalanced through enthusiasm and weight of numbers.

The jazz band grew in confidence, enough to form part of our school concerts and we were asked to play on a double bill with the Blyth-Jex Balalaika orchestra at their school. We bought colourful hats for the musicians, while a mother called Mrs Webb (whose son played trombone) made each pupil a glittering waistcoat.

The line-up I will admit was cumbersome with too many trumpets and clarinets but the audience loved it, especially the finale which was our jazz band combining with the balalaikas in 'When The Saints Go Marching In'.

We went on to play at many functions to rapturous audiences but I think the most memorable was at the Norfolk and Norwich Music Festival at Blackfriar's Hall. I did a special arrangement of 'When You And I Were Young, Maggie' in which the trumpet lead, a young lad called Stuart Childs opened with the theme played slowly like a hymn, followed by four bars from our gifted young drummer Adrian Poole which brought in the entire band swinging into the number. Snippets of solo work came from Stuart and a stunningly talented clarinet player called Harriet Ward, improvising sans music. The whole thing ended with a drum coda from Adrian and final flourish from the band which just brought the house down.

The adjudicator praised them to the hilt which made them (and me) glow with pride. Other children and their teachers congratulated us warmly with many words of praise for our performance with comments from the adults about the young age of some of the players.

I introduced banjos with the band and having purchased one for myself, taught the children as I learned too. Eventually they were featured in concerts, making quite a passable sound with a good percentage of correct chords!

I had some help with concerts from various quarters: two members of staff played the violin ~ Peter Davies and Heidi Yates (she also trained the choir). Rod Kibble was a fine trumpet player who boosted the brass in the more tricky bits and Alistair Mackie sat in for everything ~ orchestra, windband, brass group and jazz band ~ on tuba. Alistair's grandfather in Scunthorpe had some superb music banners made for the music stands in maroon and white with the letters TH entwined ~ a gift to the school.

Those summer concerts were marvellous with the orchestras, the bands, the choirs ably led by Heidi, the recorders led by Jane Reeve and later by Janet Hawes, plus solos from some very competent players. All the children were in white shirts or blouses with the school tie, looking like angels, singing occasionally like them and for the most part hitting the right notes as presumably those angels with instruments, do.

Of course, all of this cost a great deal of money as you can well imagine and certainly the PTA contribution like that of the County Hall didn't go far. I sought help from some very friendly and helpful parents, among whom were Celia Fryer, whom I had once taught and Mrs Smith who ran a Webb Ivory Christmas catalogue with 25% of the money received being poured into the music fund. Many volumes of the catalogue were given out to parents, who in turn organised sales among family, friends and people at work, boosting funds to enable me to buy instruments, music, accessories like trumpet oil (I think some children must have drunk the stuff at the rate it went), strings, reeds and of course pay for the ever-mounting repair costs.

Newspaper collection in the early years helped a bit but I think Alfred Warminger couldn't keep up with the reading or something because the bottom dropped out of the market. Rumour had it that paper manufacturers were buying pulp cheaper from foreign countries, though how true that was I can't say.

This chapter about the great music department would not be complete without mentioning exams. In music you have grades starting with grade 1 as you might expect, though in the case of woodwind and brass at that time you started at grade 3 for some mysterious reason.

As grades ascended so they became more difficult and more expensive, the fees for the Associated Board of the Royal Schools of Music being somewhat steep with some parents opting out and others mortgaging their houses.

The exams themselves were held at Princes Street Congregational Church which later became a United Reformed Church. Notices hung about saying: *'This Way To Examinations'* and *'Quiet ~ Examinations In Progress'* and best of all *'Teachers Are Not*

Allowed To Stand On The Stair To Listen At The Door' ~ well, just as if we would!

I would accompany each boy or girl for the exam down to the exam room and play for their set pieces, probably two or three and then leave them in the hands of the examiner.

Examiners came in all shapes and sizes, some male, some female and occasionally those of indeterminate gender. Some smiled at the child or me (or both), some looked grim as if anticipating a battle (which sometimes occurred), some gave a cordial greeting with a remark about the weather, while others seemed ideally suited for a part in a Hammer horror movie or even a very early silent about zombies.

There was always a great palaver about music with consternation in the waiting room when someone couldn't find theirs.

On one occasion I had to dash out to Willson's Music Shop in Bridwell Alley close by where dear Jack Ramshaw loaned me a most expensive volume, since one of my bright young stars had left his copy in school.

Another time I was in the exam room with a very gifted flute player called Meryl Dempsey, when the examiner asked her to play one of her pieces which was unaccompanied. She was very young and seemed bewildered by what was being asked of her. The kindly gentleman said, 'It's either number 19 or number 33 in your book with the blue cover.'

'Oh,' said Meryl, 'it's at home.' My heart sank but undeterred, the examiner went on, 'Was it the quick piece or the slow? Can you play it from memory?'

'Oh yes,' said Meryl and as I left the room, there came forth the most beautiful flute sounds of the set piece, played without fault, giving her a mark of distinction.

Then there were the photocopies: the what! Sh!

Due to the fact that sheet music and albums were so fiendishly expensive, music for practice purposes was photocopied to prevent appalling home accidents such as the pet mongrel mistaking it for his lunch, baby brother making confetti or being used as a substitute for Walter Raleigh's cloak.

There were other accidents and misuses but I don't think I had better go into details of those.

Suffice to say that the 'originals were kept comparatively clean in readiness for the actual examination while photocopies were kept well out of sight in a music case or instruments case. At least, that was what was supposed to happen.

On the first occasion when a boy told me he had left the music at school while he flourished the photocopy in front of me, I was in something of a dilemma. Should I have the lad hide the offending sheet inside another album or come clean with the examiner and admit what had happened?

I decided on the latter and for my honesty received a severe lecture on the subject and black mark in despatches to the Associated Board who threatened to have me struck off or excommunicated or whatever it is they do.

On the second occasion it happened, I opted to secrete the boy's photocopy in an album and bluff it out. As nothing was said I thought we had got away with it until after the very last pupil had been examined, the examiner said, 'You do know photocopies are not allowed, don't you? Please don't let it happen again.'

I didn't let it happen after that because the music department bought the exam music which I took to the examination centre to be distributed to each child.

One of the drawbacks of taking children to Princes Street was the appalling lack of parking facilities to say nothing of the cost for a long session. Invariably I would find the Monastery car park in Elm Hill full which meant dropping the pupils off at the church rooms to drive round desperately finding somewhere to put the minibus. It usually ended up at Golden Dog Lane, a good distance away where I then had to find the correct parking fee having tried to judge the length of the exams and taken into account the fact they might be running late. I would then rush back to Princes Street to find a disagreeable steward reprimanding a couple of pupils and asking where their teacher was, just the sort of thing to put you in the right frame of mind for accompanying a violin or a trumpet. I used to wonder if Gerald Moore or William Davis ever had those kind of problems.

The worst event I ever had was with the brand new school minibus.

After dropping the children as usual, I did my familiar tour of the car parks without success, ending up in desperation at the multi-storey in St Andrews. With not much thought in mind, save getting parked and back to exams, I drove the monster up the slope to the first floor and promptly struck. The ventilator on top of the 'bus wedged itself into the concrete roof with the vehicle stranded, unable to go forward or back. With the queue of cars behind me unable to do anything, the officials below soon became aware that something was wrong and as for me, I was in quite a state, both worried about my present predicament and the bunch of young musicians awaiting my arrival.

In the end, a uniformed gentleman made all the cars behind me reverse down the ramp while another one climbed into the minibus and reversed it down too with an horrendous rending of metal on top.

One of the uniformed types began to remonstrate with me for bringing in a vehicle which exceeded the maximum height. How the . . . did I know what height the minibus was? The school had only just bought it and I don't think I stopped to measure its height when it arrived.

Fortunately I knew the second man on the gate who phoned the school to explain what had happened. As I remember, Rex Hancy came down with school assistant Rosemary Elcocks who drove the 'bus away (minus an air vent) and I made the exam room.

That incident made me decided to have the exams at the school where I think you had to have twelve examinees to warrant someone coming to an individual school.

It worked quite well on the whole: I made out notices indicating *'Exams In Progress ~ Quiet Please'*, organised tea and bikkies, lunches and even, in one case a map of how to get to the A11 for the various examiners.

I remember one lady in particular who was very large and brought her cello with her. She strode along in bright green jumper, red skirt and tartan socks in a way which seemed to indicate she wore the cello in a permanent playing position.

In the lunch break she asked if she could leave her papers (which included the exam results) in my own office to which I readily agreed and, of course, you would understand that my conscience didn't allow me to even consider the merest peep.

Of all the outside concerts featuring the school orchestra, I suppose the most memorable and magical were the Cristingle services in Norwich cathedral just before Christmas with the whole young congregation carrying lighted candles set in oranges. We played for it three years running with praise heaped upon the young musicians from many important people, including the bishop of Norwich.

I was lucky enough to have a week's music course at the Royal Marine Music School at Deal, in Kent, an unforgettable visit where I saw the finest military musicians in Britain.

All of them had to play a brass or woodwind instrument of course, but as well as that had to learn a stringed one. The teaching was superb, the musicianship was likewise and the number of practice rooms countless, many equipped with high quality pianos, for I certainly heard some highly skilled pianists while I was there. The course ended with a splendid concert in Deal theatre given by the young musicians playing their stringed instruments in the first half and their wind instruments in the second.

In 1975 Stan Sinclair retired as headmaster and to mark his farewell we staged a concert with costume to include songs from three of my operettas which he loved.

The whole thing was a surprise, with Mrs Restieaux returning to train the singers, while I organised the orchestra which consisted of ex-pupils playing some of the original scores with additional orchestration added by me.

It was a highly emotional evening recorded by the local paper and I thought how the late lamented Steve Amiss would have loved it.

I have witnessed so many clever young people blossom into skilful musicians and it would be difficult to list them all.

Clarinettists I remember as outstanding were Harriet Ward and Mandy Burvill, Meryl Dempsey on the flute, Stuart Childs, Paul Flatman and Richard Leney on trumpets, excellent double bassists Karen Nevin and Elizabeth Wooding, string players Harriet Fraser,

Andrew Wickens (who also played clarinet) and Nancy Fraser with splendid percussionists Brian Savage and Adrian Poole.

Good musicians often went in families and outstanding were the Frasers, the Ross family and the Fryers but I think the most versatile young man I ever met and who went on to university music studies was Jonathan Irons.

When I was forced to take early retirement in 1989 it was Jonathan who organised the music at the party, held at Catton New Hall. He had been the star pupil at his high school (Heartsease) where he had virtually run the music department for Shirley Hallums. For my 'do' he got together ex-pupils to form a band which he led from an appalling wreck of a piano (not even 3 out of 10) which was so out of pitch he had to transpose to fit the other instruments around him!

My retirement marked the end of a 35-year career which had seen the heights and the depths, the delights and the tragedy, the years of watching young people grow into splendid musicians with my guiding hand behind them.

It was, on the whole, a wonderful experience, something to look back on and say, 'It was music to my ears' and 'Music, music all the way.'

CHAPTER 15

'That's Entertainment'
Entertaining Outside Teaching

Although I disbanded the Rémon Quartet in 1964, the year I got married, inevitably there were still enquiries for the band, despite the fact that I had now set up home with Jane at number 4 Valley Side Road, off Plumstead Road, Norwich.

It was a three-bedroomed detached house, having been previously occupied by Mark Puckle, a local television newscaster and our neighbours at number 2 were David and Phyl Flatman who had first met at the Oaks Ballroom at North Walsham where the Rémon Quartet had played many times.

To begin with we had no telephone, which meant that any enquires for the now defunct band came via my mother at Ipswich Road, who would give directions to people as how to find us.

One such enquirer who found her way to us was Mrs Gurney from Heggatt Hall what wanted to have the band play for her daughter's party, since the young lady had set her heart on having the 'band with the red jackets'.

Mrs Gurney was quite charming, describing 4 Valley Side Road as 'a dear little house' and I promised I would drag the members of the band out of retirement to play for what turned out to be a really lovely evening.

Even prior to our wedding, Jane and I had been going over to the Manor Grill at Happisburgh, a restaurant owned by a Mr Wesley Pierce in company with the people who ran the Savoy in Great Yarmouth.

I would play the piano for the diners, who occasionally got up to dance on the postage stamp dance floor, while Jane went for a walk or sat and read a book. Thinking back, it must have been terribly boring for her, although there were occasions when Mr Pierce's wife would come along and Jane could chat to her. They were, in fact, both in the teaching profession, Jane at the time at Heartsease First in Norwich and Mrs Pierce at East Ruston school, so there was plenty to talk about.

Wesley Pierce was a delightful man, deep-thinking but slow and lugubrious in action. He seemed to take to us both and asked me to organise cabaret acts at the Manor Grill on Saturday nights as well as bring along a vocalist.

Pat Swain came several times in the guise of 'Carson' the magician delighting the diners with some table magic as well as a number of illusions and I managed to get Hilton Tait along for much of a summer season to sing. Hilton would bring his wife Daphne with him which was good company for Jane.

Wesley loved the glamour of cabaret and decided to do some booking himself, persuading one or two of the London crowd to come.

I remember I had to accompany one brassy young female who produced the 'dots' (her music) in yard-length strips covered with red cues and notes. As we stuttered through one number, she turned and poked me hard in the back, hissing, 'Faster, faster.'

Now I'm usually a placid sort of guy but that kind of thing I can't take; a quiet word, yes but a poke between the shoulder blades, no. When the song ended I turned to the young lady and said; 'Don't ever do that again. If you do, I shall walk off in the middle of your act.' She got the message.

At the end of every evening Wesley would invite Jane and me to sit and talk over coffee and sandwiches. Without fail he would say: 'You can have turkey, chicken, ham or tongue' and without fail, whatever we requested came up as ham. But he was a lovely, kindly man of whom we were very fond. He and Mrs Pierce bought us a beautiful carving set for our wedding present which was typical of their kindness and generosity and I shall always look back with affection for them and the happy times we had at the Manor Grill at Happisburgh.

One evening I saw an ad in the paper for a pianist residency at the Sandringham Hotel in Great Yarmouth.

It involved the summer season with Saturday nights and the possibility of 'other nights'. Jane and I talked about it, the pro side being the money which would help pay for a holiday and the con leaving her on her own at home.

I telephoned the hotel and spoke to the owner, Teddy Lees, who asked me to come over to Yarmouth to meet him at the Sandringham.

Teddy Lees was fast-talking, quick-witted, highly intelligent and knew just what he wanted for his customers: good piano music for listening as they dined with dance tempo to follow.

'Everyone calls me Mad Teddy Lees,' he said. 'I'll play fair by you if you'll play fair by me. Be here on time, keep the customers happy and make your breaks short.' Then he added, 'Do you know a good girl vocalist?'

Yes I did: no, not Jane for though she had a good singing voice it was not of the swinging sort and besides, Jane was not really one for public performance.

The girl I had in mind was Christine Grint who worked under the name of Christine Vance and at the time of writing, still does.

She was married to a bass player from the Paul Chris band but when I asked her, she seemed very happy to come each week to Great Yarmouth to sing to my accompaniment for the summer season. Chris came to our house to run over her numbers which all seemed straightforward enough and with that, the season got underway, with each Saturday evening she coming to Valley Side Road to leave for the Sandringham in my car. Jane would spend that evening at home or visit Phyl Flatman next door, since she too was grass-widowed by her angling husband David.

Those nights at the Sandringham Hotel were hard work but good fun with Teddy Lees himself often contributing his skills on maracas and other toys. I remember that a drummer used to come for the dancing part who I think journeyed in from Caister. When the season ended in September Teddy booked me for the following summer but Christine declined as I believe she had marital problems at the time which later culminated in a separation.

Happily, not too long after she met and married Barry Mason, brass peripatetic teacher at Thorpe Hamlet who became a good friend and both he and Christine have given me their friendship in good and bad times over the years.

I did take on the following season with Teddy Lees but without Christine it wasn't the same and since Great Yarmouth was going through a bad patch, custom fell away which left Mr Lees no choice but to sell up and go. He went off to open a hotel in Aberdeen for the oil rig men and as far as I know did quite well for himself. One sad bit of news I read about some years later was that his son was murdered while on safari.

Before he left Great Yarmouth, Teddy Lees passed on my name to Percy Warnes who kept the Del Monico Hotel, a much smaller building almost directly opposite the Britannia Pier. Inevitably, Percy asked me to go and play the grand piano in his lounge for the guests on the last night of their holiday, which I did for two seasons running (after due discussion with Jane of course).

Percy was a splendid man, jovial, happy and friendly who ran a good hotel with his German-born wife who often had her 'mutte' with her (her mother).

Percy loved everything I played, singing almost every song from behind the bar as he served drinks or dried the glasses. His home was at Fleggburgh and he also had a souvenir shop in Regent Road I believe.

He was something important in the Great Yarmouth Hoteliers Association too, but his great love was golf, something he was forced to give up when he developed arthritis. I liked Percy a lot, for he was always kind, fair and generous, giving me a meal at the end of an evening without fail.

I had one experience at the Del Monico which I shall always remember.

I could never bring myself to play 'Roses of Picardy' without knowing I would break into tears, particularly as it came to the line: *'And the roses will die with the summer time . . .'*

One evening there, a lady came up to the piano and even as she approached I knew what she was going to ask for. When she did, I was about to say, 'I can't play it . . .' but she told me that her mother had sung that to her as girl and if I could play it, it would make her so happy.

With that, I cast aside my old thoughts and played it right through without a single tear.

In 1971, I told my mother that we were adding a 'wing' to 4 Valley Side Road (I was quoting from the Kern-Hammerstein song 'The

Folks Who Live On The Hill'). Mother was curious to know where we would have the 'wing' but when I told her it was to be a little human wing, she was over the moon.

So it was that in August, Jane gave birth to Elisabeth, another event which was to change our lives rather dramatically.

Even while Jane had carried Elisabeth, whenever we went to anything musical, she would have a young unborn dancing all over her inside making her musical feelings known to her mother.

As a tiny baby she practically screamed the place down when I introduced her fingers to Amyl the piano and I wondered how things would be when she grew older and made a start on piano lessons.

In fact I made a cardinal error of attempting to give her piano tuition myself, the same no-no as teaching your wife to drive. Hands crashed on to the keys, music flew all over the room and very uncomplimentary things were said about Amyl which was why we passed all those problems on to the avuncular Mr Doe, retired music master from the City of Norwich School.

In October 1973 my dear mother died, mainly from the result of a fall in a Norwich restaurant and I grieved her loss remembering the enormous part she had played in my musical career.

My father found a companion in a widowed lady named Doreen Aylett who lived at Sprowston and in due time he sold the house at Ipswich Road to buy a bungalow near her.

This was somewhat ironic, since we sold 4 Valley Side Road to move to 125 Greenways in Eaton village to be nearer to my father and Jane's parents who also lived in Eaton Rise.

My musical life had continued with my mastering the art of clarinet playing and going along each week to practise with the Norfolk TA band at Britannia Barracks.

It was all very enjoyable fun, sitting as I did in the second clarinets playing marches, selections and light music.

However, the day came when the band were asked (or probably told) to play at the opening of County Hall in Norwich by the Queen, which meant not only kitting me out with an ill-fitting uniform (memories of National Service) but persuading me to march and play at the same time.

Those who have never attempted to do this will appreciate that the biggest problem is co-ordination, the brain having to be channelled in three directions: to the legs to march ~ in step of course, to the eyes concentrating on the music perched on something called a lyre fixed to the end of the clarinet and to the fingers depressing the correct keys at the right time. I tell you now, that to begin with it was ghastly and in fact grew more so as time went on.

I put on the uniform at home to howls of laughter with the thought crossing my mind that the neighbours would have to witness my departure from the house on the day itself, an idea that filled me with dread for even as I looked in the mirror I could see the perfect prototype for the army's worst-dressed recruit. Jane had to sew on some gold braid somewhere which she succeeded in putting upside down which of course would appal the bandmaster, to say nothing of Her Majesty.

The cap I was given was, needless to say, the wrong size and when placed on my head, totally obscured my view of not only the music but the rest of the Territorials around me. With the aid of some strips of brown paper we did make it look as though it fitted me after a fashion, though it was not a 'fashion' I would take up permanently.

On the Sunday there was a dress rehearsal at County Hall where I 'marched' with the rest of them from the road leading up to the main steps but it did appear painfully obvious to me and the officer in charge that the entire band was out of step with me.

After a hurried whispered conference it was decided to place me out of sight behind one of the pillars to slip in alongside the clarinets when the band came to a static position, as it were. This was clearly done so as not to embarrass the entire company in front of the Queen who would at once note how out of step they were with me, for I believe her Majesty has a very watchful eye in these matters.

Of course, the second part of the plan was to get me to sidle behind my pillar the moment the band had to leave County Hall and march away to Mousehold or a nearby hostelry or wherever the bandmaster might lead them. With one or two bits of practice I had my sidling just right so that even the other clarinets didn't see me go, rather like the Invisible Man.

The next charade in this comedy of errors was when the band were given the opening march to play and by complete bungling, half the musicians were given Alford's 'On The Quarter Deck' while the other half were issued with Sousa's 'King Cotton'.

You can imagine the bewilderment on the Major's face as the cacophony broke forth but as a newcomer to the band I at once thought I was playing something wrong and naturally stopped. Major Thompson brought the hideous din to a halt, whereupon a massive investigation got underway with tempers becoming rather frayed.

The final farce was a full confrontation between the major and the sergeant who usually conducted band practices, the sergeant saying he would not play if the major were to conduct the band on the day.

This rife led to division within the band, most of the men supporting the sergeant and like him, refusing to play ~ somewhat like Sam and his fallen musket.

I found the whole thing hilarious but did begin to wonder what I was doing there and ought I to do a further sidle and vanish for good.

Like Wellington with Sam, the colonel was brought into the fracas and with grunts and murmurs beneath a bristling moustache, the whole business was finally settled by diplomatic means with an uneasy truce.

At the 'real thing' the sergeant conducted the band with all of us playing the same march at the same time, while the major took his place among the euphoniums. I did my sidling but without the Queen noticing and from my position among the second clarinets watched her Majesty perform the ceremony. When it was all over the major invited me to join the TA as a permanent bandsman since I imagine he had thought highly of my playing and my sidling. It was an offer which I graciously declined with the excuse of pressure of work, although I had secretly vowed that it was not for me, especially if all ceremonies were as chaotic and ludicrous as that had been.

I remember one exciting morning on a visit to Coventry Cathedral with Jane and Elisabeth, finding the entire Count Basie Band rehearsing for the evening concert with the great man himself conducting from the piano in his typical laid-back way. I was spellbound by it all, the huge overall sound, the solos and of course, the Count's piano and my only regret was not having tickets for the actual performance. Still, I suppose we had the second best thing.

I began to do some lounge work under the name of Tony Scott (my grandmother's name ~ the Scott part I mean) since the Education Authority wasn't keen on their teachers doing that sort of thing so perhaps an alias was a good idea.

I was booked to play at South Walsham Hall where there was a large bar with comfortable seats all round and the smallest grand piano I have ever seen, the property of the Swiss owner.

It was an enjoyable series of engagements with the sun streaming in from the magnificent grounds on summer evenings or the glowing cosiness of a log fire burning apple wood in the enormous hearth in the cold of winter.

I shared the month with Peter Moulding, who called himself Peter Williams, since he too taught in a local school and wanted to work incognito.

The clientele were pleasant, the staff who included Sergio, the Italian head waiter and Margaret behind the bar likewise and there were private bookings to add to the interest ~ and the income!

The Barton Angler by the edge of the Broads was another delightful spot where I played John Harrison's baby grand piano for the diners there. John was the owner, a former actor with an eye not only for business but for a touch of class and elegance.

He engaged an excellent chef called Stephen and he wanted the customers to enjoy good food in good surroundings with good music to match: hence my inclusion in his plans.

Delightful diners would ask me for things as diverse as a selection of Ivor Novello to tunes from the twenties, all of which I was able to oblige. It was a sad day when John decided to sell to leave for Sevenoaks in Kent and the Barton Angler was never quite the same again.

In the late summer of 1986 my lovely wife Jane was taken seriously ill with cancer and after several months of hospitalisation and suffering, to my great grief, died in June of the following year.

Before I returned to my teaching duties in the September I had an unexpected call from the Broadland Entertainment Agency, asking me if I would like to play the piano on Saturday evenings and Sunday lunch times at the Oaklands Hotel in Norwich.

I was alone, feeling very miserable with the sunshine gone from my life which was why I accepted the offer, particularly for something to occupy my mind and also the chance to meet people.

Under my 'stage name' of Tony Scott I played for diners on Saturday nights and Sunday lunches on a pretty awful Eavestaff upright which had seen better days a long time ago. The Saturday nights varied from a full and noisy lounge to one which was totally deserted save for the barman and me. I met some very nice people there, including Rob Jackson and his wife, he being a musician and headmaster in Norwich and I having taught their daughter music.

Adjoining the lounge and dining room was the Yare Suite and more often than not on a Saturday night there would be a private function in there with either a disco or a group for a dance. It seems generally necessary for either of these musical phenomena to produce excessive quantities of decibels to make sure people hard of hearing can appreciate their efforts and those with perfect hearing can, in a short space of time become like them.

It was partly because of this and the extremes of a rowdy lounge to a 'graveyard' that I decided to quit Saturday nights. When the disco or band were next door the incessant thumping through the walls was not exactly music to my ears as you can imagine.

Sunday lunch times were totally different with some really lovely people coming in to dine or maybe have drinks and I thoroughly enjoyed it, playing what I liked and what the diners seemed to like too. I was becoming a lounge pianist, helping to make people's lunchtime more pleasant, letting them wallow in nostalgia and on many occasions playing their requests.

Over the time I played at the Oaklands as well as other spots, I suppose the most requested numbers have been 'Smoke Gets In Your Eyes', 'Stardust' and 'As Time Goes By', the last named reminding me of the late superb lounge pianist Alan Clare who played for many years at the Dorchester in London, frequented by a great many Americans. Alan had a notice on his grand piano: *'My Name Is Not Sam'* on account of them any wits who would say,

'Play it again . . .' which, as we all know, Bogart never actually said, anyway.

I met some wonderful new friends in those first few months at Oaklands.

Margo and Derek Sayer came into my life, as they regularly came to hear my music and were so very kind to me, inviting me to their Old Catton home and later engaging me to play for Margo's retirement party ~ at the Oaklands, of course!

There were three lovely ladies who often came to have a drink there together, two widows ~ Catherine Soame-Hook and Jean Waterland and a divorcee, Norma Baxter.

Catherine always asked for 'East Of The Sun', Jean liked 'Unforgettable' while Norma would request the ever-popular 'Stardust'.

I later took up a special friendship with Catherine with nothing more than a happy companionship in mind and I can look back with pleasure at the times we spent together, at the Thorpe Red Lion Jazz nights or just out for dinner or concerts. She was a very dear and sympathetic friend who sadly died suddenly in 1995.

Mrs Rampley, a widow used to come every Sunday without fail, always requesting 'September Song' and 'Send In The Clowns' followed by a drink for me brought over by the waiter.

Brian Redfern, a keen follower of jazz and piano music would come to listen and chat, as did Les Mason, a splendid vocalist who many times urged me to form a trio with him as singer.

Then there was Oliver Scott, known to musicians as Ollie, a good pianist who would visit the lounge with his wife Janet to listen and talk 'music' in my breaks. Ollie was not in the best of health and died not longer after, Janet later on marrying again. She and her new husband Jim Barley would often pop in.

Another lovely pair were Harry Barnes and his partner Pauline who sat for many hours listening to me and did me the honour of asking me to play for their wedding reception at the Garden Room in the Oaklands on 25th January 1997.

Both were great show fans, often tripping up to London to see the latest productions.

All this time, my daughter Elisabeth was continuing with her music: she had played her oboe with the school orchestra making splendid progress from her early beginnings at Fairway School under John Burdett. There she had played a piece from ' Swan Lake' and 'Songs My Mother Taught Me' for which I played the accompaniment with her proud mum sitting in the audience.

She had continued her piano studies under Shirley Sturgeon, making excellent progress and developing into a good pianist which was to stand her in good stead later when she opted for the teaching career.

My magician friend Pat Swain or 'Carson' was a member of the Norwich Lions who had an entertainment section led by John Ward, a rep with Esso who had been an entertainments officer in the army. A few others helped John to go round to sheltered houses and other pensioners' clubs where the Lions would provide sherry, beer or soft drinks followed by fish and chips with songs and humour after that.

I was roped in to play the piano for John, Pat and others who would give their services in the worthy cause.

We had Petrina Johnson, daughter of Peter and June Johnson, up and coming young starlet who danced and sang in very professional style with numbers like 'Oom Pah Pah' from 'Oliver' and 'Let Me Entertain You' and 'Ev'rything's Coming Up Roses' both from 'Gypsy'.

Then there was the talented Neil Swain (no relation to Pat) who did splendid impersonations of well-known people such as Michael Crawford, Leonard Rossiter and the tennis player with the tantrums ~ John MacEnroe.

A good friend who came and sang was David Perkins who delighted folk with his lovely baritone voice and also featured was Sally Swain ~ Pat and Jean's daughter who played the clarinet.

In charge of it all was MC John Ward, a delightful man who would introduce artistes, tell jokes and throw away the punch-line leaving folk wondering how the stories ended and give the audience musical quizzes, often with some very ancient and obscure songs that not even the oldest residents knew. His speciality was to dance the 'Lambeth Walk' wearing a fez, with one of the ladies in the home which always went down well.

In October 1987 David Perkins asked me to be his accompanist at a concert at Cromwell House in Cecil Road, Norwich, a Methodist home for the elderly and I duly went along, David having explained that he was the guest artiste featured on the programme given by the Taverham Singers.

He and I arrived in the car park to be met by an anxious and worried looking lady whom David introduced as Miriam Batterbee, recently conductor of the Taverham Singers. Recently, because their conductor and founder Phil Richardson had collapsed and died quite suddenly on the stand at a concert and Miriam had taken over until such time as a replacement could be found.

Miriam's anxiety was that her pianist had gone sick and that she would have to play for some of the songs while the others would have to be performed unaccompanied. Did she think that David's pianist could (would) step into the breach?

Well, there was nothing else for me to do, Sir Galahad being my middle name (often spelt M-U-G) but to offer subject to the usual conditions of course ~ fee, allotted time, etc (I jest) but after I'd seen the music.

The various songs appeared to be all right at first glance and away we went into the concert with yours truly playing for both the choir and guest singer. At the interval of tea and biscuits, the choir clustered around Miriam persuading her to ask me to become their resident pianist which at the end of the evening she did. After a few question about 'terms and conditions' I agreed, which seemed to please the singers and relieve Miriam: well, I just had to say 'yes' again and in any case I've always been one to fall for a pretty choir mistress.

So it was that I became pianist for the choir and at the beginning of the following year I introduced them to Paul Donley, a musician friend anxious to become a conductor, since he had left behind an excellent choir in his native town of Northampton. Paul played clarinet and had joined John Ward and the Lions entertainers on several occasions and had also started up a jazz quartet 'Yare Valley Jazz' with me at the keyboard.

The outcome was that Paul became conductor of the Taverham Singers giving Miriam the chance to take her place with the sopranos again.

He proved himself an admirable conductor, the choir performing some splendid things at many venues and Paul introducing a touch of swing or jazz into the proceedings, appreciated by most people, shall we say.

At home in the quiet of an evening I would reflect on what had happened in my life, naturally wondering where I would go from here.

I didn't watch much television but preferred the radio or recordings, listening on the former to 'Friday Night Is Music Night', David Jacob's 'Our Kind Of Music', Benny Green, Desmond Carrington, Humphrey Lyttleton, and the lovely soft-spoken Alan Dell.

On record I would play music from my past such as Vaughan Williams' 'The Wasps' reminding me of a radio serial I once heard 'The Count Of Monte Cristo', 'Scheherazade', music used for Paul Temple and the 'Warsaw Concerto' which for me epitomised the sadness, the horror, the misery and the grief that the Second World War had brought.

As I mused upon things, I knew that my own grief lay heavily, not helped by a nagging leg pain of a less than successful operation and that a few decisions had to be made about my own future. I was finding my teaching job more and more difficult, not being able to sustain a full day without mental and physical pain and I decided to apply for an early retirement.

After various visits to doctors and consultants, the Department of Education and Science granted me a pension and in July 1989 I said goodbye to a job I had held for 35 years.

I received a cash sum from parents, colleagues, County Hall and ex-pupils which I put towards a Casio keyboard which I duly bought from Hilton Tait's shop in Dereham.

Shoals of cards of good wishes arrived including a beauty from Fred Firth, my musical 'hero' and a letter from Fred's successor, Emyr Evans, who graciously described me as a 'musical legend' in Norwich education.

I suppose my most apt and best treasured card came from two very dear friends Joyce and Hazel Fletcher who welcomed me to 'my new job'. It was obvious that my new job was to be a professional musician, one of the halves of my erstwhile dual role.

In teaching I had had the most thrilling and rewarding musical career, one that I could look back on with joy and pride for what I had achieved, a career brought to a premature end by such tragedy.

Now I had to look forward to a new career, a new beginning with new people, new things and new places.

What would my new-found career bring forth?

In that summer of 1989 I had no idea what might happen, but what actually did in the ensuing years was exciting, amazing, almost unbelievable and so filled with music it would take another volume to fill, most likely entitled:

'S'Wonderful ~ Part 2'